Cover Your Eyes

Cover Your Eyes

Adèle Geras

W F HOWES LTD

This large print edition published in 2015 by
W F Howes Ltd
Unit 4, Rearsby Business Park, Gaddesby Lane,
Rearsby, Leicester LE7 4YH

1 3 5 7 9 10 8 6 4 2

First published in the United Kingdom in 2014
by Quercus Editions Ltd

A CIP catalogue record for this book is available
from the British Library

ISBN 978 1 47129 609 3

Typeset by Palimpsest Book Production Limited,
Falkirk, Stirlingshire

Printed and bound in Great Britain
by TJ International Ltd, Padstow, Cornwall

She's there. I've covered up her reflection in the mirror but I know she's there. I'm under the blankets. I can't breathe. Am I safe here? Can she walk out of where she was and come into the room? She mustn't come closer. She mustn't. I've hung my dress over the mirror, to hide the glass, but I want to know if she's gone so I lift one corner and look. I can see the door and the rug at the end of my bed. And her. She's caught in the glass. I want to scream but nothing comes out of my mouth. Go away, I say, over and over in my head. Go away. I'm hiding my eyes and counting to a hundred and when I look again, she'll be gone. Please. Please let her be gone.

CHAPTER 1

OCTOBER

I left early that day. Everyone in the editorial office at *lipstick* knew I had permission. I'd even hinted that I was going to dinner somewhere special and allowed the others to wonder who my mystery date was. The whole way home, I was in a daydream. Simon hadn't been in the office much lately and he'd struck me as a bit distant whenever we did run into one another. I was worried he might be trying to avoid me, but then he'd phoned and asked me to dinner at Farrington's, which was the kind of formal, expensive, discreet place you don't just roll up to in the hope of a quick snack. You certainly don't invite someone there casually. He was a bit curt on the phone, but maybe someone was in the room with him. 'Don't drive,' he said. 'Take a taxi there and I'll meet you and pay for it.' He wouldn't have said that if something was wrong. He won't be distant tonight, I told myself, but how *would* he be? I'd been turning it over in my mind for days. As I let myself into my flat, it occurred to me that he might

1

have bought a ring to give me. Tonight might turn out to be the night when it happened: maybe he was going to tell me that he and Gail were divorcing. They'd consulted lawyers. Discussed everything. I could imagine Simon saying: *Bet you thought I was bullshitting, didn't you? Bet you thought I'd never have the guts to do it, but look . . . here's the proof.* I imagined the ring exactly, lying in a small box lined with dark blue velvet . . . diamonds clustered round a square-cut ruby.

I spent ages in the bath. I put on sheer black tights and my favourite LBD: smart but not too dressy, and tried to stop myself wondering what might happen after dinner. Would he come back here? Would he spend the night? Maybe he'd already told Gail that he was going to be away. I was almost lightheaded with happiness as I sat back in the cab on the way to the South Bank. Did I have time to email Jay? She'd been my best friend since college. Her real name was Julia but she refused to be called that. We'd been on a gap year together, first to the Far East and then to New Zealand to see my dad, who'd run away to the other side of the world the minute he and my mum divorced. Nowadays he and I Skype and email and Dad could easily be in Scotland or somewhere, but back then, I missed him and felt the distance keenly. Jay and I had a blast and it was hard to leave New Zealand and come back to college. After graduation, she got a high-powered job in a finance company in Manhattan

2

and I went to work on my local paper. Although we didn't see each other that often we were always chatting or emailing. I'd been at the local paper for a few years – graduating from editorial assistant to feature writer – and was thinking it was high time I got out of that office. I had my own perfectly okay, if tiny, flat, but all the time I was longing to get to London and to a real job on a proper paper or, even better, a fashion magazine. I saved as much as I could of my salary every month. Then I saw an ad in the *Media Guardian* and answered it. The job was assistant to the fashion editor at *lipstick* magazine, and definitely meant for someone much younger than me, but I was so desperate that I didn't mind a cut in pay.

The fashion editor didn't look a bit like my idea of a fashion editor. I wasn't sure what I'd been expecting, but Felix Priestley looked more like a bank manager: a tall, rather skinny man with horn-rimmed glasses and thin hair, wearing what I later discovered was something like a uniform for him: dark suit, white shirt and a tie so nondescript as to be practically invisible.

'Come and sit, Megan,' he had said to me. 'Or should I call you Miss Pritchard?'

'No, Megan is fine,' I said. He smiled and that transformed his face. He instantly looked mischievous and fun and I could see him as he must have been when he was a little boy. He started to explain to me what I was going to have to do once I'd started at *lipstick* and after a bit, I interrupted him.

'Excuse me, but aren't you interviewing other people? What you're saying makes me think that perhaps I've got the job.'

'Oh, of course you've got the job. No point interviewing other people if I'm happy with you, is there?'

'Well,' I murmured, not really sure of what I ought to be saying.

'And do call me Felix. We can't be having surnames if we're going to be working closely together. I'll just get Simon in here so that you can meet him. He's the editor, but I can't see him objecting to you if I'm happy.'

Simon Gradwell came into the room. His eyes were so blue that I thought he must have been wearing contact lenses. He had a slight Scottish accent, which made every word he said sound reassuring.

'You've come down from Nottingham, haven't you?' he said,

'Northampton.'

'Oh, I'm sorry . . . well, not as far to travel and no need for any Robin Hood references, either.'

After a bit of conversation, he said, 'Well, Megan, I know that Felix is keen to have you. As far as I'm concerned, that's fine. Start as soon as you like.'

'Thank you.' I said. 'I'm going to love working here, I know, and I'll start as soon as I've sorted out somewhere to live . . .'

4

'That's great. We . . . Felix and I . . . are both looking forward to working with you.'

'Thanks. I'm looking forward to it too. It's the kind of job I've wanted for ages. I'm really excited . . .' I stopped then, not wanting to appear too eager, but I was telling the truth.

The *lipstick* job was exactly what I'd wanted. Felix is a lovely boss and we get on well. I loved going to work every day, still do. But then I fell in love with Simon, and things got slightly more complicated.

I've been in love with him for nearly a year. We've been lovers for six months. I've done something I never thought I'd do: stepped into the kind of scenario I'd have told all my friends to avoid. Falling in love with your boss is the worst sort of cliché and I've become the other woman in a love triangle that's beyond banal.

I sometimes wonder if anything would have happened between us if my mother hadn't died suddenly a few months after I came to London. Her best friend, Anita, phoned me while I was sitting at my desk, copy-editing a rather lacklustre spread about the latest beauty products. She told me the news. Mum had been on her way out of the door to the shops when she'd had a heart attack. Her next-door neighbour found her only a short while later, but she was already dead. At first, Anita's words were nothing but squeaks in my ear. I couldn't move; couldn't speak. Anita kept saying: 'Megan? Are you okay, Megan? Do you understand? She's dead . . . so sudden. She can't have suffered. It must have been so quick. That's what the doctor said. I'm sorry to ring you at work only I had to tell you at once, didn't I? I phoned your poor dad and woke him up . . .' She laughed and her laughter sounded weird mixed in with the tears. 'I forgot he was in New Zealand . . . poor man.'

I found my voice then. 'Thanks, Anita . . . it's good of you,' I started to say and then I was crying too, all over my work, holding the phone to my ear with one hand and wiping my eyes with the other. Tanya, sitting across the room at her station, noticed something was wrong and came over to me. I waved her away and went on crying and listening to Anita talking about arrangements for funerals. Suddenly, I couldn't bear it.

'I can't, Anita. I don't know what to do. I've never arranged a funeral . . . Oh, God, I'm so sorry, I'm being pathetic, only—'

'Don't fret, darling,' Anita said. 'You come down and stay with me for a few days and we'll arrange everything together. I've contacted the under-takers already . . . don't you worry about it. You need time to grieve. Such a terrible thing. She was too young . . .'

I put the phone down in the end, thinking that I would now be able to pull myself together somehow, but the opposite happened. I felt something like a tidal wave of tears rising through my whole body.

'What's the matter, Megan?'

Simon was standing in front of me, looking worried. I couldn't speak. He came round to my side of the desk and took both my hands and, speaking over his shoulder to Tanya, said, 'Can you get us a couple of cups of tea or something? With sugar, please.'

To me he said, 'Come and talk to me. Tell me what's the matter.'

When we got to his office he sat me down on the comfortable chair and stood beside me. He put his hand on my shoulder and I can remember thinking: *Please don't take it away,* wishing he would go on touching me and then crying even more because how come I was thinking about this when my mother had just died?

Tanya brought the tea. I managed to pull myself together enough to stop crying and drink some of it. When I'd told him about Mum, I said, 'I'm afraid I'll need a few days off, to arrange things . . .' My voice failed me and tears came to my eyes again at the thought of never seeing my mother ever again.

'Here's what we'll do,' he said, quite calmly, handing me his own hankie. 'We'll go round to yours and pick up your stuff. Then I can drive you there . . . where is it? Northampton, right?'

I told him yes. I couldn't get over how kind it was of him to offer to drive me home. I put the sodden hankie to my eyes, suddenly over-whelmed by grief again, feeling all on my own, with my father so far away. As soon as I get home,

I told myself, I'll phone him. He'll make me feel better.

We left the office together. I could sense Tanya and the others looking at us. When we got to my flat, Simon waited in the car while I went inside and stuffed some things into a bag. He got out of the car to put my bag in the boot. As he opened the passenger door for me, he touched me again, on the arm, and asked if I was okay.

Driving is like being in a moving bubble. There's nothing else, just the scenery unscrolling outside the window, the rest of the world somewhere far away. You're with another person and you could be the only two people on the planet. We didn't say much to begin with, then he started asking me stuff. Normally, I hate talking about myself, but in the separate world of the car, I didn't mind. 'Tell me about your mum, Megan,' he said.

'She's very . . . it's hard to say what she is,' I said. 'Quiet. She doesn't usually show her feelings very much, but she's kind. She was, I mean. She used to be a nurse, but she's retired now. Was retired. Oh God, I can't get used to talking about her in the past tense. Dad's in New Zealand. They divorced years and years ago.' I remembered that I had to phone him. I'd Skype him when I got to Anita's house.

'Brothers and sisters?' Simon asked.

'No. My parents had me when they were quite old. At least, quite old for those days.'

He turned his head briefly to smile at me.

'Well,' he said, turning his attention back to the road. 'I expect being an only child has its advantages too. My brother's a bit of a pain, if I'm honest.'

It was dark by now. 'I'm really grateful, Simon. I don't know what I'd have done without your help.'

I had the sudden mad feeling that the car was driving towards some kind of precipice. The air between us felt thick with unspoken thoughts, his and mine. I couldn't guess at his but mine were tangling themselves in my head. *Had he told Gail he was driving me all the way to Northampton? Would she mind?*

'That's okay,' he answered. 'You've just lost your mother. It was the least I could do.' I began to wonder about what would happen after we got there. Would Simon just turn round and drive straight back? Wouldn't his wife worry about him if he didn't? What had he told her?

When we were nearly there, I said, 'D'you mind stopping at my mum's house first? Before you drop me at Anita's? I just want to—'

'No need to explain. You can phone Anita from there and tell her when to expect you.'

I let myself in. The house was cold and dark and still smelled of the lavender furniture polish that Mum always used. It was tidy, as always. I went through to the kitchen and found a cup and saucer on the draining board, and automatically I picked them up and put them away in the cupboard, hearing my mother's voice say, as she must have said to me a million times: 'That cup is neither use nor ornament by the sink once it's dry. Put it in the cupboard, Megan!' How many times had I sat at the kitchen table after school, doing my homework till Mum came home from work? I walked into the sitting room and noticed how small it seemed, how old-fashioned the television was. When I asked her why she didn't get a modern one, she said, 'What's the point of that? I can watch what I want to watch perfectly well on this one. I've got better things to spend my money on.' Looking around, I wondered what those things might have been.

Simon hadn't followed me but was waiting in the hall when I said I was ready to go.

'I'll phone Anita and tell her we're on her way,' I said.

We drove away from Mum's house in silence.

'I am so grateful,' I said to Simon when we pulled up outside Anita's.

'No worries. You look after yourself. Take care.'

I'd already half turned to open the door when he reached over and touched my hair, stroking it like my mother used to stroke it when I was about five. Don't cry, I told myself. Not now. I stepped out of the car and closed the door. Simon raised his arm in a wave and I watched as his tail-lights disappeared down the road.

Anita showed me to the room I was going to be

sleeping in. Although she'd sounded so calm and supportive on the phone, now I could see that she was so obviously upset, I felt I should have been looking after her.

'Will you be all right, Megan?' she asked, tears in her eyes.

'I'm fine, Anita. Thanks. I don't know what I'd have done without you. I'm going to Skype Dad now. I haven't had a chance to talk to him yet.'

'I'll let you get on, then,' Anita said and left the room, closing the door quietly behind her.

Everyone looks like a zombie on Skype. My dad, when I got through to him, looked much the same as he always did, which wasn't brilliant, but he peered at me, too close to the computer he was using, making him look monstrous and out of proportion.

'Megan? You okay, darling? Your poor mother . . . I don't know . . .'

'Not really, Dad.' A sob caught in my throat. I started again. 'It's so awful. It was so sudden. And I hadn't spoken to her for a couple of days. I never said . . . well, I never said any of the things you're supposed to say but I didn't expect—'

'Darling, she knew you loved her. She did . . . and she loved you better than anything. You know that too.'

I nodded. I had been trying not to cry in front of him but this was too much for me. I burst into tears again.

11

'Oh, Megan darling, don't cry. Do you want me to come over? I could fly over . . .'

'No, no, Dad. Honestly. There's no need. I'm okay. I'll be fine.'

We talked for a few more minutes but we kept coming back to Mum and the death and her funeral and in the end, there was nothing more to be said. I considered Skyping Jay and then thought better of it. I was exhausted, and tomorrow there would be so much to do. I went downstairs to join Anita.

When I came back to *lipstick* after the funeral, Simon was very kind to me. About three weeks later, at the end of a long day when Felix and I had been working on a particularly complicated article, he put his head around the door.

'Haven't you two got homes to go to?' he said. 'Come on, Felix, you must let Megan go home at least. It's almost nine.'

'Time flies when you're having fun, didn't you know?' Felix replied but added, 'Yes, you go on now, Megan. It is a bit late and I want you to be fresh tomorrow.'

'I'll give you a lift home, Megan,' Simon said. That was the beginning. When we got to my flat he asked, 'You going to be okay, Megan? Got any food in?'

'Oh, yes, I've always got something,' I said. I fumbled about in my bag for the key. 'I'll make some pasta. Like some?'

We didn't get to the pasta. Before I could turn the light on, he took hold of me gently by the shoulders and turned me towards him. Without saying a word, he kissed me and my legs almost gave way. I clung to him in the dark, and felt something inside me falling. The door to the bedroom was open. He took my hand and led me there. We held one another and I was trembling. We didn't say a single word while he undressed me, and as he made love to me for the first time I thought ridiculously that this must be what dying was like. I could hear us crying out together and he was kissing me, and the warm glow from my bedside lamp fell on us both. I had no idea of how much time had gone by. I think we must have fallen asleep. It was after midnight when we woke up.

Almost as soon as he'd left, the guilt arrived, so strongly that I could almost see it: a kind of thickening of the air, filling my nostrils, misting my eyes. I didn't know how to deal with it. I felt bad, imagining him going home, putting myself in the place of the immaculate Gail, whose photo I knew so well because it was there on his desk at the office. I was desperate to tell Jay what had happened but I stopped myself that night. Later on, after one particular evening when the guilt was weighing me down worse than ever, I emailed her and told her everything. She answered in a way that was typical of her.

FROM: jay2375@gmail.com
TO: meganp84@gmail.com
Subject: HMMM!
Well. Can you hear me taking a deep breath? That's cos of not wanting to say the wrong thing. I'm happy for you and worried for you at the same time. Make any sense? Not much help I know but I'll Skype you later and hold your virtual hand, kid. Chin up, eyes front. That sort of thing. Chat to you later. xx

She did, too. We spent hours on Skype, and she made me feel better. I thought I detected some disapproval but she denied it. Said it was just that a married man wasn't what she'd hope for me in an ideal world, but she could see how far gone I was. I knew she'd be on my side whatever happened, and she has been.

Simon and I quickly fell into a routine. On days when I knew he was coming round, I'd leave the office a bit early, then he'd get to mine about six. He'd go at eight or thereabouts and my whole life shrank into those two hours we had together. We made love, over and over again, and the more we did, the more we couldn't stop. The more I loved him. The more I wanted him to leave his wife and marry me. Live with me for ever.

The time we've been together, I've been happier than at any other time in my life. I feel bad admitting this. I should have gone on feeling guilty. But

14

the truth was: I'd got good at managing the guilt. Other things mattered more to me. My own feelings. What Simon told me. I knew that what I was doing was wrong. There was nothing I wanted more than to be with Simon, so I perfected a sort of conjuring trick. I made his wife disappear: from my thoughts, from my dreams, from every part of my life and naturally, as his wife vanished, so did my guilt. I loved being in the office and knowing that only he and I knew our secret. I loved the hours and hours of sitting in meetings thinking about the last time we'd been together, and the time before that and dreaming about the next time and the time after that and what he'd said and what he'd do when we were alone later on until my face burned with the heat generated by what I was remembering and every single nerve end was twitching with desire.

While the cab was stuck at a traffic light that didn't seem to want to change, I texted Jay: *On my way to dinner with S. Excited. Xx.* We'd talked about what might happen tonight for ages. She knew what I was hoping for. The reply came back almost at once: *Don't get your hopes up. Might just be a good meal. Xx.* I looked out of the window.

My first article for *lipstick* was appearing in the next issue and I wondered whether celebrating that might be a good enough reason for dinner at Farrington's. The Eva Conway piece came out of an editorial meeting earlier in the year. I'd only vaguely heard of her, but Felix was dead set on our having what he called 'a proper piece' about her in the magazine.

'You can't ignore her, Simon,' he said. 'She's the designer's designer. Just scratch any one of the recent flavours of the month and you'll see her influence. All of them: McQueen while he was alive, Westwood, McCartney, Prada and Armani even . . . they all bow the knee to Eva Conway.'

'Well, I don't,' Simon was dismissive. 'Do we really want to go with this? She hasn't been around since . . . I've forgotten since when, but ages, in any case.'

Felix raised an eyebrow. 'American *Vogue* had a kind of *Where are they now* piece a while ago and they rather went to town on Eva Conway. She did this astonishing collection in the early seventies. We're coming up to the fortieth anniversary. After that, she left the designer world behind her and disappeared.'

'Well, perhaps she ought to stay disappeared?' Simon laughed. Felix tried one more tactic.

'You ought to give it serious thought, Simon. We'd be ahead of everyone else. *Vogue* and *Harper's* and all the rest . . . they'll probably not even realize the anniversary is happening. We'll be ahead of the curve.' He wrinkled his nose a little, as if the phrase was one he wasn't quite used to saying out loud.

'Okay, okay. I give in. I can see I'll never hear the end of it from you, Felix, if I don't. Where does she live?'

Felix, who was now allowing himself a smile at the idea of the article, said, 'She doesn't see anyone from her old life, apparently. Lives out in the country somewhere not too far from London. I'll find out the address. I know someone who knew her long ago. It'd be best, I think, for us to send someone to interview her.'

I was about to say that I'd find her, when Simon looked straight at me. 'Julianne'll write it up, of course, but Megan could help her? Do the research? Possibly go along to the interviews too? Seeing as how Julianne's baby's nearly due?'

How did Simon guess that I wanted to do it? I looked at Felix. He nodded.

'Good idea, Simon. Nice one for Megan to get involved in.'

My luck got better. Julianne had to leave work sooner than she'd wanted to, because of complications with the pregnancy, and they let me cover for her, officially, while she was on maternity leave. I even got a raise. I was determined to do the best possible job so that Simon and Felix would see that they could trust me. Then maybe he'd promote me to junior features editor and I would not be just an editorial assistant after she came back.

That was something like what happened. Julianne left and Simon said I could take her place as maternity cover. I got to write the piece about Eva Conway. I was thrilled with myself. Thrilled to be allowed to interview her on my own, enchanted by the house she lived in, and by her.

17

Far from being an ancient crone, she turned out to be an elegant woman who seemed much younger than her seventy-eight years. Her ash-blonde hair was up in a French pleat and she was wearing clothes that clearly cost loads and were more stylish than anything I'd ever seen on someone who wasn't actually modelling them for a photo shoot. I was grateful to Simon that he'd trusted me to do the interview; ecstatic that he liked what I wrote; excited to think that I'd see my words in print when the magazine appeared at the end of the week. Maybe Simon had an advance copy. The nearer I got to the restaurant, the more convinced I was that this was going to be a double celebration: his divorce and my first publication.

Simon was waiting on the pavement. He paid the driver and then kissed me briefly. He wasn't smiling.

'Hi, Megan,' he said, and we went into Farrington's without another word. Something was wrong. The place was almost empty, which maybe wasn't surprising early on a Tuesday evening. As we sat down opposite one another, at a table near the back of the room, he looked away suddenly as if he wanted to be anywhere but where he was. Then he recovered himself a bit and smiled at me, but I knew in an instant that something was different. He wasn't like he usually was. From the moment I'd stepped out of the taxi, I'd been aware of a lack of warmth about him. If you've done nothing

18

for the past six months but interpret looks and actions and words, you know instantly when something isn't as it should be.

He was stiff and polite. I could have been someone he'd only just met. I told myself: he's got to be formal. He can't be all over you in public. What if someone he knows is at this restaurant? Lots of media people go to places like Farrington's and everyone knows the editor of *lipstick*, who is famous for being just as good-looking as most of the male models spread across its pages.

It struck me that this restaurant wasn't a place to have a romantic meal together – it was a place where the person you were with couldn't make a scene. No one would dare to shout or weep around people who might recognize you; among the crystal glasses and the starched white napkins in a room where the walls were covered in silky, dark red wallpaper. A chill came over me. He wasn't going to tell me about his divorce from Gail. I think part of me had known that from the moment I sat down.

The food came but I had no appetite. I left most of it on my plate. My stomach was in a knot. Thinking back, I can't remember what we spoke about. Nothing important. It was like having a meal with an acquaintance. I was longing to put out a hand and touch his, but I didn't. He hardly smiled when he spoke to me and by the time the pudding arrived, I felt as if every nerve in my body had been stretched as thin as a thread.

The words, when he spoke them, fell like blows, even though I'd been half-expecting them.

'Megan, love, I don't know how to say this. I'm not good at this sort of stuff, but, you know . . . I have to say it. I have to. I don't want to, but it's no good. We've got to stop seeing each other. I should have stopped it long ago, but it was so hard. Now, we've got to put an end to . . . well. We've got to draw a line, that's all. I hate it, but there it is,' He paused. 'Aren't you going to say anything?'

I took a sip of wine. *Love.* How did he dare to call me *love*? And he hates it . . . how much can he really he hate it if he's doing it, I thought. I must have stared at him. He went on: 'Don't look at me like that, Megan, okay? I can't bear it. It's not . . . I mean I don't want to, you must know that, but I've got to. Stuff has changed, I'll be honest with you. It's not the same any longer.'

'I'm exactly the same. What's happened to you?'

'I'm . . . we're . . . that is, we're expecting a baby.'

The inside of my head seemed to swell and all of a sudden, my eyes were full of tears and I picked up the heavy damask napkin and dabbed at them and left mascara on the white cloth. A baby.

'When's it due?' I said. I couldn't say what I wanted to say. I wanted to shout: *How dare you lie to me about your marriage being over?*

'Early spring,' he said. I took a long sip from the wineglass and considered throwing the rest in his

20

face. Instead I put the glass down and counted backwards. Gail was probably four months pregnant. Simon and I had been sleeping together for six months, almost to the day. Bastard. Bastard to me and to her as well. Spring could be any time from February. I felt quite sick. How had I swallowed his lies? He'd let me think that sex with his wife was a thing of the past. He didn't do or say anything that might have made me think differently. That was one of the reasons I really did believe he might choose me. I knew – everyone *does* know – that men always stayed with their wives. That they always go back to their homes in the end. Simon and I, I was convinced, would be unlike the rest. Not having sex with his wife was part of that. Had he actually *told* me they weren't? It was hard to go back over the months and all the times we'd been together, but I tried. I only remembered words: *You're the one. You're the only one. It's never been like this with anyone else, ever, my darling. Not ever. Just killing time when we're apart.* Lies like that. It came over me slowly that no, he'd never actually said: *I'm not sleeping with my wife.* I believed what I wanted to believe. I was stupid. Deluded.

'You should have said. I wouldn't have slept with you if I'd known you and your wife . . .' My voice petered out and I stared at the ends of my fingers, curled round the stem of the wineglass.

'Wouldn't you? Really? You'd have said no, that first time?'

21

I thought back to the first time. 'Maybe not,' I admitted. 'But there wouldn't have been a second time, not if you'd told me.'

'I don't believe you.'

'You can believe what you like,' I said but he was probably right. Being with him became an addiction almost immediately.

'I'm sorry, Megan. I really am. I didn't . . . I mean, I wouldn't . . . I wouldn't dream of hurting you but you can see I can't leave Gail now, when our baby's on the way. It wouldn't be fair to make a child grow up without a father.'

I should have said: *Pity the poor brat with an unfaithful bastard like you for a dad*, but I didn't. I said: 'I'm going home. I won't come into the office tomorrow. In fact, I won't come into the office ever again. You can send my stuff to my flat. I'm leaving *lipstick*.'

'But Megan, you love it . . . I'm sure it'd be—'

'Sure it'd be what? Fine for me to be in the office with you there, even though you've dumped me? Are you serious?' My anger flared up so suddenly that for a moment I no longer felt as though someone had been beating me up from the inside.

'And what about serving out your notice?' he asked.

'I don't give a shit about that. I'll starve rather than work anywhere near you.'

I did give a shit. What about my career in journalism? I had ambitions. I wanted to succeed.

'No, Megan. No, you're right. I'm so sorry. Of

course you won't starve. I'll send you a cheque, don't worry. You'll need something to tide you over till you find a new job, right? And I'll give you a glowing reference, naturally.'

'Naturally,' I said, and added, 'you can stuff your glowing reference.'

Hush money, blood money, I said to myself but I didn't say no. I should have said: *Keep your money, you condescending prick,* but he was right, I would need it, so I didn't mention the cheque and bent down to pick my bag up.

'I'll come out and get a cab for you,' Simon said. 'Here's a bit of cash for that, too.'

'Thanks.' I was taking money from him again. I should have torn it up in front of him but I wasn't thinking straight. The thought ran through my mind: *He's buying you off. Like a whore.* I said, 'Don't come with me. I want to be on my own.' I sounded almost normal. I told myself: *If I can get to the door. If I can go up the stairs to the street and find a cab and go home, I'll be okay. I must hang on till I'm on my own.* I stood up and started walking out of Farrington's.

'Wait, Megan. Please wait. I want to . . .' He wasn't speaking loudly enough for his voice to carry very far. By the time I'd reached the door I couldn't hear him. Would he come after me? Would he pull me back and say: *Don't go. I'll leave her. I'll leave everything and come with you.* I knew he wouldn't.

I held it together in the cab. I didn't want the

driver to see me falling to bits. All the way home I fought back tears. I paid the driver and stumbled up to my flat. Once inside I went into the bedroom. I flung myself down on the bed and began to cry at last. I don't know how long I went on sobbing, but eventually it was as though the whole of my body had been hollowed out. My eyes burned, my mouth was dry and I felt nauseous and sore all over. I was shaking with cold, even though the heating was on. The thought of Simon and his wife together, as he and I had been together: the image which hadn't worried me in the last six months because I'd conveniently eliminated Gail as any kind of sexual competition flared into life and branded itself into my head . . . how long would it be before I would stop seeing it?

CHAPTER 2

'The board's going up in the next couple of days, Ma.'

Eva Conway looked at her daughter and wondered for the millionth time why it was that with such great raw material at her disposal (good hair, good skin, fine blue eyes) Rowena managed to look so ordinary. She wasn't unattractive, but there was something bland about the way she dressed and Eva felt a small twinge of disappointment every time she looked at her. Guilt followed. There wasn't a law that said Rowena had to be stylish or striking. She was smiling at her mother from the other end of the table and saying something. Eva tried to concentrate on the words.

'Ma, you're not listening.'

'I'm sorry. I was miles away. But you said . . . a board going up.' Eva shrugged. 'I don't quite understand, I'm afraid.' She picked up her spoon and began to stir the coffee in the cup that Conor had just put in front of her. As she didn't take sugar and her son-in-law had already kindly added milk for her, it was something to occupy her while Rowena spoke.

25

'I'm sorry, Ma,' she said. 'I'm afraid we've instructed the estate agent. They're going to put the board up outside the gates soon. Possibly even tomorrow and I didn't want it to catch you by surprise. There's been some interest already . . . Nick . . . you met him, do you remember? When he came to value the house . . . Nick says he's got a couple of buyers who are eager to look around.'

Eva blinked. She did remember Nick. He was a tall young man with a head like a hard-boiled egg. A boiled egg with spectacles. He had walked around Salix House in his pale grey suit appraising everything and Eva had suddenly seen clearly the shabbiness and tiny inadequacies that she normally didn't notice. Take a deep breath, she told herself. Don't get too angry. Her heartbeat was speeding up. She felt as though she were being dragged along by a tide of something; events that were nothing to do with her. Now, irritatingly, she was beginning to tremble and she dug her nails into her palm to stop herself from shouting at Rowena. 'So. Let me understand you properly. Selling the house, I understand, is now a *fait accompli*. But I don't want to leave it, Rowena. Couldn't you wait till I'm dead and then sell it?'

Rowena burst out, 'Of course not. You'll live for years and years yet, I'm sure. You're not even eighty. No age at all.'

'If I leave Salix House, I'll die within months,' Eva said, matter-of-factly.

'Oh, don't be such a drama queen, Ma. Honestly.

As if you'd die. You *must* know how mad that sounds. You're healthy; you're busy with the costumes for the Belstone Players . . . what's going to happen to the Christmas production of *The Boy Friend* if you decide to die? What a thing to say! You're always in the garden, or going out to lunch with this friend or that. You hardly ever have a free day. You'll be perfectly fine. We've been through the whole thing over and over, haven't we? We've spoken about everything. You *know* we can't go on in this way. It's just getting . . . too difficult.'

'In what way?' Eva leaned forward a little and tried to look as receptive and interested as possible. It was true that they'd talked about this subject before but Eva was determined to spin the process out as long as possible. And I've got a right to, she thought. This is my house. They're selling my house. How do they dare to do such a thing to me?

Rowena sighed and began to list the ways in which things were getting difficult. She ticked them off on her fingers as she spoke, which annoyed Eva so much that she had to look at the framed photograph on the wall behind her daughter's chair to keep from saying something she'd regret.

'First of all, there's the money,' Rowena said. 'That's the main thing. We simply cannot afford to keep up Salix House any longer. As it is, it's beginning to eat up your savings as well as every bit of our income. We've had to let several people go who used to keep it looking good. Even with everything you do, I don't see how the garden can possibly stay as nice as it is without getting some more help and the money just isn't there. The fabric of the house isn't in a terrible state yet but it very soon will be. We can do paint cover-ups till we're blue in the face but that doesn't alter the fact that there's structural things that need doing to the brickwork, the chimneys, and so on, not to mention the wiring. I dread to think about the wiring, Ma. It's ancient. The house could go up in flames at any moment.'

'What nonsense!' Eva laughed. 'I admit, the house is a little . . . well, *shabbier,* than we'd like, but I'm sure that we can do something about that, can't we?' She turned to Conor, appealing to him. Sometimes he took her side in arguments.

'No, Eva, Rowena's right. I'm afraid we can't. We don't have the financial resources. That's the top and bottom of it.'

Rowena hadn't finished. 'And that's not all, Ma. I've been offered a promotion at work—'

'Which will mean a little more money, no?'

'A little more, yes. But also a great deal more work, I'm afraid. And that brings me to something else that I should have told you about earlier. I'm sorry. I don't know if I'm coming or going, half the time. The thing is: we're both going to be so busy with selling the house, buying another and the hassle involved with that, as well as with my ordinary work, that I've advertised for a mother's help. Someone to stay here with us, deal with the girls, take them to school and bring them back and generally see to them when Conor and I can't.'

Rowena could, Eva noticed, afford to pay someone to look after the girls. There always seemed to be enough money to do what Rowena thought was necessary. How quickly the young decide things, Eva thought. How definite they are about everything, and how optimistic.

'You've got money to pay what's in effect a live-in nanny, but not to do anything to save Salix House?'

'Because it's only temporary. Only till we move,' Rowena said. 'It's not an ongoing expense, like everything about this house. My raise will just about cover her salary.'

Eva said, 'Is the commute getting too hard to do? You've never complained about it before.'

'Because I'll have more responsibilities. I'll need to work later. Get there earlier. And you're right, the commute is hard. It's ridiculous and expensive to commute to London every day. Conor can work anywhere, with his computer consultancy, of course, but we've both agreed that what with the house being so hard to maintain and Dee coming up soon for secondary school and frankly, there not being a decent school within miles of here, that this is the right time to sell Salix House and move to London.'

The kitchen around Eva seemed to shrink and then stretch as though she were in some mad version of *Alice in Wonderland*. It took a while for her brain to arrange the words in her mouth but at last she said, 'And what will happen to me?'

'To you?' Rowena seemed genuinely puzzled. 'You'll move to London too, of course. We'll find you a lovely little flat, very near us. Or maybe we'll get a house which has a granny flat already as part of the property. Or you could go into sheltered housing, if you'd prefer to do that. You won't be put anywhere you don't want to go, Ma. I promise you that.'

'I don't feel as though—'

'As though what?' Rowena was frowning.

'As though I've been properly consulted.'

'Oh, Ma, how can you say that? We've spoken about this dozens of times. You know we have. Whenever we've spoken about it I've tried to find out what you think, but you don't want to know. You just change the subject and hope the whole problem will go away.'

That was true. She *didn't* want to know. 'I wish there was a way I could truly not know!' she said. 'I can't bear the thought of—'

'You'll soon get used to somewhere else, you know,' Conor said helpfully. The man was a fool. Eva debated saying so and thought better of it. To her it was obvious. How could she leave Salix House when every room, every corner of every room, every picture, every plant in the garden, was like a part of herself? She and Antoine had built it up from the ruin it was when they first saw it more than forty years ago, into something different.

Unusual. Not like any other house she'd ever seen. She loved it, but that wasn't the only reason she didn't want to leave it. She felt bound to the house by ties that no other person would understand. No one could. She was attached to it by things that were (how could she express this even to herself?) more than physical. Ties of guilt and shame and memories. Things had happened here, words had been spoken here that had entwined themselves into her soul and Eva felt unable to imagine leaving. She couldn't say this to Conor and Rowena. To them, Salix House was a property. There would be other properties somewhere else. She understood that, but she would find it hard, to say the least, if they sold it and banished her, exiled her to another home altogether.

'Well,' she said, finally, 'just because the house is yours technically, that doesn't mean it's yours *emotionally*. You must see that I still think of it as mine. Even though it's not.'

Rowena sighed. 'Ma, we can do this the hard way, or the easy way. It was a wonderful thing you did, passing the ownership of the house to us.'

'I only did it to avoid death duties,' Eva said. 'I didn't realize anything like this was going to happen.'

'But you must be able to see why it is, Ma,' Rowena was trying to be calm and speak kindly but she was, Eva knew, getting more and more exasperated. 'I've told you. We'll find you a really good place to live. How could you think that we

31

wouldn't? But Salix House is no longer viable. You must see that.'

No longer viable. There was nothing to say to that. Rowena and Conor had come to live at Salix House when Dee was born. In those days, neither of them was earning a great deal. They had a tiny flat in Amersham and when Eva proposed that they move in with her, they accepted at once. The burden of childcare was shared and it made Eva happy to have a baby in the house. The irony wasn't lost on her. She'd been terrified throughout Rowena's early childhood, but this little scrap of a girl was different. After Bridie was born, Eva made up her mind that here were two sisters who'd be friends for ever and she made every effort to encourage them to like one another, to do things together. And it's worked, she thought. They get on beautifully. How will it be if they're not living with me any longer? Will I be able to make sure they're all right?

Everything had changed in the last year. Rowena had found a job with another accountancy firm and started to commute; Conor's web design consultancy began to be profitable; and now Rowena had been promoted. And still, Eva thought, there isn't enough money to ensure the survival of Salix House. She'd already lived long enough since putting the house in Rowena and Conor's name to be sure of avoiding any death duties on it and she'd never, up to now, regretted making that decision. But if I'd kept it in my name, would

Rowena have gone on giving me large sums of money for its upkeep? The truth is: she wants to move to a place that's more convenient for her work and the girls' schooling and the small part of me that isn't entangled with Salix House can see her point of view, even if it isn't one I share. My own daughter is contriving to make the rest of my life different; to take me from somewhere that's part of the fabric of my life and put me in a place I don't know. She pushed her chair away from the table and stood up.

'I'm going to my room, now,' she said. 'I can see that you must do whatever you want. It's not for me to stop you.'

She tried to leave the kitchen with a firm stride, her head up, as though she were on an imaginary catwalk. Walk like a young woman, Eva, she told herself. She went straight to the study and sat at her desk, staring at the dark wood, not seeing it, but remembering the first time she'd set eyes on Salix House.

1967

In October, Antoine had been commissioned by *Vogue* to photograph a spread of Eva's latest dresses. 'Wait till you see the location I've found,' he told her. 'You'll love it. A Queen Anne house in the middle of nowhere and absolutely falling to bits. Practically a ruin. It's just what I wanted.'

Salix House was exactly as Antoine described it.

Eva went with him to look at it on a grey day a week or so before the shoot. The estate agent showed them round.

'It used to be a school,' he told them. 'Been on sale for ages and going at a knock-down price because it's such a wreck.'

'It can't always have been such a wreck. How long's it been on the market?'

'Two-and-a-half years.'

'It's not exactly on the main drag. Who'd want to live out here? Four miles out of a small town.' Antoine said this as he wandered round the entrance hall and looked up at the broken windows in the cupola.

'It only took us an hour or so to drive from London,' Eva said. 'It's a beautiful house. You can see that it used to be beautiful, I mean.'

'And now it's derelict,' Antoine said. 'Which is just what we want, isn't it?'

'Oh, yes,' Eve said. 'It's perfect.'

That spread – which appeared in the *Vogue* issue of April 1968 – was one of Antoine's triumphs. The clothes were beautiful, and the models included Lissa, the sixteen-year-old who was as sought after as Twiggy and Jean Shrimpton. On Lissa, Eva's clothes looked other-worldly, and what Antoine photographed that day became known as the *Ghost* collection. Falls of crepe and chiffon in grey, taupe and storm blue; lace blouses with ruffled collars; silk shirts with fine pintucks worn with tight trousers; an evening gown that fell in a thousand opalescent pleats from the shoulder to just above the knee, made from thin silk in the palest pink imaginable; chiffon skirts that moved like smoke against Lissa's legs: Eva was happier with these garments than with any she'd created before.

Antoine placed Lissa in an empty classroom, leaning against the skeleton of what once was a desk; sitting on a wooden chair near a blackboard that had come adrift from whatever had kept it on the wall, looking out of cracked and grimy windows; under a salix tree, her thin face surrounded by a halo of pale, pointed, fragile-looking leaves; standing by the gate posts at the bottom of the drive gazing up at the flying eagles; looking lost under the domed roof of the hall.

After everyone else had gone home, Eva and Antoine drove to the estate agent's office to return the keys.

'I'm going to buy it,' Eva said. 'Salix House.'

'Come again?'

'You heard me. It's going so cheap, Antoine. I love it. I've fallen in love with a house . . . can you believe it?'

'You're mad. You've taken leave of your senses. Think, Eva. It's a wreck.'

'It doesn't have to be. We could do it up.'

'We? I'm not ready for this Eva. Really. Do think before you do anything rash.'

'It's not rash.' Eva had never been so sure of anything. 'It's an investment. It'll be beautiful.'

'It'll be crippling, financially.' Antoine was beginning to waver, Eva could hear it in his voice.

'And if I told you it wouldn't? If I told you I could afford it, all on my own even if you don't want to come in on it, what would you say then? If money wasn't an issue?'

'You're determined, aren't you?'

'You're beginning to agree with me, aren't you? I can tell.'

He smiled. 'You know me too well. But okay. The place is certainly . . . well, I'm the one who found it and told you about it. I think you're right. I think it could be fabulous.'

'Then let's make it fabulous. Help me with it, Antoine. Please.'

He put out a hand and stroked her knee. 'How can I refuse you, Eva? You must have anything you want. If you can. You know I'll help you. Though what's going to happen to our flat? And how can you work from the middle of nowhere?'

'Oh, God, don't be a killjoy! We'll sell the London flat. We could get a much smaller place to stay in when we need to, but why would we? Why not work from here?'

'Because it's the middle of bloody nowhere.'

'Anywhere outside a three-mile radius of Piccadilly Circus is the middle of nowhere to you. This place is fine. Only an hour or so to town. And look how cheap it is. Have you ever seen a house like this at such a price?'

'It's not a cheap house, Eva,' said Antoine,

pulling up outside the estate agent's office. 'It's an incredibly expensive ruin.'

'But it'll be *our* ruin,' Eva said, happy that he'd come round to her way of thinking so readily. 'And it won't be a ruin for very long, I promise you.'

Eva sighed and turned her mind deliberately away from thoughts of the past. For the last ten years, she'd been designing and sewing the costumes for the local amateur dramatic society's annual spring production. The Belstone Players were a good company, and it gave Eva satisfaction to know that her costumes had added to their reputation. She enjoyed the challenge, loved being able to draw something different every year, choose the fabrics, sew them, be praised at the first night and mentioned in the local paper. Musicals were a speciality of the Belstone Players. Eva opened her sketchbook and began to draw a pretty twenties dress for one of the flappers in *The Boy Friend*. So far away from the dark memories that seemed to overwhelm her more and more often these days.

CHAPTER 3

I wasn't allowed to ring his mobile. That was the rule. From the beginning he'd emphasized that I could text him but not call. *No way of knowing who's in the room, right?* he'd said. Especially at night, hey, Simon? I imagined him lying there in his bed, all crisp white sheets and lacy pillows, next to Gail, and I couldn't bear it. I was a bit drunk, but I *did* know what I was doing. I wanted to wake him up. I wanted him to suffer a bit. I imagined him saying to himself: *I got through that okay. That went well, all things considered. She didn't throw a wobbly. She'll be okay.* Well, fuck him, I thought. I'm going to wake him up. It's the least he deserves. The thought of them lying there together, maybe even touching, was too much for me. I wanted to spoil the night for both of them. I wanted them to lose sleep. I didn't care if they never slept again.

'Hello? Simon?'

'Who's that?'

'Who the fuck d'you think it is? It's me. Megan. Remember?'

'It's three in the morning.'

'Can't help that.'

'Can we talk tomorrow?'

'No, I want to talk now.'

'I can't do that.'

'Why not? Is she there? Next to you in bed?'

'Go to sleep. You'll feel better in the morning.'

'No I won't. I'll feel worse.'

'I said: I can't talk now.'

'Is she getting suspicious? Is she looking at you? Thinking: who's this ringing up my husband on his mobile at three in the morning?'

'I'm going to hang up now.'

I sat there with my mobile in my hand, trembling. She must have heard. She'd have a couple of questions to ask him, about who was phoning him in the middle of the night. For a few moments I allowed myself to imagine a fight so dreadful between the two of them that he'd walk out of his house and come straight round here saying: *Forgive me, Megan, you were the right one all along and I've behaved so badly. What can I do to make it all up to you?* I felt disgusted with myself for being such a self-deluded idiot. I must really be pissed, I thought, if I can believe even for a second that he'd do anything like that. I put the phone down and went into the tiny kitchen of my tiny flat and made myself a cup of coffee.

As I drank it, I tried to work out what would happen next. No Simon, no job, and no idea what I wanted to do beyond crawl into my bed and never come out. 'Bastard,' I said aloud. He could have timed it differently. He could have waited a few days and allowed me my bit of glory in the office later in the week, with everyone saying nice things about my Eva Conway article but no, he had to mess that up as well. He knew how much it meant to me and how I was longing to see my name appear in bold type at the top of the page. Now I could never go to that office again. Someone, probably Tina, the current intern, would be given the uninspiring job of taking everything out of my desk, putting it in a box and bringing it round here. Maybe I'd phone in the morning and tell them to bin the bloody lot. Yes, maybe I would.

I went back into the bedroom and lay face down on my bed. I wanted to Skype Jay but she'd be in the office, not able to speak properly. I could smell Simon on the pillow. Could I really? I fell asleep before I decided.

Eva was wide awake in the middle of the night. There was something comforting about thinking of everyone else fast asleep. A dim light was always on outside the girls' room and downstairs, the spaces that were filled with voices and light during the daylight hours collected shadows and whispers that Eva was never able to identify. Was that old woodwork contracting in the colder night air? Or was it faint traces of everyone who'd ever lived here, the distant whisperings of ancient voices, audible in the dark? It was easy at such times to imagine that Rowena, Conor, Dee and Bridie had vanished altogether. Salix House became truly hers again. She could, if she felt like it, go from room to room and see it as it used to be when Antoine was alive. Or when they'd first found it. At that time, the gateposts at the end of the drive were entirely covered in ivy. The salix trees, after which the house was named, had almost disappeared in the undergrowth that had sprung up around them.

Eva sighed. She could go over in her head the thousands of decisions they'd made as they restored the house, about what colours the walls ought to be, where this or that piece of furniture should go or was that the right picture for that space? Sometimes, she amused herself by mentally rede-signing parts of the house. Shall I change my red velvet sofa for a black one? What about the hall table? Is it too much? Until the last few weeks, her home had been at the same time a source of happiness and a repository of memories, many of which made her shiver even now. She sometimes felt that the walls were impregnated with them, or with her feelings. Were all houses like that: haunted not only by what had happened in them but by what people had *felt* in them? Did tears and anguish and arguments stay there, for ever, absorbed into the very fabric of the place? Well, she thought, Rowena's put paid to that. When she considered the possibility of living somewhere else, part of what she felt was guilt at leaving behind her all her past selves, every Eva she'd been since she first came here.

41

Old people were generally supposed to be bad sleepers. For the first time in my life, she thought, no one is surprised when I tell them how much of the night I spend reading or listening to the radio. She'd never slept well. As a girl, she used to read novels under the blankets by the light of a torch. Agnes Conway would have been shocked if Eva had turned the light on and left it burning half the night. She'd have felt personally responsible if she'd known that her adopted daughter suffered from insomnia. She'd have assumed that the fault was hers, that she must have done something wrong.

1938

Eva was four years old when she arrived in England on a dark, cold December afternoon. She stood in the village hall with a few other children and wrinkled her nose at the smell of damp clothes and old wood. She had a small suitcase at her feet and all around her huge adults moved about, speaking a language she didn't understand. She'd stopped crying hours before, realizing that tears wouldn't help her. Nothing could change what she'd done. It must have been something dreadful, or why would she be here by herself? Being here must be her punishment. Whenever she thought about her sister, a freezing terror seized her and her mind wrenched itself away from Angelika and concentrated on these people

– who were they? What would happen to her while she was here?

A lady came up and spoke to her. Eva couldn't understand what she was saying but she heard 'Agnes Conway' said over and over again and real-ized that it was the woman's name. She wasn't pretty like Mama, but she had a kind face and a brown coat. The woman looked at Eva and took her hand and led her out of the hall and to a small house. They'd had to walk quite a long way down a dark street. When they came to the house and the woman opened the door, it dawned on Eva for the first time that this was now where she would live. She burst into tears on the doorstep and she went on crying all through supper. At bedtime, she was still hiccupping from the tears she'd shed, and wondered if she'd go on crying all night long, but at last, she fell asleep.

When she was young, Eva had long red hair which hung in a plait down her back. The red had turned to grey some time ago, to which she had added ash-blonde highlights, and now she put up her hair during the day, but at night she plaited it again, just as she'd done as a child. Agnes was kind to me, Eva reflected. She did her best and looked after me as well as she could.

The darkness didn't frighten Eva. When they'd first moved into Salix House, in the days before the work had been done and it was still nothing but the shell of a building, she used to imagine the night settling over the house like the folds of a soft, dark blue blanket. Now she moved through the rooms, liking the silence and noticing, as she had almost stopped doing, the high ceilings, the wide windows, the way the stairs from the ground floor curved up from the square hall to where the bedrooms were on the first floor, arranged along three sides of the house. The banisters became a kind of gallery. Eva smiled at the thought of how Dee and Bridie loved sitting there, peering down at the hall through the bars outside their room whenever guests came to dinner or a party.

She glanced at her dressing table, checking that all was well with the mirror. It looked safe enough: carefully draped with a selection of scarves which hung down from the top of the frame and covered up the glass. Dee, who was nine now, had asked about it once when she was much younger. 'Why, Granny? Why do you cover up the mirror?'

'I've always done it, since I was very young. I feel a bit funny about mirrors, that's all.'

'You *could* not have a mirror in your room,' Dee said, sounding a little doubtful.

'Unfortunately I need one because I'm vain,' Eva told her. 'I like to see that my lipstick is on my lips and not my chin. And that my hair is properly brushed. You know . . .'

'But you have to move the scarves whenever you want to look at yourself,' Dee said, and then another thought occurred to her. 'You could call me and I'd tell you if your lipstick looked nice.'

'Well, that's very kind, darling, but what if you're

at school? Don't you worry yourself about my mirror. I'm used to it being covered up.'

Eva had avoided mirrors for most of her life. Even though her work had involved much looking, pinning, draping and rearranging of garments; even though she'd spent hours re-doing hair or fiddling with accessories, tying scarves and adjusting hemlines, most of the mirrors she'd encountered during her long career were public ones. They were in her studio, backstage at fashion shows and, for the most part, there were so many other people crowded in front of the glass alongside her that what she tried to avoid seeing had scarcely any opportunity to float on to the silver, to hover and shiver in the background. She'd hung scarves and necklaces over the corners of every dressing-table mirror in every bedroom she'd ever slept in, so that most of the surface was obscured. Anyone who came in and saw them assumed that such decorations went with being a famous designer given to extravagant effects. What a lot you can get away with, Eva thought, if you have a reputation for being artistic!

And all of this because of something that happened when she was seven. She knew it was a ridiculous prohibition she'd laid on herself, after just one bad experience, but there it was: she didn't like to see herself reflected because of that summer evening, so long ago. There had been other bad experiences, but this was the first: the one that set the pattern.

The mirror in Eva's bedroom was fixed on to a stand and could swivel right round and Eva loved it. She used to like making it swing backwards and forwards to catch the early evening light that fell through the window as she was getting ready for bed.

One summer evening, after a particularly sunny day when she'd been playing with her friends in the field that lay behind the hedge at the bottom of the garden, Eva went up to her bedroom feeling hot and tired. Agnes had bathed her, in luke-warm water, only an inch or two deep, on account of the War. After the bath, she'd put Eva to bed as usual, kissing her goodnight and telling her not to let the bugs bite. Then she went downstairs and Eva was left alone. As soon as she heard Agnes walking about downstairs, Eva got out of bed. She knew that the trees at the edge of the field would be spreading dark shadows on to the lawn and she wanted to see them. She stared at the garden in the last of the sunshine. She pushed aside a corner of the black-out curtains and stood there for a few moments.

Then she'd turned to get back into bed, and caught sight of someone reflected in the mirror. Something that was not Eva was there in the glass.

She wasn't scared at first. She didn't know what it could be. Then the shape moved in the glass and turned into *someone*. There was a girl reflected

46

in her bedroom mirror, but even though Eva saw her through a kind of thin mist, she knew it was her sister. Her hair was red, like Eva's, and she was wearing her dark brown hat and coat which Eva recognized. She trembled. She had no need of those details like clothes or hair to tell her it was Angelika in her mirror. She knew her sister in her flesh and her bones.

She whirled round towards the door to see whether by some magic her sister *was* truly present, but no one else was in the room. Eva searched the glass. That's where Angelika was and she would never leave. She put her hand on the mirror and stroked the cool surface and found nothing. She was still awake and trying to make sense of what she'd seen when Agnes looked in on her as she always did, to check that all was well before she went to bed herself. Eva pretended to be asleep. After Agnes had gone, Eva got out of bed and found her school summer dress on the chair. She hung it over the mirror so that none of the glass was showing.

That was more than seventy years ago, Eva thought, and I'm still unwilling to take the risk of facing my mirror directly.

The window was closed, she was sure of that. It had been a frosty day and the night was chilly but Salix House was always warm. She got out of bed and went to take her dressing gown from the en-suite. As she was crossing the carpet she saw the curtains move a little: a small pushing forward

47

of the fabric as though someone were hiding behind them. Eva stood very still. No one. No one was there, or could be there. That would be impossible. The girls had gone to bed hours ago. Still, Eva thought, I should make sure, or I won't sleep. She took a deep breath and parted the pale green silk curtains and all she saw was her own reflection. Me, Eva thought. No one else. So why, *how* had the movement happened? There wasn't the least breath of a draught in the room. Quickly, she thought, and she felt her own heart beating too loudly in her chest. She pulled the curtains closed again at once. It had to be done immediately, as swiftly as possible, in case something else were to appear suddenly, gathering in the darkness to imprint itself on the black glass. *Not something*, Eva thought, shivering. *Someone.*

CHAPTER 4

'**G**o away, Felix. Please. I can't face anyone just now. I don't feel like seeing anyone.'

'But I've got some of your things from the office, Megan. Please, open the door. Come on, please.'

'I don't feel well. I don't want to see you, okay?'

'I'm afraid not. Decidedly not. I must see you.'

'Leave the stuff outside. I'll get it later.'

Silence for a bit. Had Felix gone? I lay there, my mouth dry and foul from the wine I'd drunk last night and feeling as though my head was being slowly squeezed in a nutcracker. What was Felix doing here? Didn't he have better things to do with his time? What *was* the time? I glanced at my watch and saw that it was almost four. Couldn't be four in the morning so must be four in the afternoon. As near as I could calculate, I'd been out for the count for about nine hours. I heard him speaking again. Trying a different tack this time. Not so strict but softer and more sympathetic than usual.

'Dear Megan, please open the door. I'm not going away, you know. I'm now going to sit down outside your flat for however long you continue to be so obstinate.'

I groaned, then pushed back the bedclothes and went to the door, walking very slowly. I was still in the dress from last night and I didn't care. I knew that Felix would sit out there till I let him in.

At first he said nothing, then: 'Oh, poor Megan, you look like you've been in the wars.'

'I'm fine, Felix. Can you just give me the stuff and clear off, okay?' I was trying to annoy him. I wanted him to go. I wanted to be left alone.

'Certainly not.' He carried the box through to the sitting room and put it down by the window. I leaned against the door.

'Right, thanks, Felix. You've brought me my stuff now you can go. I'm very grateful.'

He didn't say a word, but led me, as though I were a small child, to the bathroom.

'My advice, Megan, is take a shower,' he said to me. 'When you've showered, I think you should change into some comfortable clothes. I never thought the day would come when I'd be recommending leisurewear, because as you know I detest the very concept, but if you have such a thing . . . tracksuit bottoms or something . . .' He almost pushed me into the bathroom. 'I shall go and put a pot of strong coffee on.'

'You won't find one. I've only got instant.'

'Never mind. I'll manage. I think you should eat, too. In my experience, breaking up with someone always makes you feel hungry.'

I did what he said. It was easier than fighting him. I couldn't imagine Felix in the midst of anything like an emotional crisis. We'd always got on very well at work, but he managed to keep his private life to himself and I realized that I didn't really know all that much about him. He never spoke about his personal life. I'd already stepped out of the shower when it struck me: how did he know that I'd broken up with someone? I hurried to get dressed and went into the kitchen as quickly as I could.

'Excellent!' he said, in his most encouraging tones.

'Stop talking to me like I'm a sick kid, Felix.'

'Please sit down and eat your omelette, Megan.'

I was impressed. He'd found the two eggs and the brown paper bag of slightly shrivelled mushrooms and turned them into something delicious. I was just about to say so when he sat down opposite me at the tiny table in my kitchen and said, 'You look surprised. I'm a good cook. Admit it, that's a damned good omelette, isn't it?'

'It is, Felix. Lovely. And thanks for bringing my stuff. I'm sorry I made you wait. I just didn't feel like seeing . . .'

At this point, words failed me and I began to cry again. Felix jumped up from his chair and came to put his arm around me. Kneeling by my side, he said, 'Oh, dear, you have got it bad, haven't you? Poor Megan. Come and sit on the sofa. I can't cheer you up in this undignified posture.'

I didn't want to be cheered up. I deliberately hadn't rung anyone except Jay. I had no intention of putting anything about my feelings on Facebook or Twitter. I'd keep on ringing Jay and crying on Skype and the rest could wait. 'I don't want to be cheerful. I want to disappear. I want to stop hurting, Felix. It hurts so much.'

'I know it sounds unlikely to you at the moment, but you will feel better soon, I promise.'

How could he say that? He had no idea what I was feeling. I hadn't told anyone, not even Simon, the reason why his wife's pregnancy had hit me so hard. I could go for ages without thinking about it but then something happened to nudge my memory and I'd be back there, in the bad time, and it would come into my mind and make me feel once again the guilt and anguish that I'd felt when I was sixteen. Stop thinking about that, Megan, I told myself. Haven't you got enough to be miserable about without dragging all that up again now? I let Felix lead me to the sofa where we sat side by side and he took my hand between both of his.

'Now, Megan, I'm very sorry to have to say this, because as you know, I avoid clichés like the plague . . . ha! ha! But he isn't worth crying over, really.'

'As you don't know who it is I'm crying about, you have no idea if he's worth it or not,' I said. A silence followed and I began to mop at my eyes and nose with a screwed-up tissue I'd found in the pocket of my trackie bottoms.

Felix looked down at his hands and sighed. 'I *do* know, actually. Don't look like that. No one else does.'

I was too stunned to cry. I sat there with my mouth open, astonished. I'd been so sure that nothing, nothing I'd done could have given away my secret. I said, feebly: 'How? How do you know? When did you find out?'

Felix said, 'Well, I don't know why everyone else in the place is so unobservant. I noticed how you kept your eyes on him at meetings. You blushed every time he walked into the room. You said his name as often as you possibly could. Do I have to spell it out?'

'You must think I'm—'

'No, I don't. I also noticed something no one else seems to have grasped.'

'What's that?'

Felix stood up. 'I'll just go and get myself another coffee, if you don't mind. Won't be long.'

'Don't go. Wait. Get your coffee in a second. Tell me first. What do you mean? What did you grasp?'

He came back and sat down next to me. 'I mean . . . I've been at *lipstick* longer than Simon. I was there when he was appointed editor and I know him pretty well. He's always been Mr Cool and Uncaring before but with you—'

'What, what with me?'

'He unbent. He was almost tender with you. I don't think anyone else saw it but I did.'

I thought: *tender.* I changed him from Mr Cool

to someone *tender*. Felix carried on as though we were having an ordinary conversation. As though he'd cheered me up and we were gossiping about someone we both vaguely knew. He couldn't possibly have known what his words were doing to me. He took my hand in his and patted it. He said, 'He obviously didn't think as much of you as you did of him. You're far, far better off without him, you know. Good riddance, I'd say.'

I felt bruised and raw all over.

'Is it true, Granny? Are we really going to have a nanny? Like in the olden days?' Dee and Bridie were sitting on the red velvet sofa in the study. The children called it a squashy sofa and that described it well. Eva had had her fill of hard armchairs in Agnes Conway's house. She made sure that any sofa she ever bought was one you could sink into, and had lots of cushions piled on to it as well. Bridie was hugging one of these now. She was probably, Eva thought, pretending it was a creature of some sort. The child had a repertoire of complex imaginary games and was good at keeping up the pretence. Dee, who was much more practical, had tucked her long legs under her and was fiddling with one of her red-gold plaits, looking worried. 'Like Mary Poppins or Nanny McPhee?'

'No, nothing like them, I'm sure,' Eva answered. The girls often came to see her in the morning before they went to school. Eva looked forward to this time, between the end of breakfast and before they left the house with their father. He worked from home but Eva didn't take too much of an interest because the whole subject (IT and everything that went with it) bored her, but she was glad to have him around. She was even more glad that he spent most of his time in his own study, a purpose-built shed (far too big and grand for a real shed but that was what Conor always called it) erected in a distant part of the garden. As for Rowena, what she did in her accountancy office was even more mysterious. Eva imagined her adding up numbers but of course that was ridiculous. She'd be dealing with people's tax problems and the kind of fiscal complications that made Eva's eyes water. She'd relied on her accountant for many things but it was hard to imagine other people being so dependent on Rowena. She clearly had a talent with numbers. Perhaps my father was an accountant, Eva thought. The last time I saw him I was too young either to know what he did or to care very much.

Rowena would already be on the train to London. For a split second, Eva saw the morning through her daughter's eyes: how horrible it must be to get up before anyone else and leave the house while it was still dark for much of the year. The very next instant she thought: I did it. While I was still working in London, I did it and never complained. *But it wasn't for long and it wasn't easy*, said an inner voice which Eva chose to ignore. She went on talking to the girls.

'Your mother and father will find a nice young woman to look after you. Just till they settle what's going to happen about finding a new house.'

'But I like this house,' Bridie said. She was six years old, a solemn, sturdy, dark-haired child with a round face and a neatly cut fringe which gave her the look of an animated doll.

'So do I, darling. So do I. Now, isn't it time you went and found Daddy? You don't want to be late for school. Come and give me a kiss goodbye.'

'Will we be able to choose the person?' Bridie asked. 'The one who's going to look after us? That'd be fair, wouldn't it?'

'I'm sure your mother'll consult you,' Eva said and made a note to remember to mention that to Rowena. Bridie was right. It would never do to appoint someone the girls had never laid eyes on.

After Dee and Bridie had gone, Eva went to sit at the desk under the window. The monkey-puzzle tree which grew a little too close to the house was just outside and to the left. It was the first thing you saw when you looked out at the lawn, which sloped away to the laburnum and magnolia trees fringing the edge of the property. The window had been quite small when they first moved in, but they'd had it enlarged and now it occupied almost the whole of the west-facing wall. She looked out at the long border. It had taken years to create the tapestry effect she'd wanted: dense, subtly coloured and ornate but she'd achieved it at last and now she would have to leave it to someone else.

For years, Eva had worked in the garden along-side a couple of young men she'd found in the village who used to come in and do the heavy work. She'd turned it, not quite single-handedly, into the beautiful place it now was. It had taken hours of poring over catalogues and visiting nurseries, as well as thousands of drawings almost as careful as the ones she did when she was still designing clothes for someone other than the Belstone Players, to get it to this point. Almost the worst thing about leaving Salix House would be leaving the garden behind. Wherever I go, she thought, I'm not likely to have anywhere like this to play with. I might get a nice little patio on which to make a minimalist Japanese-style garden. The trouble was, minimalist was the exact opposite of what she liked, but she determined not to worry about such things until she could no longer avoid it.

I can't fight to stay here, she thought, because Rowena is determined and perhaps she's also right, and it's impractical and ridiculous to want to hang on to the past. But she had made this place herself. Everything in Salix House was there because she wanted it to be there. Everywhere else, since she'd arrived in this country as a small child, was some-where foreign, someone else's idea of a house and she'd had to become a person she wasn't: someone put together from different bits of herself, but missing an important truth. She had always, from the moment she'd opened her mouth to speak her first English word, been part of a terrible lie. *She came to England all by herself,* Agnes used to tell her friends. Only Eva knew that Angelika had started the journey with her. *Poor little thing,* they would say and make 'tsk' ing noises with their teeth and pat Eva on the head or hands. Since speaking of her sister to the woman on the train, she had never said one word about her and no one, not Agnes nor anyone else, had ever guessed at her existence. Eva shivered to think of what she'd done.

CHAPTER 5

Time goes by so slowly when you're unhappy that it's exhausting. I couldn't do anything after Felix left yesterday. I haven't been able to do anything today either. Jay and I had a long conversation on Skype almost as soon as she'd got back from work. My eleven thirty at night.

'All things considered,' she said gently, 'you don't look too bad.'

'I feel bloody awful.'

'It's not death, Megs. It's grim for a bit but it'll get better. You'll meet someone else.'

'I don't want anyone else.'

She sighed, but not in an impatient way. More regretful. 'That's now. You can't imagine anything else in the world but things change and they get better and you'll find another job and meet other people and then . . . you'll see. You're not going to be single for ever you know. Statistically, that's just unlikely.'

She looked so earnest that I smiled. 'Oh well. Statistics have always been a great help in situations like this.' She opened her mouth to say something but I interrupted her. 'I'm sorry, Jay. I really am, only there's no one else I can talk to like I can to you. I'm loading you down with my stuff. You've got stuff of your own and I never even ask you about it. Soz.'

I looked at my friend in her smart Manhattan flat . . . apartment . . . I took in the suit (either Donna Karan or a good imitation. Probably the former), her very fair hair cut in the sharpest of bobs and her wide mouth, still immaculately lipsticked even though it was quite late in the evening. Stylish, that's what Jay was. Would always be. I couldn't imagine her falling to pieces over any man.

'I don't have time for love. Scarcely have time for sex, if I'm honest. Statistics have their downside, right?'

After I'd spoken to Jay, I made the mistake of turning on my phone and reading the messages from people in the office, expressing surprise, friendship, solidarity. Telling me to get in touch. I cried over some of them but I wasn't strong enough to reply. There wasn't a message from Simon and as I turned off my phone again, I knew that I'd only turned it on hoping that there would be. Some magic words, some spell that would make everything okay again. Nothing.

I was still, after more than twenty-four hours, feeling stunned. Tender, Felix had said. I'd turned Simon into someone tender. He couldn't have been the way he was with me and not loved me a little. *But he never said he loved you,* I thought.

Not even once. He hadn't needed to. I told myself that actions speak louder than words. They might do for all I know, but the words mean something too. I could imagine him thinking to himself: *Well, I haven't lied to her. I never said I loved her.* The fact was, by the time I started needing to hear him telling me he loved me, it was too late. I was besotted with him. Besides, every time we were together he proved how much he loved me. That's what I thought, at least.

But it was my fault. I knew he was married and I could have had a bit more sense and self-control. Instead of doing what I did: trying to make him notice my eagerness for work and my enthusiasm for staying late at the office.

When I first came to this flat, I used to jump when the post was delivered because my flap made such a loud noise. I soon got used to it and now no longer noticed it. If I heard the noise in the afternoon and evening, it was generally a flyer from a takeaway joint. But because I was just sitting there, feeling unhappy and not doing much else, the noise of something being pushed through my letterbox caught my attention. Whoever was there was taking rather more care, as though trying to make as little racket as possible. I went to the door, and instead of a pizza flyer or a sheaf of coupons for unmissable offers at Asda, I saw a long white envelope. I could see my name written on it. *Megan* – not typed but handwritten. I recognized Simon's writing and my heart began to beat alarmingly fast. Pick it up, you idiot, I told myself. It'll be the cheque. The money he's paying you for leaving *lipstick*. For throwing in the job you loved. I held the envelope in my hands and took it back to the sofa, wondering why I was making such a fuss about a perfectly business-like communication, which I'd been expecting. There was no stamp. He must have walked up to my door. He must have stood out there, while I was in here, and he hadn't knocked. He didn't want to see me. He couldn't have made that any clearer. I took a deep breath and tore open the envelope.

The cheque was there. It was surprisingly generous. I read the letter that came with it about five times, trying to find a meaning in it that just wasn't there.

Dear Megan

(after all this time all I merited was a *Dear*. Fuck him.)

Here's the cheque as promised. I'm more sorry than I can say that you've left lipstick. *I hope you'll get the kind of job you deserve and as I said, any time you want a reference from me, just say.*
Love, (not really love. Just the convention. He might as well have put *luv* like in a text.)

Simon.

Not worth keeping. I put the cheque in my wallet and tore the single page of the letter across and across again and dropped the pieces in the bin.

I slept badly that night and woke up very early, but as soon as I was sure that the newsagent down the road would be open, I went out to get the latest issue of *lipstick*. It was out today. At least I have that, I thought. My article about Eva Conway. My name in print.

A thin drizzle was falling as I walked. I was completely exhausted. Maybe it was because I was tired; maybe what had happened with Simon was bringing back the one thing I tried hard not to return to. Everyone, I told myself, has something in their life that they keep firmly under control. The last few months had been so busy that I'd managed not to think about my particular secret for a long time but now it had returned to the top of my thoughts. I thought I'd almost scrubbed it from my mind for ever, but no. *For God's sake, Megan*, I told myself, *anyone would think you were the only teenager ever to have an abortion.* It had been my decision and I could've changed my mind, right up to the last moment. Matters weren't helped by the fact that my parents disagreed about what I ought to do.

My father and mother married late. He was well over forty when I appeared, and already going grey. He looked more like my grandfather by the time I got to school and this embarrassed me a bit but I loved him. Mum was a Catholic but I had no idea that her religion meant anything to her until I got pregnant. She never said so, but that was what really split them up. Dad thought Mum was getting at me, trying to force me to keep the baby, and he hated it. He's not an easy person to row with, but after it was all over, he quietly announced that he was leaving for New Zealand.

'You've found someone else,' my mother fumed at him. 'How can you just abandon us? What'll we do?'

He deliberately misunderstood her. 'We'll divorce. Lots of people do it. No need for dramatics. I think we'll both be happier if we did. Megan can come and visit me, can't you, Megan? You'd like New Zealand.'

I didn't say a word. Part of me *did* feel abandoned. He was the parent I loved best: how could he just let me carry on here without him? Still, what he said was true and I could see why he wanted to go. There'd been a coolness between my parents for years. My pregnancy turned it into a battle.

My mother begged me, pleaded with me, to have the baby. She said she'd look after it. She said the birth didn't have to spoil my life, spoil my chances. She didn't quite say that the child would be far better off with her as a mother instead of me, but she thought it. I know she did. My father simply said: 'You should let Megan decide what she wants to do. It's really none of our business.' He looked straight at me and smiled. 'I'll help you, if you want to have an abortion. Of course I will. Financially and in every other way.'

I was so grateful to him. My mother tried a different tack.

'What about the father?' she asked. 'You won't tell me who it is, but doesn't he have any say in the matter?'

'No,' I answered.

'That's disgusting. That's immoral.' She was almost spitting at me.

I said nothing. I didn't want to dignify the person who'd fumbled clumsily with me during a drunken party with the title of 'Father'. I felt ashamed at my own behaviour. I hardly knew the boy and that was what he was: a boy. We were both sixteen. He was the cousin of someone at school. Neil. For twelve years, I've made an effort to not think about him – to push his name down into a dark place in my head where it doesn't disturb me. If I met someone called that now I'd be okay, I think, but for a long time I dreaded coming across a Neil and having to speak the word aloud.

To give her credit, my mother did help me in the end, when she saw I wasn't going to give in. She knew Dad wouldn't be of any practical use whatsoever. She dealt with the medical stuff; she took me to the clinic. She brought me tea, cup after cup. Then two things happened; three, if I count my father and mother divorcing and him leaving.

The first was that I felt that my mother loved me less because of what I'd done. She withdrew a little. She wasn't exactly the most demonstrative person before, but afterwards, she seemed to become detached from me. That was how it felt anyway. I should've spoken to her about it, I can see that now, but I didn't because part of me was happy not to have her on my case, nagging and reproaching. Her coolness *was* a reproach, but I could deal with that better than I could face constant yattering on about how I'd ruined my life. I told myself it didn't matter. I'd be away at college soon. I wasn't going to live at home after graduation. The paper that took me on (and I knew I was lucky to get a job, any job) was in my home town. So, I found myself a tiny flat to rent – not much more than a bedsit really – even though my mother thought I was mad not to come and sleep in the bedroom I'd had since I was three. I went to visit her of course, but I was getting more and more desperate to leave Northampton, to go to London and part of that was wanting to be a journalist, longing to write. More than anything I dreamed of getting on to the staff of a magazine. I was sick of covering school events and local sports and petty criminal stuff, but I knew that I'd also be much happier a bit further away from my mother, a little less liable to get a visit from her whenever she felt like it.

The worst thing, though, the second thing, was what happened to me after the abortion. When I first discovered I was pregnant, I was surer than I'd been of anything in my whole life that I was doing the right thing in having an abortion. So where did the guilt come from? Because it came, and back then it was like a creature fastening itself to my heart. I began to look at babies. Little kids too. I started to imagine what this child of mine might have been like. What sort of a mother would I have been, given the chance? It was easy to spend hours tormenting myself. In the end, the guilt faded, but I was left longing for a baby. Whoever I fell in love with, he became a part of the fantasy of our future: the children we would have together. Now Simon was having a baby and not with me. He'd dumped me, and that was bad enough but he also destroyed my dream of a child. I felt despair mixed in with the guilt. Mostly, I managed to live with it, not notice it so much, especially when I was happy with other parts of my life. One way I did this was by keeping it secret. I'd never told a soul about what happened to me when I was sixteen. It was my private pain and I wasn't about to share it. Even Jay didn't know that about me, though I'd often been on the point of telling her. Until the other night, I really thought I'd beaten those feelings into a kind of submission, but here they were again and I suspected they'd keep on coming back.

I bought *lipstick* and walked home. I was determined to take pleasure from my article.

I read it. Then I read it again. Then I sat at the

table with *lipstick* spread out flat in front of me and read it for a third time. My first paragraph wasn't there. It had been cut. The second was there, but all through the piece, small groups of my words had been altered. Anyone else, maybe even people in the office who'd seen the original article, wouldn't even realize that things had been changed. He (I knew at once that it must have been Simon) hadn't rewritten my article from scratch, he'd done something much subtler, the kind of thing which he could justify by saying he'd *edited* it. A phrase added here. An adjective put in there. A trite, much-used expression substituted for one I'd tried to make fresh and original . . . I was stunned and even wondered whether I was the one who was mistaken. Maybe I *had* written this dross, because that was what it felt like to me. Not mine any longer but ordinary, boring, media-hype kind of dross.

Check, Megan, I told myself. Before you start going ballistic, just check first. I opened my laptop and went to my Eva Conway file. I was right. I'd known I was right from the moment I'd started reading. I made myself a cup of coffee and sat down again, trying to think straight, working it out. Today was 12 October. The magazine went to press two months before publication day. So . . . 12 August. If he'd made changes to my text, he'd have done it before that date. Bastard, I thought. He must have worked it all out. Changing my piece before then meant he had two months and not a day more before I discovered the extent of his editing. Why hadn't he told me how much he'd changed it? Perhaps it was Felix who'd done the editing but I remembered him okaying the piece. I rang him.

'No,' he said, sounding very confident about it. 'I sent it through to Simon with no changes. What's happened?'

'Nothing, Felix. No worries . . . I've got to go. See you soon.'

So Simon had changed it. He'd edited it after it had been passed by Felix. Well, he was the editor, but why hadn't he discussed it with me? What was he afraid of? He was my boss . . . It was his job to make everything that appeared in *lipstick* as good as it could possibly be and if a junior reporter had cocked it up, there was nothing wrong with him saying so and making some agreed changes. But I hadn't cocked it up. He'd told me how good my story was. He hadn't needed to say that, but he'd said it. He probably thought I loved him so much that when the magazine came out, he'd have been able to convince me that everything he'd done was an improvement. He hadn't told me two months ago because it was easier not to say a word. We'd been happy together in August. Why rock the boat? We'd been closer to one another than ever. We'd gone to Paris for the weekend. Gail was away at a conference and I could hardly believe my luck. I'd thought that those two days were the best days of my life. I'd come back to

London quite sure that our relationship was not common or garden adultery, but a true love affair which would end with Simon and me, together for ever. *4ever*, like something scrawled in black marker pen on a filthy wall.

Now I could see what a coward he was. He must have thought: *Oh, I'll deal with Megan and any tantrums when the November issue comes out. She'll forgive me, I'm sure. She'd forgive anything I did.* Which was true at the time. He might not have been able to persuade me that his version was better than mine, but he'd certainly have been able to sweet talk me into not caring very much. Now, though, I cared a lot. He was probably heaving a sigh of relief right at this very moment. *Thank God I don't have to explain the edits*, I imagined him saying to himself. *Megan's not my problem any longer.*

But Eva Conway: what would she say? She'd approved my copy. I'd sent it to her and asked her to change any inaccuracies or mistakes and she'd been very kind. I still have the handwritten postcard. Her italic writing was thick and black on the cream card. '*This is a very generous and flattering article. Thank you for letting me see it. I look forward very much to reading it in print. Yours ever, Eva Conway.*'

There was *lipstick*, lying on the table. I had nothing to do. I had no work to go to. The walls of my flat were beginning to press in on me. I picked up the magazine and put it in my handbag, went into the bedroom and began to sort through the clothes in my tiny cupboard. It wouldn't do to go and see Eva Conway in trackie bottoms and a fleece. Making the decision to go and see her didn't take long. Hadn't I promised to get a copy to her as soon as it appeared? Now more than ever, I wanted to explain to her how my work had been altered . . . wanted to reassure her that the changes had nothing to do with me. I'd sent her my original text and she might notice that this version was different. I could drive down to Salix House after lunch and give Eva Conway the magazine myself. I thought, for the millionth time how lucky it was that Dad had left me his old car when he moved to New Zealand. I'd never have been able to afford one on my salary. Simon wouldn't have arranged for her to get a copy, I felt sure, and she lived miles away from the nearest newsagent. Yes, I'd drive to Buckinghamshire and surprise her. I felt pleased with myself for having sorted out what to do to occupy myself for at least the next few hours.

CHAPTER 6

Some days were harder than others. There were mornings when the dreams Eva had during the night stayed with her throughout the morning. Last night, she'd been back there, in the old flat in Berlin, with her parents. With her sister.

1938

From the moment she could understand anything, Eva loved Angelika better than anyone else in the whole world, except Mama. Angelika was four years older and wore her long red hair in two neat plaits tied up with ribbon for special occasions. Eva had red hair too but her eyes were like greenish marbles while Angelika's were dark brown. Everyone patted Angelika on the head and said, 'You're so like your beautiful mother!' and it was true. Angelika was beautiful and Eva knew she wasn't. She wasn't jealous, but she was full of admiration for her lovely sister and tried to imitate everything she did. She knew Angelika hated to be followed around, but Eva couldn't help it. She added herself to the dolls' tea parties and came to sit alongside Angelika on the dressing-table stool while she played with Mama's old jewellery and scarves.

'Go away, baby,' Angelika always said, but one day, she actually pushed Eva off the stool and made her cry. When Mama came to see what was wrong, Angelika told her.

'She's a baby. She can't play properly. She can hardly talk properly. You said she'd be better when she got bigger, but she hasn't got better at all. She's still a squawky, crying baby. You used to love me and now you don't. You love *her*. It isn't fair.'

Angelika stamped off to the bedroom and Mama went after her. Eva, still following and unable to stop following, listened at the open door and heard what they said.

Mama spoke first: 'You should try and understand Angelika, since you're eight years old, and a big girl. There's nothing to be sulky about. Eva loves you and needs you. You're her favourite person in the world.'

'Well, I wish I wasn't. You're always busy with her. When she was a baby you did nothing but feed her and look after her but before that you used to play with me and dress me up and take me to the park and the lake and sometimes to the café. Since Eva was born, you play with me less because you love me half as much.'

'What nonsense, Angelika! Of course I don't love you half as much. I love both my children exactly the same but Eva's younger. She can't do as much for herself as you can. You have to look after her.'

'But I don't want to,' Angelika whined. 'And I don't want her playing with my dolls and I don't want her following me around. Oh, I wish we lived in a really big house like Inga's and then we wouldn't have to share a room.'

'Be thankful for your good life, Angelika, and don't be so unkind. I don't want to have to tell Papa how you've been behaving,' Mama said, and started walking towards the door. Eva fled down the corridor but she could hear Angelika shouting after Mama.

'Why is it always me? Why don't you tell Papa how Eva's been behaving? I'm always the one to be told off. It's not fair.'

Mama must have thought Angelika's behaviour really dreadful because she *did* tell Papa about it. Eva knew that this meant trouble for her sister. Papa never normally bothered himself with such matters. He was too busy, that was what Mama said. Eva never knew what he was busy with, because he went to an office somewhere quite far away.

'You are never,' Papa said to Angelika at dinner-time, in front of Eva and Mama, 'to be so unkind to your sister again. We're a family, Angelika, and that means something. Yes, it means something. Promise me you'll never be so unsisterly again.'

'I promise,' Angelika said, and tried to look as though she really meant it, though Eva could tell that she didn't. Not really.

Even though she was young, she knew something that Mama and Papa didn't know. Angelika didn't love her. Not a bit. Not even a tiny scrap. Once, at bedtime, before Angelika came into the room, Eva had whispered to Mama, 'Angelika hates me.'

'Oh, my darling child, never say that!' Mama cried out. 'I can see that it must look like that to you, Eva, but truly, truly she loves you. It's just . . . well, it's hard for you to understand but before you were born, I used to do everything with her and she's . . . she'll get used to it. She's not used to sharing me, you see. It's hard for her.'

Mama passed a hand over her eyes. Maybe, Eva thought, she wants to cry. But I'll make her feel better. I'll tell her I don't mind.

'Don't be sad, Mama. I'll try and behave better. I'll try not to follow Angelika so much.'

'Thank you, my baby. You've taken a weight off my mind. You'll grow up together and you'll be the very best of friends, I know it.'

After her mother left her, Eva considered what she'd said and sighed. It's not true, she thought. We'll never be best friends because I know Angelika doesn't like me. It's not just that she wants Mama all to herself. She doesn't like me. I can see it when she looks at me. This thought made Eva feel so sad, so cold and sick, that she started shivering and bit her lip to stop herself from crying out. She pretended to be asleep when Angelika came to bed and she did fall asleep in the end, but it took her a long time.

Then, one day, Mama and Papa called Eva and Angelika to the dining room. The table was spread with a lace cloth. It was Friday and the silver candlesticks were on the sideboard, ready to be lit at dusk. Mama and Papa were sitting in their places, as though they were about to eat.

'Angelika, Eva,' Papa spoke solemnly, 'Come and sit down, both of you. We've been thinking very carefully, your mother and I, and we've reached a decision.'

Eva listened, and tried to work out what Papa was telling them. She didn't understand most of it, but in the end she realized that Mama and Papa were sending them away to England. On a train. She and Angelika were to go there without Mama and Papa. Angelika asked, 'But who'll look after us there? Till you come and find us?' Papa had been quite definite about this: they'd only be alone in England for a short while and then Mama and Papa would come and find them and the whole family would live together again, only not here. Not in Berlin. Not anywhere in Germany.

As they lay in their beds that night Eva dared to ask her sister to explain to her once more what was going to happen.

'You're a baby,' Angelika sighed. 'It's no use telling you anything. They think we'll be safe in England and that's why they're sending us, only I don't want to go. How can we live in England? We don't even speak English. And they say kind people will look after us there but how do they know that? Perhaps the people will be cruel and wicked and lock us up in dark cellars. How can Mama say she loves us so much and then send us away?'

Eva said nothing. She was frightened of stopping the flow of Angelika's words. This was the first time her sister had ever spoken so many words to her all at once. And not shouting at her, either. Not telling her she must go away and play somewhere else. Eva couldn't help feeling a little happy, and she fell asleep while Angelika was still speaking.

Enough of such thoughts, Eva told herself. What's the point of going over the past again and again? She sighed and picked up her cardigan from the back of the chair. It was time to go downstairs.

Rowena was standing in the hall next to a tall man. 'Ma, do you remember Luke Fielden?'

'Of course,' Eva said. 'You were here the other day, viewing the house.'

'Luke . . . Mr Fielden . . . has come to have another look around.'

'Lovely,' said Eva.

'It's a great pleasure to see you again, Mrs Conway,' Luke Fielden said. He was probably in his late thirties but looked younger because there was not a single thread of grey in his hair. 'I've admired your designs for years. My mother used to love your dresses. She waited for every collection, to see what you'd do.'

Eva bowed her head and smiled. She never quite

knew what to say when paid a compliment. Antoine, years ago, had told her: *just thank the person. That's it. No need for anything else.* So obediently she now said: 'Thank you very much.'

Men could be classified into animal types; she'd thought that since she was very young. Most of them were either bears, foxes, horses or pigs. This one, however, was a wolf: dark with yellowish-brown eyes set at a slanting angle in a dark-complexioned, longish face. A thin nose, which made almost a perfect triangle in profile. Good teeth. She'd often noticed this type of face in the latest fashion spreads. She had determined to be out when people were looking around Salix House but today she hadn't quite managed it. Was Luke Fielden going to buy it? Rowena said: 'We must get on, Ma . . . maybe see you later.'

Rowena was leading Mr Fielden down the corridor to the dining room and drawing room when the doorbell rang again. Eva called out to Phyllis in the kitchen: 'I'll get it. I'm in the hall,' and she walked to the door and opened it.

'How do you do?' she said, smiling at the young woman standing in the portico. 'Have you come to look around the house too? Do come in out of the cold. I'm sure my daughter won't be long, she's showing a man round at the moment.'

The woman looked vaguely familiar: dark and pretty, with a good figure and even better skin. Grey eyes. She was wearing a scarf in a pleasing mixture of reds and mauves wound round her neck. It'll never leave me, Eva thought. This instant weighing up of everything a person is wearing. The young woman said, 'Oh, no, I'm not here about the house. In fact, I had no idea it was for sale. It was quite . . . well, it was a bit of a shock to see the board.'

Eva remembered her then. 'I'm sorry,' she said. 'You must forgive me. I'm getting old. You're the young woman from *lipstick*. I'm afraid I can't recall your name, though of course once you started to speak, I knew immediately who you were. Come in, come in. It's very chilly. I'll ask Phyllis to get us a cup of tea and some biscuits.'

They went into the kitchen. Phyllis was preparing supper but broke off to say:

'Oh, hello Miss. How very nice to see you again. Miss Pritchard, isn't it?'

'Megan, please,' said the woman. 'I've come because the issue of *lipstick* with my article in it came out today. I've brought it to show you.'

'How kind of you!' said Eva but thought: why has she driven all this way? She could easily have sent the magazine through the post, or rung up and told me about it.

'I promised I'd bring it,' Megan said. 'Do you remember?'

'That's true,' Eva said. 'Now that you mention it, only you'd be amazed how many people promise things and then forget entirely.'

The woman – Megan – nodded as she sat down opposite Eva at the kitchen table. She said, 'I came because I wanted to show you what's happened to the article.'

'Nothing bad, I hope?' Eva was surprised at how excited she was. She'd been in magazines all the time in the fifties and early sixties and in American *Vogue* earlier in the year and yet it seemed as though the thrill never disappeared. I'm still vain, she thought. I still want good press. She knew this article was good because Megan had already sent her the text to approve.

'Well, I'm cross about it but I hope it won't spoil your pleasure,' Megan said. 'The editor has changed it, altered things without consultation. I wanted to explain before you saw it.'

'Come in. Come and sit in the study. Phyllis, can you bring the tea through there? Thank you.'

Eva led the way.

'Do sit down, my dear. We'll be more comfortable here. There was no need to come all this way and bring the magazine yourself. It's really very kind of you.'

'I'm so sorry. About the changes, I mean . . . here you are.'

Eva took the copy of *lipstick* from Megan and went to sit beside her on the sofa. The door opened.

'I've brought some Melting Moments too,' said Phyllis, putting the tray carefully on the coffee table.

'Lovely,' said Eva, 'thank you!' Phyllis left the room and Eva picked up the teapot and began to pour. To Megan she said, 'Do have a Melting Moment. I'm sure that'll cheer you up.'

Megan took a biscuit and smiled. 'I expect you think I'm mad. No one in their right mind would care so much about edits someone had made to an article.'

'If I were a writer,' Eva said, 'I probably would. I hate anyone interfering with anything I've made. Let me read the piece and we'll speak when I've finished. All right?'

Megan nodded. 'Page forty-three,' she said. Eva opened *lipstick* and at first sight, she was very pleased with the look of the thing. The photographs were not Antoine Bragonard, but they were good of their kind and Salix House was as photogenic as ever. The study, with Eva herself looking not too bad on the scarlet sofa and the wall of books in the background. That teal silk shirt was a good colour with her hair. She didn't look too ancient and it crossed her mind that airbrushing might have been used. *Well, why not?* she thought. Antoine used to say that the camera always lied to some degree, so why not do everything you can to make people look better? There were good pictures of the hall and the dress room, where one of her designs from the *Ghost* collection was up on a dressmaker's dummy. The silver grey chiffon with satin-trimmed sleeves. Yes, it looked good. She smiled at Megan and said, 'Well, I haven't read it yet but the pictures are lovely.'

Megan said, 'Yes, I know. And the article's

probably fine too. I'm sure I'm making a fuss about nothing.'

Eva read the piece, conscious of Megan waiting; conscious of her unhappiness. Surely no one could be so wretched simply on account of an editor's changes to her text? But as she read, she could see that there were places where the piece had been cut. There was almost nothing about her coming to England as a child on the *Kindertransport*. The paragraph she remembered about finding the house with Antoine and how they had done it up together was missing as well. The editor, whoever he was, had been a bit savage, but still, the article read well and Eva was happy to be able to say so honestly.

'You mustn't worry, Megan, 'she said. 'It reads very well. Whatever the editor deleted or changed, only you and I will notice, so there's no harm done.'

'There *is* harm done,' Megan said. She stopped abruptly as if there was something she wanted to add. Eva looked at her, surprised.

I didn't know what to say to Eva. I sat on the sofa and stared out of the window at the monkey-puzzle tree. She got up and placed the magazine on the desk. She turned to me and said, 'Dee and Bridie will enjoy seeing the pictures. They'll think I'm quite famous.'

'You are,' I said. 'You'll probably have other journalists ringing up and asking for interviews now.'

'Really?' She looked alarmed so I added, 'But of course you don't need to see anyone if you don't want to. Just get anyone who answers the phone to say that you're giving no further interviews.'

'No one would come to Salix House, would they? Doorstepping? Is that what they call it now?'

I laughed. The idea of a bank of paparazzi standing in the drive to catch Eva as she came out of the house was incongruous. I said, 'No, don't worry. Dead lazy, most journalists are. It might have been different if you'd been living in London.'

Eva shook her head. She was sitting at the desk now, facing the sofa, looking at me searchingly. 'I don't care, actually,' she said. 'No one is really interested in me, I know that. I thought it was a little strange that *lipstick* was so keen on a feature like this.'

'Our fashion editor, Felix, is a huge fan of yours. It was his idea, at the beginning. Now you'll have a whole lot of new fans, at least.'

'Well, I'm most grateful to you, Megan, and I'm very happy with the piece, even with changes. And I know you're hurt by them but that's not the whole reason you're so upset, is it? And if you don't wish to tell me, then of course I wouldn't dream of prying.'

Should I say something? Why burden Eva with my problems? Yet she seemed so sympathetic.

'I'm no longer working there,' I told her.

'Oh, no! But why? You seemed so happy working for *lipstick*. And besides, you're good. I think you are, anyway. What happened? I'm being too nosey. I'm sorry.'

'I decided to leave. On Tuesday night, actually.'

'Just a few days ago?'

I nodded. I could almost see the word *Why?* hovering in the air above Eva's head, but she was too polite to say it out loud. 'I've been seeing my boss for the last year. I was in love. He's just dumped me though and I didn't want to keep bumping into him at the office, so I left.'

'He was married?'

'Yes. I feel . . . I feel horrible about that.' I imagined Eva thinking: *If you feel so horrible why do it?*

What Eva actually said was: 'It happens. It happens very often. There are many different reasons for such affairs and I don't, I *really* don't think you should torment yourself. You've lost your job . . . that's quite bad enough to be getting on with, without adding retrospective guilt. Is he feeling bad? Your boss?'

'I don't know.' This was true. In one way, he was probably glad to be rid of me. Perhaps I'd been becoming more and more of a problem for him.

The door burst open and two small girls came rushing into the room.

'Granny!' said the younger one. 'Can we come in here? Daddy says there's a man looking round the house and we aren't allowed to rampage around.'

'Yes, come in, girls,' said Eva. 'I've got something to show you. But first you must meet Megan.'

84

'Hello,' I said, trying to look happier than I was feeling. 'I'm Megan Pritchard.'

'Hello,' said the elder girl, holding out her hand for me to shake. 'I'm Dee . . . well, Deidre really but everyone calls me Dee and that's Bridie, my sister. Bridget really.'

I shook Bridie's hand as well. Dee looked like Eva's daughter, whom I'd met briefly when I came to the house the first time. I guessed Bridie was like her father. She was dark and plump where Dee was skinny and fair. They both stood staring at me, not knowing what to say but before I could think of something, Eva chipped in.

'Come over here, girls, and have a look at this. Megan's written an article about me and it's in a magazine.'

They pored over the pages of *lipstick* together, exclaiming and asking all sorts of questions like 'Did you write all these words yourself? How long did it take you?'

I answered the girls as best I could. Dee was obviously reading *lipstick* for herself. Eva looked over her shoulder, helping her with the occasional word she didn't understand. Bridie came to sit next to me on the sofa. She turned and stared at me and for a few moments she didn't say anything and I was frantically searching my mind for topics of conversation suitable for a small child you'd never met before. Then she said, 'Are you going to be our new nanny?'

What was that about? Where did she get that idea?

'No, I'm not. I'm just here because I brought that magazine to your granny.'

'Oh.' Bridie thought for a moment. 'Only Mummy said we're getting a person to be a nanny. And then here you were so I thought it was you.'

'No, I'm afraid not. I'm just visiting.'

'I could ask my mummy, if you want. If you'd like to be our nanny.'

I couldn't help smiling at Bridie. Since I'd decided not to go back to *lipstick*, I hadn't given any thought to what I was going to do next. What I felt like doing was getting in my car and driving as far away from London as I could go. Abroad. I could go abroad and never come back to England. I could go and see Dad in New Zealand. He'd take me in. But I didn't want to do it because I knew it wouldn't work. I wouldn't magically become another person just by leaving my flat.

'Thanks, Bridie. I hadn't thought of being a nanny.'

Dee had finished reading and came over to sit down next to her sister. She said, 'Bridie's worried about getting a nanny. She thinks she'll be like Nanny McPhee, with warts on her nose.'

'No, I don't, silly!' said Bridie. She turned to me. 'You'd be a nice nanny. I wish you could come and look after us.'

'Bridie!' Eva said. 'Stop nagging Megan, please.'

I was just about to tell her not to worry about it when the door opened and Rowena came in.

'Hello, darlings!' she said to the girls. 'I was

86

wondering where you were, Ma. Luke wants to leave now but he can't move his car . . .'

'Oh, that must be me,' I said. 'Boxing him in. I'm so sorry.'

I followed Rowena into the hall. A man, presumably Luke though Rowena obviously didn't think introductions were necessary, was standing by the round marble-topped table. I said, 'I'm terribly sorry. I'll move my car.'

He didn't say: *That's okay*. He tried a smile but it didn't quite work. He was clearly pissed off. He looked . . . I found it hard to work out what he looked like but his expression made me think he fancied himself and didn't have that great an opinion of anyone else, least of all me. I dashed out to my car and reversed so that he could get out.

'Much obliged,' he said, bending down to speak through my half-open window. His eyes were strange: a kind of light orangey brown, like an animal's eyes. He was handsome in a chilly sort of way. Most people, I thought, would have been okay with 'Thanks'. I decided he was stuck-up as well as self-satisfied. He didn't look obliged at all. Maybe he was in a rush or something. I said, 'Sorry to have held you up.'

'Not a problem,' he replied and waved a hand as he got into his car and whooshed away down the drive. I would have followed him but I hadn't said goodbye to Eva and the girls, so I got out of my car and walked back towards the front door, thinking about the man I'd just met. Was he really interested in buying Salix House? The idea of him owning it, the idea of Eva's lovely dresses taken out of the wardrobes in the dress room and packed up in storage boxes or given away or sold, depressed me. I couldn't imagine Eva anywhere else. He could be, I thought, a speculator. A developer, who'd tear down Salix House and put up ten little box-like structures in its place. I really, really hoped he wasn't.

My phone rang just as I stepped on to the porch. I'd forgotten it was in my jacket pocket and the ringtone startled me. I didn't look to see who it was but held it to my ear and said, 'Hello?'

'Megan?'

Simon. I felt winded and turned towards the car again. I should put the phone down. I can't speak to him here. These half-formed thoughts flew through my mind. I didn't hang up. I walked back to the car and got in, still holding the phone to my ear. I hardly heard what Simon was saying, so shaken was I by the fact that he'd rung me.

'Hi, Megan,' he said and I could tell just from those two words that he was drunk. He had a particular way of drawling, of not exactly slurring but stringing out his words a bit more than usual when he'd had a glass or two. Perhaps he'd had a boozy lunch and not bothered to go back into the office. 'Just touching base. Seeing if you're okay. How you are, I mean. And how are you?'

'It's none of your business how I am, Simon.' I tried to keep the emotion out of my voice.

'No need to be shirty,' he said. 'I still care about you, Megan, in spite of everything.'

'Care about me? I don't know how you have the nerve to ring me up.'

'Come on, now, be fair! I explained everything, didn't I? I know I did.'

I lost it then. 'And that makes it okay, does it? Well, get this, Simon. I don't want to hear from you ever again and if you try and phone me, I won't answer.'

'How dare you yell at me!' he shouted.

I flinched, but quickly recovered.

'Stop it!' I shouted back at him. 'Fuck off, Simon. Just fuck off and let me be. Go back to your precious wife and your precious baby and I hope you're all very happy together.'

'Well, there's not going to be a baby—'

'What? What do you mean?' He was almost panting at the other end of the line, like someone who'd just run a race. If I'd been feeling angry before, this enraged me so much that I found it hard to breathe.

'You told me you were expecting a baby. What happened? Or were you lying about your wife being pregnant?"

'No, no, of course not. There *was* a baby . . .' He sighed. 'There's no baby any more. She's lost it. Bet you thought: *Let's see if I can get something really really bad to happen.*'

'Hang on,' I said. I needed time to think about what he'd said. 'Are you saying your wife had a miscarriage?'

'Yup, that's exactly what I was saying.'

'Simon, you're pissed. I can hear that you are. Do you know what you're saying at all?'

'Of course I do! Gail lost the baby. Him. It was a him. No more baby.'

'And you're saying it's my fault?'

'If the cap fits . . .'

Bastard, I thought. What was he doing? What was he accusing me of? Killing his child? No wonder he wanted to phone me. *Why should we be the only unhappy ones? Megan can suffer too. Right. Brilliant.* I was almost sure that he'd wake up tomorrow with no memory of even having spoken to me. I wanted to cut him off but I managed to blurt out some kind of apology.

'Simon. I really am so . . . so sorry. That's if I had anything to do with it.'

I snapped my phone shut. I didn't want to hear his reply. But could it be true? Everything except the shock of what I might have done left my head. I forgot that I was there, in the early evening darkness in front of Salix House. Eva, Rowena, the girls, the article, everything that had been in my head before I spoke to Simon seemed to contract into a hard knot of anguish.

I don't know how long I'd been sitting there when the knocking came on the window. Eva. Oh, God, I thought. What'll I say to her? How can I explain? I blinked, realized I'd been crying, scrabbled in my glove compartment for a tissue and blew my nose. It occurred to me that I could drive off, never see Salix House or Eva or anyone ever again. But I'd left my things in the study and Eva was standing there, looking concerned, so I wound my window down.

'I'm sorry,' I said, before she could ask me. 'I'm sorry you've had to come and find me like this. I had a phone call . . .'

'From him? The one you were telling me about?'

'Yes,' I said. 'I'm sorry. I shouldn't have let him get to me, but he did.' I wasn't about to tell her what he'd said.

'Come back inside. Come and sit for a while. Have another cup of tea or something stronger.'

'Thank you. You're being so kind.'

'You will get over it, you know,' Eva said as we walked up to the house. 'It's a cliché and everyone always rushes to say it but it's true. Doesn't mean you don't go through hell first, of course, but you do get over it in the end.'

I tried to smile. When we reached the hall, I said, 'I'd better go home now. You've been so nice. But I really should go. If I could just wash my face a bit, before I set off. I'll go and get my handbag. I left it in the study, I think.'

'Of course.' She pointed to a door. 'You remember where the downstairs loo is? Come and get your things and I'll see you when you're ready.'

The downstairs cloakroom was off the corridor

leading to the kitchen. My make up, I knew, would have disappeared and I imagined my face must be a mess. As soon as I went in and locked the door behind me, I wanted to open it again. I had no idea what it was about the room but it was very cold and I felt suddenly uneasy. Pull yourself together, Megan. It's the poshest downstairs loo you've ever been in. Fluffy dark blue towels. L'Occitane soap. One of Eva's designs – her own original drawing – on the wall to the right of the basin. A white china bowl of pot-pourri with a fragrance of vanilla and roses on the wide window sill.

I calmed down after a bit. Maybe I was uncomfortable here because I was feeling so rotten in general. The mirror was set too high up on the wall: that was the only thing wrong in the whole room. Eva must have put it up there to suit her son-in-law.

After I'd washed my face, I put down the lid of the lavatory, and sat on it. Then I fished around in my handbag and found my hand mirror and a lipstick. For the thousandth time, I promised myself that I'd try to become the kind of person who carried everything she needed for a make-up repair job in a neat, zipped-up case. I squinted into the mirror, moving it around so that I could see all of my face. As expected, I looked as crap as I felt and there wasn't much I could do about it. I focused on my mouth and began to apply my lipstick and then the mirror fell out of my hand

and I scrabbled round on the floor and picked it up and thrust it into the depths of my bag. I opened the door as quickly as I could and came out on to the corridor.

I could hear childish voices coming from the study. The girls must be in there with Eva, I thought. Looking to my right, I could see up the corridor to the hall. There was the vase, on the table, full of silk flowers. The grandfather clock in the corner outside the dining-room door. *I must have imagined it*, I told myself. *There was no one in the loo with you, Megan. You are seriously losing it. Seriously.* I took two or three deep breaths and reckoned I was okay to go back to where Eva was. There was no way I could have seen anything else reflected in my small, inadequate mirror. But I had. I'd seen something. Someone. A bit of some-one's face. *It must have been a bit of your face, you idiot. Maybe you turned the mirror in a funny way without thinking about it.* But it wasn't my face. It was a face I had never seen before and didn't recognize. It vanished as soon as my eyes fell on it, but it *had* been there. I could have sworn that something had been there, a kind of shadow moving across the glass.

I returned as quickly as I could to the study. As soon as I came in, Bridie jumped up and took my hand.

'I like you,' she said. 'Don't go home yet.'

'I like you too,' I said to her and found that I meant it. I liked having her hand in mine.

Dee, anxious that her younger sister was getting all the attention, wasn't going to be left out. 'I like Megan as well,' she said to Bridie, frowning a little.

I was just about to proclaim my devotion to Dee, too, when Eva spoke: 'I'm sure it's time for your tea now, girls. And I'd like a word alone with Megan. Say goodbye now, please.'

They said goodbye and I kissed each of them in turn. On their way out of Eva's study, they were whispering to one another but I couldn't catch what they were saying.

'Megan,' Eva said, 'You'll forgive me for saying this, but you look dreadful. I've had a word with Rowena and she agrees. We think you ought to stay here tonight. We'd really love to have you, you know.'

I opened my mouth to say no, that wasn't necessary and I was perfectly fine but suddenly I felt weak and wobbly and I could feel tears coming to my eyes again. I said, 'I'm okay, really. The tears are because I'm so . . . well, because you're being so kind. I don't know if . . .'

'*I* know if,' said Eva firmly. 'Of course you're an adult and I don't want to make you feel . . . but I'm sure it wouldn't be sensible for you to drive all that way in the dark when you're upset. Everything always looks better in the morning. Come with me, and I'll show you where you'll be sleeping. It's the smaller guest room, but it's pleasant enough. I've lent you one of my night-gowns and there's a new toothbrush in the en-suite.'

I nodded. There was so much I wanted to say to Eva, but I couldn't. I didn't think that the morning would necessarily make me feel any better but she was right that I was too shaky to drive now. I said, 'You're being so kind to me, Eva. I'm really grateful. Thanks.'

As we went upstairs, she said, 'I'll send Phyllis up with a tray for you later on. Is that all right? Or would you rather come down and eat with us?'

'A tray. Thank you. That'll be good.' I didn't feel at the moment as if I'd ever want to eat again but I knew I'd probably be hungry later on.

'It goes without saying,' Eva went on, 'that if you want anything, anything at all in the night, just come down to the kitchen and get it for yourself. I walk about at all hours, these days. All right? You're to make yourself completely at home.'

'I will. I'm really grateful.'

When Eva left me in the small guest room, I sat on the bed and wondered how I'd fill the night hours. I didn't think I'd be able to sleep. There were books in a small shelf beside the bed; there was a radio on the bedside cabinet. My iPad was in my handbag: plenty of things I could do, but I didn't feel like doing any of them. I lay back on the bed and looked around. Red curtains, made of velvety stuff with a raised pattern on it. Thick, beige carpet. Not a proper dressing table but an ordinary pine table with a swing mirror on it. I didn't have the energy to explore the bathroom.

When Phyllis brought my supper on a tray, it

looked so delicious and I was so hungry that I ate it at once: mushroom soup and toast, some smoked salmon sandwiches and a fresh fruit salad. I hadn't had anything to eat since early morning, apart from half a Melting Moment.

When I'd finished eating, I put the tray outside the door. I could hear voices coming from downstairs. A bit earlier on, I'd heard the girls going to bed; saying goodnight and then their dad's voice answering them. In the end, the house fell silent and my breathing was the only sound in the room. You might as well undress and go through the motions of going to bed, I told myself, and I got into Eva's nightie, which was like a long-sleeved white T-shirt. It was soft and smelled of something lovely and covered me up almost to my ankles. I went to brush my teeth. I didn't have any make up left on my face after crying so much but I washed my face anyway, scrubbing away at my eyes, making them even more scratchy and sore than they were before.

I turned out the light and lay in bed staring at the ceiling. Darkness was good. Darkness was what I wanted. I don't know how long I lay there, but eventually I fell asleep.

I woke up quite suddenly and for a second I didn't know where I was. There's an eye-blink of time when you feel okay, and it's morning, or nearly morning, but then you remember the bad things and you want to go back, back into the night. I looked at my watch and saw that it was five o'clock. Two hours at least before I could get up. Whatever Eva had said, I didn't dare to go down to the kitchen. Instead, I lay in bed and tried to go back to sleep. I must have drifted off, I think, or at least, had some kind of waking dream. At first I thought it was the girls, Dee and Bridie, up early and chatting but I knew this room was nowhere near where they were sleeping. It couldn't be them. Also, they sounded too close to me. I heard whispers. Someone was whispering somewhere. I sat up at once and looked around. Nothing. No one in my room. I glanced over at the table, at the swing mirror and saw a flicker of white in the glass. I turned cold with fear but then realized that it must have been me, my face and upper body in Eva's white nightie, reflected there. I lay down again. Of course it's me, I thought. Who else could it possibly have been? Still, I didn't want to look at the blank silvery surface and I closed my eyes tightly, with my face turned into the pillow.

'I hope you slept well,' said Eva. 'You look a little better, I think.'

'Yes, thanks,' Megan answered and smiled. Eva could see that the smile was an effort for her. She was just about to say something else when Dee and Bridie came running into the kitchen.

'Megan! You're still here. Mum told us you were staying the night,' said Dee. 'Will you play with us after breakfast?'

Megan shook her head. 'I'm sorry. I can't. I've got to go home now. It was very kind of you to let me stay but I have to get back to London.'

Rowena followed the girls into the kitchen and sat down opposite Megan. 'Good morning, Megan,' she smiled. 'Ma showed me the article you've written about her. It's really wonderful. You must be so proud. I'm sorry I was busy with Mr Fielden yesterday and didn't get a chance to speak to you properly. I hope you slept well?'

Megan nodded and said, 'Yes, thanks very much.' For a few moments the only sound came from everyone helping themselves to cereal and milk and coffee. Then Bridie spoke. 'Do ask her. Please, Mummy,' she said.

'Yes, please, Mummy,' Dee joined in.

Rowena sighed. She took some butter and began spreading it on a piece of toast. 'Oh, Bridie, honestly!' She turned to Megan. 'I was moaning at supper last night about the trouble I'm having finding a nanny for the girls. They both want me to ask you if you'd be up for it. I told them I was sure you had better things to do than be their nanny.'

'I haven't,' Megan replied immediately. 'Actually I've recently left my job, it didn't work out. So I'd be free.'

'I told you that,' said Eva. She took a sip of coffee.

'Well, you did tell me but I can't have made the connection. I don't for one minute suppose you'd fancy coming to be a nanny here, would you? To these two? You can't believe how awful everyone I've interviewed has been. Just—' she spread her hands and shrugged her shoulders and sighed '—hopeless in dozens of different ways.'

Eva watched Megan. The girls were silent, looking at her, tense at the thought of what she would say. Would it be a good thing for them? Was Megan capable of looking after two children, the state she was in at the moment? Maybe it would be good for her; to put her somewhere far away from the things that were troubling her. Megan was intelligent and sensible. She seemed to like the girls. And after all, it would only be until they moved out of Salix House. Eva found herself hoping, almost as hard as the girls, that Megan would say yes. Megan looked up from her plate at last and said, 'Well, that would be . . . it would be strange for me, because I don't know how good a nanny I'd be, but I haven't got anything else to do right now, so I don't see why not. At least for the time being.'

Before Rowena had a chance to say anything, Dee jumped up and grabbed hold of one of Megan's hands and Bridie took the other and they both started squeaking and jumping up and down.

'Let go of her, girls, please,' said Rowena, 'Megan'll change her mind about looking after you.'

'You won't, will you?' Dee said. 'We'll be ever so good, promise.'

'No, I won't.' She smiled at them. Rowena said,

99

'Okay, kids, if you've had your breakfast, go off and play. Megan and I have to sort out the details. Come into the drawing room, Megan, and we'll work everything out. Thank you so much for doing this. You've rescued the girls and me from a whole series of Nannies From Hell. How soon can you start?'

CHAPTER 7

After I drove away from Salix House last Saturday, I spent a long time thinking about what Simon had told me. I felt sick at the thought that it might be true. Now Eva and Rowena had given me a way of leaving London, leaving everything behind. I could live in Salix House. I loved the house, although I had found that first night creepy. And what about what happened in that small downstairs lavatory? Was that only a product of how I was feeling? Aside from all that, which was probably just a product of my overactive imagination, could I be a nanny? Did I even like kids enough to spend hours looking after them? It wouldn't be many hours. They were at school for most of the day. At least I'd be away from London and a long way away from Simon. If I were here, wouldn't it be easier not to think about all the things I wanted to avoid, and work out what I wanted to do next?

I started making arrangements. From first thing on Monday, I was cleaning and tidying my flat. I wanted to leave it ready for the agent who was going to sublet it while I was away. I didn't know how long I'd be working at Salix House, but I was sure it wouldn't be all that long and I had every intention of continuing to look for work as a journalist and of moving back to my flat sometime. But looking after two children was different from anything I'd ever done, and it was a good way of not going over and over in my mind everything that had happened with Simon. I thought a lot about Eva, and what a shame it was that she was going to have to leave Salix House. There was something about the place now that hadn't been there when I'd first gone to interview her. I'd been impressed then. I thought that everything I looked at was artistic and unusual and touched with a kind of *difference*. It was a special place. The first time I went there, Eva had shown me round the garden. We'd walked across the lawn and sat on the bench near the monkey-puzzle tree and Eva had seemed happy. She explained to me that making the garden was a kind of substitute for making the clothes. It gave her something creative to do and I could see she was proud of what she'd achieved. I was absolutely sure she didn't want to leave the house. Now, maybe because both of us were unhappy, it felt as though the combination of our moods had had an effect on the fabric of the house. After spending more time there, I was thinking of it as slightly shabby and also a little unwelcoming. But what on earth did I mean, *unwelcoming?* Grow up, I told myself. The house was fine and you were just being stupid. Everything will be better once you're there, once you're busy with the girls. I moved in the following Sunday.

My bedroom in Salix House is practically the size of my whole London flat. When Jay first caught sight of it on Skype, she said, 'God, Megs, you've landed in the jam. It's stunning.' And it is. I can see the drive from my window, edged with the pretty trees the house is named for, curving down to the gates. It is late October and a few pale green leaves are still clinging to the red twiggy branches. I've got a bed, a little sofa, a colour television, a dressing table and more cupboard space than I need. There's also a chest-of-drawers and an en-suite bathroom. On the wall above the bed is a large still life of a white jug with some apricots lying next to it.

I liked the room as soon as Rowena opened the door to show it to me. I was relieved about that because the moment I arrived in the house, I sensed again that the atmosphere *had* changed. It hadn't been my imagination. Now, especially at certain times of the day, I have the feeling that I'm missing something; that there are conversations going on where I can't hear them. I feel unsettled and awkward when I'm alone in certain rooms.

Fortunately, that doesn't happen very often. Someone walks in and dissipates whatever it is that's odd about the atmosphere. Bad vibes are here, somewhere, and it worries me that I can't quite pin down where they're coming from or why. At my most paranoid, I think: it's me. They're attached to me, somehow. I've brought them to Salix House. It was perfectly okay before I came but now that I've moved in, things seem not to be exactly as they were before. But I feel fine in my room.

The girls were happy to see me. Eva seemed pleased too. I haven't a clue if I'm capable of being a nanny but, for the moment, I've decided to put my journalistic ambitions on hold, while I deal with everything that's happened recently. The pay's decent and I get bed and board, no rent to pay. I like the girls. The job isn't very hard and I don't have very much to do. I have to take them to school, fetch them at the end of the day. I help them with homework if they need it. I like Eva especially and it makes me happy to think that I'll get to know her better. Perhaps I'll even be able to help her when it comes to leaving Salix House. And I'm far away from Simon and everything that reminds me of him, which is good, even if there's no way I'll be able to escape from his terrible accusation.

During the last few days, I've learned certain things about this house and about Eva and her family. However carefully you've interviewed someone (and I thought I'd done a thorough job of it) you can't know what their lives are like. Not really. Not until you share a house with them.

On my first night here, I couldn't sleep. Something woke me up. I opened my eyes in the unfamiliar bed and listened. Houses make strange noises. People often put the sounds down to plumbing: the pipes are heating up or cooling down or something. But this was different. I thought it might have been a floorboard creaking. I checked the time, thinking that perhaps it was someone waking up extra early. One of the girls, maybe, up before daybreak. But it was two in the morning. It couldn't have been the girls.

I got out of bed and put my slippers and dressing gown on. The house was silent now but I knew I wouldn't be able to fall asleep again for a while. I'll go downstairs, I thought, and get myself a hot drink. I opened my door as quietly as I could and stood at the top of the stairs. A draught was blowing round my ankles and I looked down, astonished. This was the best insulated house I'd ever been in. I already knew that Eva liked warmth and in any case, where would any draught be coming from, up here? There were no windows opening on to the landing on the first floor. The front door was shut and so were all the hall windows. And then the draught stopped, just like that. It disappeared as suddenly as it had come. I puzzled over this as I crept downstairs, treading carefully on the carpeted stairs, but then I noticed that a light was on in the kitchen. Someone else was up. For a second, I froze on the bottom step, wondering if I had the energy to make conversation with one of the family at this hour. I was working out what to do when Eva came out into the hall.

'Ah! It's you, Megan. I thought it must be. Nothing wakes Rowena up but sometimes Bridie has a nightmare . . .'

'I'm sorry,' I whispered.

'No need to apologize. It's often hard to relax on your first night in a new house. Come and have some camomile tea. That's very good for getting you to sleep.'

I followed her into the kitchen, and wondered how I could get out of drinking camomile tea. She must have read my mind because she turned to me and smiled.

'That's if you feel like camomile tea. Hot chocolate is also good.'

'Thanks, I'd much rather have that. Would you like something? I can make it.'

She waved in the direction of the table. 'I have my coffee already. Decaff at this hour, of course, but always coffee.'

As Eva showed me where to find what I needed, for a moment I had a strange feeling of being in someone else's life: *I'm in Eva Conway's kitchen making hot chocolate*, I thought to myself. It was like acting in a film when I didn't quite know my part. I waited for the milk to heat up.

Eva said, 'You don't have to stay and talk to me, you know. You can take your chocolate back to your room if you'd like to. I often wander about in the middle of the night. Old people need less sleep, they say.'

'That's okay. I'd rather stay here, if you don't mind.'

'Not at all. It's a funny time of the night, isn't it?'

'The house feels a bit different.' I was thinking of the draught around my legs and I nearly said something about it and then didn't. Eva looked much older in her nightclothes. She was wearing a greyish hooded velour robe which I recognized from the White Company catalogue. I'd wanted the very same one but could never afford it.

'The girls are so excited that you're going to be taking them to school tomorrow,' Eva said.

'I'm a bit nervous, actually. Maybe that was why I couldn't sleep. Mr Fitzpatrick's coming with us, to show me the way and what to do when I get there.'

'Mr Fitzpatrick? Conor, surely. Eva, Rowena and Conor from now on. *Mr and Mrs* sound so formal.'

Rowena had made a point of telling me that too. Calling the girls' father by his first name was going to be hard for me till I'd got used to it. Even saying *Eva* and *Rowena* sounded funny, like using the first names of your teachers at school. We sat in silence for a few moments and I felt more and more as though it was up to me to find a topic of conversation. In the end, I said, 'Dee and Bridie seem to get on very well, don't they?'

'They do!' Eva smiled. 'Well, that's important, I think. I told Rowena when they were both very young that it was the most important thing . . . sisters. They should be friends. Look after one another. Rowena was an only child but as soon as Bridie was born, I did everything I could to make sure that the two of them got along well together.'

'Not all siblings do, though, do they? Get on, I mean.'

Eva didn't answer this but asked, 'Do you have brothers and sisters yourself?'

'No,' I answered. 'I'm an only child.'

'Awful. It's not good being an only child. I've always thought so. Sisters . . . well, that's a very special relationship, isn't it?'

'Have you got a sister?' I asked. Eva looked at me with an expression I couldn't decipher. She didn't answer me. I didn't feel I could repeat the question and was just about to say I was going back upstairs when she said, 'No. No, I certainly don't have a sister.' She was almost whispering, as though she didn't want anyone else to overhear but there wasn't anyone there except me. She'd chosen an odd way of saying something simple. What was the 'certainly' about? It was almost as if having a sister was disgraceful.

She added, 'I'm going to bed now, I think. Do stay and finish your hot chocolate. And help yourself to biscuits or something if you're hungry. And could you turn out the light in here when you leave? We always leave the one on the landing on. Bridie likes to see it shining under the door. Goodnight, Megan.'

She left the kitchen, walking slowly. Once she'd gone, the silence that fell was broken only by underwater sounds coming from the enormous fridge. I looked at the dresser, where a collection of blue-and-white china was displayed; at a fruit bowl sitting on a marble work surface, at the clean white doors of the cupboards and nowhere could I see any sign of anything as mundane as a biscuit tin. What did a designer biscuit tin look like? In the end, I opened several cupboards before I remembered the pantry. Hadn't Phyllis gone in there to fetch cakes and things when I first came to interview Eva?

I opened the pantry door. There, right on the shelf facing me when I came into the room, was half a chocolate cake on a cake stand under a clear plastic dome. I didn't dare cut myself a slice of that. What if Phyllis was keeping it for a special occasion? I decided not to risk it and almost as though I was being rewarded, I noticed a tin on the shelf above the cake stand. I took three oat biscuits and went back to eat them at the table.

I hadn't had more than one bite when I suddenly felt uncomfortable, as though someone I couldn't see was watching me.

'You're being a bloody idiot!' I said aloud, thinking that hearing my own voice would make things seem more normal. It was the silence, weighing down on me, that was what was freaking me out. As soon as I heard myself speak, I'd be okay, I was sure. Only I wasn't. The feeling of being watched persisted and I turned round abruptly and looked to see if the curtains at the windows were drawn. Sometimes being in a lighted room when it's dark outside makes me feel as if I'm on a stage with an unseen audience staring at me, but this room had curtains. No one could possibly see in. *But what if someone is out there anyway? Not seeing me, but looking at the other side of the curtains?* I wasn't going to stay here. I put the biscuits in my pocket and turned out the light. I almost ran across the hall and went up the staircase as fast as I could without making a racket. When I got to my room, I glanced back downstairs, almost expecting to see someone following me. *There's no one following you,* I told myself. *You're just tired, that's all.* The flowers in the vase on the hall table seemed to glow pale in the surrounding near-darkness. The hall was quite empty.

'Come and meet my teacher. He's called Mr Shoreley,' Bridie said, dragging me by the hand into her classroom.

Mr Shoreley looked up when we came in and said, 'Hello, Bridie. Is this your new nanny?' To me he said, 'She's been telling me all about you.'

'I'm Megan Pritchard. It sounds a bit odd to hear myself called a nanny.' I wanted to add that I was a journalist but stopped myself. Instead I said, 'It's a super classroom.'

Bridie had gone over to talk to her friends. Mr

Shoreley was quite nice-looking. If you needed a teacher for an advertisement, you'd probably have chosen someone exactly like him: tall, with blue eyes and wearing narrow rectangular glasses in silver frames. He was wearing a sweat shirt and trainers, which surprised me a bit. The dress code had clearly changed since I was at school.

'Bridie loves coming to school,' I said. 'She was waiting by the door today, in her coat long before we had to set off.'

'She's a pleasure to have in the class. People are fooled by her quietness, but she's often thinking, about stuff you wouldn't expect. I think she's a bit . . . overshadowed by Dee but deep down, I reckon she's got a good opinion of herself. Quietly confident.'

'Thanks,' I said to him. 'I don't know either of them very well, not yet.'

'Well, Bridie's a bit of a dark horse. Dee's such a star and so I sometimes think that she gets kind of overlooked. Did you know she's learned her telephone numbers by heart? Her mother and father's and she'll soon have yours, no doubt. Tables are in her head already. Maths and Science are my subjects, so I try to make sure she's progressing at her own rate. It'd be a shame if she got bored and turned off . . . right?'

I nodded. He was smiling at me and for the first time since before I met Simon, I felt . . . *something*. A kindness coming from him. And I knew, because you can tell, that he was attracted to me. It was like moving into the range of a warm fire, after standing in the cold for a long time. As for me, I was pretty sure that his face wouldn't linger in my mind for too long after I'd gone home but I did know that I liked him.

CHAPTER 8

'Well, Ma? What do you think?'

Eva didn't know how to answer. The house Rowena and Conor had made an offer on, the house that they'd brought her to see, was elegant and attractive and just what they'd been looking for. And Eva hated it. She said, 'It's a lovely house, really. I think . . . well, I can see that it will suit you perfectly. Very near Dee's school, too, didn't you say?'

'It is. It's near both their schools. We pointed them out on the way.' Rowena's voice was tight.

'I know,' Eva said. 'I remember. But I wasn't paying too much attention. Still, it's a nice street.'

That was also true. There were trees planted at intervals in the pavement outside, which was more than could be said about a great many London streets. The house was tall and narrow. Four floors . . . she couldn't imagine a life in which she'd have to go up three flights of stairs to get to the sitting room, but if she agreed to live in the basement then that would be exactly where she'd be put.

'You haven't seen the best bit yet,' said Rowena.

'The granny flat. I've deliberately kept that for last. Conor, you don't have to come down with us.'

'Give me a shout if you want me. I'm going to look at the garden.'

Transparent, thought Eva. She wants him out of the way for some reason. Maybe because he's more likely to sympathize with me if I make objections. She won't be able to bludgeon me so easily with her logical arguments.

'Come on, then, Ma,' Rowena said. 'Follow me down.'

Following Rowena involved holding on to the hand rail very tightly indeed. The staircase down to the flat was almost a spiral. The drop between each step was incredibly deep, much more so than Eva was used to. I'd never be able to relax. I'd have to be on my guard constantly in case I fell down them, she thought. She could manage now, just about, but what if she lived another ten years? More?

'What do you think of the bedroom?' said Rowena. 'See, you've got a window that lets in the light and you can see the railings on to the street. Plus, there's a little paved bit out here which we could turn into a kind of garden area for you, if you'd like that. Hang baskets up and things.'

'Mmm,' Eva answered, so as not to have to say anything else. How odd, she thought. The ceilings in the rooms upstairs, because it was such a tall, skinny sort of house, were, if anything, too high. She'd felt a little lost in each one. Even the kitchen seemed a bit cavernous. This basement made up for it. The ceilings were depressingly low, the window was tiny and the light wasn't good. I'd have to have the light on during the day, she thought. What kind of electricity bills would that mean?

'Come through and see the sitting room. And the bathroom. You've got a really lovely bathroom.'

'Yes,' said Eva, wandering from the very small sitting room (with its very small window on to a yard-like space and some treacherous-looking stone steps leading up to the back garden and not a hand rail in sight) into the admittedly luxurious bathroom. With no bath.

'There's only a shower here,' said Eva. 'You know I hate showers. I have a bath every night.'

'Don't worry, Ma! Of course we could put in a bath for you. That'll be no problem.'

Eva said nothing. I don't like it, she told herself. I don't want to live here, but if I say that now, if I tell Rowena that I'm not prepared to go up all those stairs and be crammed in a dark basement, she'll start on about sheltered housing and who knows if that would be better? Eva had two scenes in her head. In one, she was in among the rest of the old people in a beige sitting room with the television blaring because some of the ancients were a bit deaf. In another, she was in a room on her own, with no one visiting her and unable to go and talk to Rowena or the girls or Phyllis. Which would be worse: to be lonely, or to be among people you didn't know and might not particularly like if you did know them?

'You're not saying anything, Ma. Does that mean you hate it?'

For a moment, Eva considered lying. Wouldn't everything be easier if she simply gave in? But then she'd have to come and spend the rest of her days in this basement and how could she bear that? 'Yes,' she said finally. 'I'm afraid it does. I can't live here, you know. I'm very sorry.'

'But why? It's perfect. I don't think you're approaching this in a very positive spirit, honestly. You just said upstairs that it's an ideal house.'

'For you it is. For you and Conor and the girls, I can see it is. But it isn't an ideal house for me.'

'I don't see why not. You'd be completely independent and right with us at the very same time. How come that's not good enough for you?'

'It's not that it's not good enough, Rowena. As far as it goes I can see it would be a very convenient arrangement. Of course I'd be happier living with my family than stuck by myself in a home or something but you *must* see that it's impossible. The stairs would kill me. I'd have to go up three flights if I wanted to sit with you. I'm fine at the moment, obviously, but I won't always be and this is not designed for someone old.'

'Oh, come on, Ma! You've said it yourself. You're years and years from being like that, so don't go playing the old lady card now. You've still got the use of your legs. You drive. You're perfectly healthy. It's just that you're being stubborn about Salix House and you really can't afford to be. Luke

116

Fielden might make an offer. He's coming round again later on this afternoon. We're going to sell the house at some point and whether it's to Luke, or someone else, we're going to accept it so you'd better get used to the idea.'

'There's no need to be angry, Rowena. You asked me what I honestly thought and I've told you. I won't be able to live here. If you want to buy this place you're most welcome but I'll have to find somewhere else.'

'Okay. Okay. I'm sorry. And you're right. I did say we'd find you a place you liked. I did say that.'

'Have you got any more ideas?'

'There are a couple of possibilities very close by. I'll arrange for us to go and see them soon. We'll find somewhere. You mustn't worry, Ma.'

'I shan't worry,' Eva said, wondering whether it was true that as long as she hadn't found somewhere to live, they couldn't be evicted from Salix House, even if it was sold, either to this Luke person or someone else. She decided that for now, she would let Rowena do the worrying. Normally she was good at not letting unpleasant thoughts affect her, although recently she'd had difficulty in pushing them aside. Sometimes there was nothing she could do to stop them coming.

1938

This was what Eva knew: she was four years old. Her name was Eva Bergmann. She had to be good.

117

She had to obey Angelika, who was older. She knew how to speak. Mama and Papa often called her a chatterbox. But now the words had gone suddenly, every one of them. She couldn't remember how to say anything. She opened her mouth, wanting to speak, wanting to tell them what had happened and there was a great black space in her head and a silence filling her mouth. She knew she was tired. She felt sad and frightened but somehow she couldn't cry. She thought: Why can't I? What's happening to me? Where am I? Eva was burning hot and whenever she moved, it hurt all over her body.

She was in small room with a wooden floor. There was a rug with orange flowers on it. Someone was kneeling next to her. Holding her hands. Stroking her brow with cool fingers.

'Eva Bergmann,' this person said. Eva nodded because that was her name. The woman, who was wearing a navy blue skirt and a pink blouse, kept on stroking her hand and smoothing her hair back from her forehead. She said something, but Eva couldn't understand. These words were different, just as Mama and Papa had told her they would be. She couldn't remember the name of this place, but she knew they'd been sent far away from home. *So that you'll be safe,* that's what Mama had told them. This must be where she meant. She'd warned Eva and Angelika about the funny words. *'Maybe you'll be lucky,'* Mama said *'and there'll be someone there who speaks German.'*

A man did come who said things Eva could understand. He was a doctor. She had been taken ill, he said. He told her the lady's name: Agnes. He explained that Eva would be living with Agnes. Eva didn't care. She didn't care about anything. She was tired. She wanted to do nothing but sleep and sleep.

Eva was ill for a long time. It was only much later, once she'd learned those strange words, that she realized quite how long. She lay in bed and there were bad dreams which she tried to forget when she was awake. This was hard. The worst bits clung to the edges of her thoughts and she spent the time when she wasn't asleep looking at the room she was in. There was a big window. There was a chest-of-drawers with a mirror on it and you could see tree branches and bits of sky in the glass and Eva liked looking at it. When she heard Agnes moving about downstairs, in the kitchen, banging saucepans, Eva tiptoed from her bed and looked out of the window at the garden. A big square of grass. Sometimes the grass was frosty. Trees were black and spiky and Eva wondered what had happened to the leaves. There was no music. Eva longed for the sound of Mama playing the piano. She longed for Mama. And Papa. She tried to remember what their faces were like and it was hard to picture them and this made Eva cry. She tried hard not to think about Angelika because when she did, it was difficult for her to breathe and Eva's heart began to thump too hard, so hard that it hurt her and she wanted to vomit and sometimes she did and that was horrible and stinky, so she stopped. Whenever her sister came into her head, Eva would close her eyes and hold her breath and push her to the very edges of her mind and then she'd fade away and be forgotten till night time. There were bad dreams then, but during the day, Eva began, bit by bit, to stop thinking about what had happened.

Eva refused to speak. For weeks not a word had passed her lips, even after she began to feel better, less tired, less hot. Even after she'd grown used to Agnes looking after her, even after she was allowed out of bed and downstairs.

Then one day Agnes came into the kitchen, carrying a basket. Eva was at the table, being looked after by Mrs Gregg from next door.

'Look, Eva dear,' said Agnes, opening the basket. 'I've brought us a sweet little kitty.'

She picked the kitten up and held her out to show Eva. The cat was white and ginger with a tiny pink nose and was so small that she fitted easily into Agnes's cupped hands. Eva looked at the creature, who suddenly leaped out of the basket and landed on her lap. Amazingly, the kitten settled down at once and fell asleep. Eva thought: she knows I love her. I haven't said a word and yet she knows I love her. The almost imperceptible weight of the kitten on her legs had warmed her, and she stroked the pale fur with one hand. Then, without even thinking about it, she repeated Agnes's last word: *Kitty*.

'That's right, Eva,' Agnes's voice shook. 'Kitty. Good girl. Kitty. This is a cat. Can you say cat?'

Eva said, obediently: 'Cat.'

That was the beginning. Agnes said, 'Oh Eva, darling. This is so exciting. You're *speaking* again! You'll soon be able to say everything. Anything you like. You'll see.'

Kitty grew into a plump ginger-and-white cat. It was taken for granted that Eva loved her, but no one knew exactly how much. Nor exactly why. Telling would have been embarrassing and others wouldn't have understood that she was more than a mere animal. She'd been Eva's way back to life, back to normality, from the dark place in which she'd found herself when she first came to Agnes Conway's house.

CHAPTER 9

I was getting out of the car outside the girls' school when my phone rang. I scrabbled in my bag and fished it out as I crossed the playground. I would have left it to go to voicemail but it was Rowena so I answered it.

'Hello?'

'Oh, Megan, so glad I've got hold of you. You must be at school, right? Sorry to ring now but I've got a massive favour to ask you. We're stuck in traffic on the way home . . . driving in London is a complete nightmare . . . and I'm not sure I'll be there in time. Could you possibly see to him without me? Just give him a cup of tea or something and tell him I won't be long, okay? Only I said five and it's not going to be five.'

'Sure, 'I said. 'No probs. Only you haven't told me who's coming. Who am I meant to be looking after?'

'Sorry, sorry. Luke. Luke Fielden. I should've said. He does seem keen on Salix House so I want to encourage him as much as possible.'

'Okay, not a problem. Best get on; the girls'll be out in a moment.'

'Thanks so much, Megan.'

I sighed. I really didn't relish the thought of this. Would it be okay to give him a cup of tea and leave him in the sitting room by himself? Probably not. Just thinking about someone other than Eva owning Salix House made me feel sad for her, so I didn't imagine I was going to have too much fun hearing how much he was looking forward to moving in.

Dee came running out to find me.

'Megan, can you come? Bridie's crying in the cloakroom.'

I set off after her. 'Why's she crying?' I asked.

'She's lost her hat. Mr Shoreley's helping her look for it.'

Mr Shoreley and Bridie were waiting for us.

'Found it!' Bridie said, happily. She ran up to me and hugged me. 'I was very sad. I thought it was lost.'

'Even if it was lost,' I said, hugging her back, 'it wouldn't have been a disaster. We'd have got you another hat, Bridie.'

'But I like this one. Granny made it.'

She pulled it on to her head and I saw what she meant. It was only a simple knitted hat, but the pretty pink flower stitched to the side of it did make it special.

I turned to Mr Shoreley. 'It was kind of you to help look for it.'

He smiled. 'I'm good at looking. I've got X-ray eyes.'

'He hasn't really got X-ray eyes,' Bridie explained. 'That's a joke. He's always joking.'

I laughed and said, 'Well, X-ray eyes or not, thanks very much, Mr Shoreley. It would have been a shame to lose this nice hat.'

'Tom,' he said. 'Please call me Tom.'

'Right,' I said. 'And I'm Megan. Now, let's get home, girls. We've got a visitor coming in a while.'

'Okay,' said Dee. 'Bye, Mr Shoreley.'

A chorus of goodbyes went on then. Dee and Bridie to Mr Shoreley . . . Tom . . . and him to them and me to him and him to me. At last we were in the playground. Dee was skipping.

When we got back to Salix House, I gave the girls a glass of milk and a biscuit each while Phyllis cooked supper, and put them in front of the television in the sitting room. Just before five, I went upstairs to comb my hair and put on a bit of make-up ready for Luke Fielden's visit. You could go to the downstairs loo, I told myself, but I knew that I wasn't going to step into that room if I didn't absolutely have to.

The doorbell rang as I was crossing the hall. I went to open the door and there he was, smiling. To be fair, the smile didn't leave his face when he saw that I was neither Rowena nor Phyllis.

'Hello, Mr Fielden, do come in,' I said, stepping back into the hall. He was tall, I noticed.

'Oh . . .' He only hesitated for a moment. Then: 'It's you. You very kindly moved your car for me.'

'That's right. I'm Megan Pritchard. I'm working

here now, I look after the girls.' As we walked towards the sitting room I said, 'Rowena's been delayed in traffic but do sit down in here, she won't be long. I'll get you a cup of tea.'

'That's okay. A cup of tea would be great. Can I help?'

'No, thanks, that's fine. I won't be a moment.'

He sat down and I went to the kitchen. I'd just got everything together when my phone pinged to announce a text message.

'May be further delayed. Do show LF round yourself if he doesn't mind. He wants to go over house once more before offer. Thanx.'

They left the London house in Conor's car. Eva hated being driven, she much preferred being in the driver's seat but the firmness and determination with which both Rowena and Conor had insisted on the big car indicated to Eva that they didn't really trust her behind the wheel. Perhaps they thought she was too old to drive but that was nonsense. Her eyesight was excellent and so were her reactions. Still, if she was insisting that the stairs in this London house were going to be beyond her, then she'd better also accept that she'd be demoted to a mere passenger.

Eva closed her eyes and tried to breathe evenly. She had no intention of continuing her argument with Rowena on the way back, and the best way to avoid arguments in a car was to go to sleep. If you couldn't really fall asleep, because you were churned up by what you'd been doing all day long, then you pretended and no one was any the wiser. Rowena and Conor wouldn't mind. They began to talk about the house. They were excited about it. They won't discuss what to do with me, Eva told herself, even if they do believe I'm truly asleep. It occurred to her that they probably knew she was putting it on as a kind of avoidance strategy. Maybe she wasn't as good an actress as she thought she was, or perhaps they could tell from her breathing that she was simply opting out of conversation.

The rhythm of the car must have lulled her properly to sleep because after a while she felt herself jolting awake and Rowena was saying, 'Are you okay, Ma? You were talking. I couldn't understand what you were saying . . . you must have been dreaming.'

'I'm fine,' Eva said. 'Just dozed off for a minute.'

Forcing her eyes to stay open, Eva looked out at the autumn landscape sliding past the windows at high speed. I can't even enjoy the trees, she thought. The dream is still there. She didn't have to make much effort to recall it because she'd been having the same dream, on and off and in one form or another, for as long as she could remember.

There was always a space. A wide, dark space. It had a vaulted wooden roof. A grey floor stretched out in front of her for yards and yards. In the early days of the dream, Eva didn't know where it was but then there was a train somewhere, so she assumed it was a railway depot of some kind.

126

She knew the train was there, even though she couldn't see it. The floor was grey concrete. Darkness surrounded her, and rose into the roof. The strange light, bright and white, came from round lamps, like the headlights of a car. Bitter, deadening cold. Eva was squashed in somewhere. The space above her head was nothing but black. She reached out her hand and felt rough wood. Then she curled herself up behind something, some kind of crate. She hated the scratchiness when her fingers touched the wood. She wanted to cry but knew she mustn't. She heard words and they sounded funny. They were in her ear, whispering, but they came from far away, too. Eva had forgotten most of the German she'd known as a child and she'd been careful about never relearning it. During the War, it had been a form of self-defence: if you didn't know any German words, no one could say you were German, could they? No one could even *think* you had anything to do with the enemy. Still, she knew what the words in the dream meant. She remembered the voice clearly. A girl's voice saying: *Deck deine Augen.* Cover your eyes, that meant. Each time she heard it the phrase went to her heart and settled there. *Cover your eyes*, the voice from far away always said to her. *Zähl bis hundert.* Count to a hundred. In the dream, she thought, we were playing hide-and-seek.

We'd had a cup of tea together in the sitting room and I did try to be as friendly as I could. I couldn't

127

say I liked Luke any better than I had the first time we'd met. There was something about him that made me feel on edge in some way: uncomfortable. I suppose he couldn't help how he looked (as though the rest of the world was somehow failing to meet his expectations) but his voice and manner made it worse. He seemed impatient at being kept waiting and obviously would have rather Rowena was the one showing him round. Well, I thought, that makes two of us. He drank his tea quite quickly, I noticed, so I thought, okay, you've made it clear you don't want to sit and chit-chat with the hired help, so I'll offer to speed things up.

'Rowena just texted me,' I said. 'She's asked me to show you round, if you don't mind.'

'Would you? Really? Only it'd be a tremendous help to me. I'm in a bit of a rush.'

'Okay, that's fine. We can start whenever you're ready.'

He stood up. 'That's great.'

'I'm happy to take you round, of course, but I've only been here a very short time so I don't know much of the history of the house or anything.'

'That's no problem. Tell me about yourself instead. Rowena told me you were a journalist. Hadn't you written something about Mrs Conway?'

It sounded funny, hearing Eva called that. Did I want to tell him about myself? He was at least being polite, asking me questions about myself. I said, 'I used to work at a fashion magazine, but

I was only an editorial assistant. I've left there now.'

Would he want to know why? I was already framing a reply when he said, 'Do you come from round here?'

'I'm from Northampton.'

'Do you get to go back very often?'

'Not that much, any more. Actually, my mother died quite recently and my dad lives in New Zealand.'

We were already walking around, and although he'd seemed preoccupied with what he was looking at and appeared not to be paying attention to what I was saying, he stopped when I said that and turned to look at me. 'I'm sorry to hear that,' he said and for a moment his light brown eyes looked kinder in the long, rather forbidding face.

We moved on to the next room and I was glad he didn't ask me any other questions. He was busy now examining everything. Tops of doors. Corners of floors where they met the walls. I must have seemed a bit bemused because he said: 'I've got some experience of looking at property. You'd be amazed how few people notice things like the slant of a floor. The fact that door frames aren't straight. That sort of stuff.'

'Are you a surveyor or something?'

'Used to be. Run a property development company now.'

What I said next came out before I could think

about what I was saying. 'Are you going to develop Salix House?'

'I certainly am, if I buy it. I reckon it'd make a really interesting and unusual small hotel and spa. Or a really wonderful private house. I can see all sorts of possibilities. What do you think?'

I couldn't tell him what I thought. I said, 'I'm sorry. I shouldn't have asked you in the first place. It's not my business.'

He smiled at me and said, 'Shall we go upstairs now? I'm sorry if you don't approve but I fell in love with this place the moment I saw it. I intend to improve it, you know. I'm not a vandal. Also, please call me Luke.'

'Right. I'm Megan.' I shut up after that. We went from room to room, speaking very little. It felt rather personal, showing him the bedrooms. I'd never been in some of them myself. Eva's was decorated in shades of olive and rose. Her mirror was hung with so many scarves and necklaces that you couldn't see the glass. Rowena and Conor's room was mostly cream and grey with touches of dark red. Luckily my own room was tidy. When we'd been round every room on the first floor, he started down the corridor towards the stairs leading up to the dress room. Of course, I told myself. He's got to see that too. There's nowhere in this house that's out of bounds.

I knew that the cupboards were full of Eva's dresses. She'd brought me up here the first time I came to see her and shown me some of them, taking the hangers carefully off their rails, hooking some on to the open doors and draping others over the chaise longue which stood against one wall. A long mirror on a stand near the door had been covered with a sheet then and was still covered, I noticed. I sat down on the chaise longue and waited as Luke walked about, thinking that for someone in as much of a rush as he'd said he was, he was taking his time.

'I should go back down,' I said. 'The girls'll be wondering what's happened to me.'

'Okay, I'm sorry. Let's go. I've seen what I needed to see.'

He went out first. On his way out, he must have caught his foot on the edge of the dustsheet covering the mirror and it slid down to the floor.

'Let me fix that,' he said.

'It's fine. I'll do it. You go down,' I told him. I'd already picked up the thick, chilly sheet in my arms and I turned away from him, ready to drape it over the mirror again. What must have been his reflection, as he left the room, moved across the glass and I rushed to cover it. I had the sensation of muffling something with the cloth. That's ridiculous, I told myself as I followed him out of the room, making sure to turn off the light. I don't know what made me look behind me, but it seemed, as I glanced over my shoulder, that the mirror and the sheet flung over it were glowing a little in the dark, as if the tall, white-draped rectangle was itself a source of light. *You're off your*

131

rocker, I told myself, but all the way downstairs, I felt unsettled. Scared. *Pull yourself together*, I told myself. *What you're thinking is impossible. Completely ridiculous.* By the time I got to the hall, I'd almost convinced myself that what I'd really seen was light from the corridor shining on the dustsheet. But I didn't seem able to shake the feeling that I'd been stifling or somehow silencing something when I placed the dustsheet over the glass. It was as though there was energy there, some kind of life or movement in the mirror, and the sheet was there to hide it; to cover something up.

'Here we are,' said Conor as they drove through the gates and up to the front door of Salix House. The eagles perched on the gateposts were wreathed in mist but it seemed to Eva that their stone eyes were following the car as it passed, spreading their wings to protect her. Eva blinked away tears. How was she going to leave this place when coming home to it was such a solace? She opened the passenger door and stepped out into the chilly, damp air of an early evening which seemed like the middle of the night.

'Mummy! Daddy! Granny!' The girls were on the doorstep, and behind them Eva could see Megan, holding the door open.

Once she was out of the car, Rowena didn't draw breath, letting out a stream of words that lasted all the way into the house. 'Gosh, girls, go inside at once. It's freezing. Hello Megan. I'm exhausted.

Are you okay? Was Luke Fielden all right? I'm sorry to land that on you, but the traffic was ridiculous.'

'It's all fine. Don't worry. Come in and have something to eat. It's waiting in the kitchen, all you need to do is warm it up. I'll go and get the girls into their night things and we'll come down.' Megan turned to Dee and Bridie. 'You'll get a slice each of Phyllis's apple pie if you're really quick in the bath.'

Megan went upstairs with the children. Eva wondered if she could plead tiredness and go off upstairs too. But she'd slept in the car and Rowena and Conor would realize that she was trying to avoid a post-mortem on the London house. Better face it all over the kitchen table.

Rowena warmed the soup. Conor got the baked potatoes out of the oven and poured the dressing on the salad. They were speaking to one another as they prepared the meal, but Eva tried to pretend that she was somewhere far away.

There was something about coming home late to Salix House, heating up a meal prepared long before, and sitting round the kitchen table which reminded her of the days when she and Antoine lived here by themselves. Rowena hadn't been born then, she thought. We used to sit in here when we were working late on a collection, or a photo shoot. There were times when the kitchen table was the only place in the house where you could put something down. Every other surface was covered in lengths of fabric, bits of paper, pins, drawings, Antoine's photographic equipment. Boxes full of buttons, cards with lace wound round them, feathers, sequins and ribbons spread themselves into every room in the house.

Antoine had been dead for years but there wasn't a day when Eva didn't ask herself if she hadn't made a terrible mistake, investing her love in someone who couldn't love her with an equal passion.

1965

She'd never been very good at falling in love. Perhaps, she used to tell herself, it was her early childhood, the way she'd been wrenched away from everything she knew, which made her so hard to please. She loved some of her friends, and had slept with several men, but she hadn't experienced true sexual love. It was obviously possible to exist without it but somewhere, buried so deep within her that she could go for a long time without even thinking about it, was the awareness of *something*: lost, missing for years but there, at the very limits of her consciousness, like an underground lake: love, waiting to rise up from where it had been lying for as long as she could remember.

When it happened, Eva wasn't ready for it. She was thirty-one. Surely that was a bit late for it to appear for the first time? It hasn't happened up till now, she reasoned, so that's likely to be that. I'm on the shelf. She wasn't even very upset at this thought. She had a career, a reputation, a following and the Conway look was being imitated.

Antoine Bragonard wasn't world-famous when she met him. They spoke about him on the fashion grapevine, but he and Eva had never managed to be in the same place at the same time. Then, one day, there he was, commissioned to take the photos for a spread in *Harper's Bazaar* which included a Conway dress.

He was pale, with dark hair and a long, rather Roman nose. Someone once remarked unkindly that he looked like a bird of prey. 'If they ever make a film of Edgar Allen Poe's poem, you know, the one about the raven knocking on the chamber door, Antoine would be perfect. Even his hair looks like feathers.'

That, Eva thought, was jealousy. The man who spoke in these terms was almost bald and was clearly envious, she decided, of Antoine's thick, dark, shiny hair. He wore it cut short. He dressed in black trousers and white shirts, always. While she was married to him, Eva tried to persuade him into colours, patterns, something other than his uniform, but he was stubborn. In the end, she settled for varieties of fabric: shirts in linen, cotton, silk and soft wool; trousers in corduroy, serge, twill, denim, anything she could think of. The style never changed. You wouldn't complain that a tiger looked the same every day. The creature was simply, most beautifully, itself. That was true of Antoine. The way he looked pleased Eva in ways she didn't quite understand. When they first met she found herself drawn to him, attracted by his looks and his charm, but perhaps, she thought, he isn't into women at all. It didn't take long for the two of them to discover that they liked one another. He understood what she was doing with the clothes she made. He knew how to arrange the models so as to bring out the theatrical element in Eva's designs. The greatest part, Eva often thought, of their relationship was that: they understood one another. Eva never had to interfere. During the time they worked together, she saw, over and over again, the care that Antoine took to light a garment, pose a model in ways that took your breath away. The photographs appeared everywhere. Antoine became better and better known and editors demanded more and more of his time, but he always stopped what he was doing to come and take photographs of the latest Conway collection whenever Eva said she wanted him.

'Of course she comes first,' he said in an interview in the *Observer*. 'Yves Saint Laurent and Chanel are who they are, and of course I'm honoured to work with them both, but Eva Conway is my dearest friend.'

The first time Antoine kissed her, they were clearing up after a catwalk show. The models had left, it was empty backstage and most of the clothes had been packed away. Eva was looking round the cavernous dressing-room, gathering together hairclips and fallen powder puffs and a couple of bras

. . . how could you leave your bra behind? She bent down to pick up a pink affair which was mostly lace and as she got up again, Antoine's arms were round her and before she knew what was happening, he was kissing her. She felt as though she'd been asleep and had suddenly woken up. She allowed herself to be kissed and then she moved to bring herself closer to him, kissing him back, wanting to absorb him into herself, wanting to be sheltered, wanting the kiss not to end.

'Come back with me,' Antoine whispered in her ear, kissed her neck. 'Come back to my place.'

'Yes,' Eva said. 'Yes, I will.'

She hardly noticed her surroundings; was only dimly aware of white walls with huge photographic enlargements on them. They went straight into his bedroom, and Eva, dizzy with longing, felt herself pushed back on the bed. She raised her arms and pulled Antoine to her. 'Wait,' he said and undressed quickly. She had a glimpse of his smooth chest and white skin and closed her eyes as he removed her clothes, carefully, tenderly. He said, 'I want us to be naked. I want to see you . . . see how lovely you are.'

Eva said nothing in reply. They made love for what seemed to her at the same time an eternity of almost agonizing pleasure and something that was over far too soon, and afterwards, when Antoine was already asleep, Eva lay awake for a long time wondering why she suddenly felt a little sad. I'm imagining it, she told herself. There was nothing in anything

Antoine did or said that was not exactly what I wanted, needed to hear. Still, she had the idea, which she couldn't shake however much she tried to, that she was the more passionate one; the one who lost herself in sensation; who forgot everything; who felt herself overcome with emotion, and she was uncertain about the strength of Antoine's feelings. In any case, by the time they woke up together next day, Eva was lost. She loved him. Even if he was not in love with her, she wouldn't mind. What did they say? That there was always someone who loved and someone who was loved? She would be the one who loved. She felt safe with him. Protected. Maybe she'd even tell him her whole story one day – talk about the things she'd never confessed before. Would he forgive her? And if he forgave her, was there a chance that she'd forgive herself?

Everyone in the fashion world assumed they were an item. Eva did nothing to contradict the gossip, because she revelled in it. Antoine, too, didn't seem to mind his name being linked with hers in the papers or in Jennifer's Diary in the *Tatler*. They did everything together: ate, worked, travelled, so that when he suggested that they live together, Eva was overjoyed. She'd been living in a small flat in Chelsea, which was slowly filling up with her possessions.

'It's like a basin with the tap left running, Eva,' Antoine said. 'One day you'll get back from somewhere and find stuff seeping out under the front door. Let's get somewhere bigger? Together. We can live together . . . I want to be with you, Eva.'

For a moment, Eva was speechless. He was serious. He wanted to live with her so that must mean . . . She couldn't help smiling. She hadn't ever been so happy before, but she said as calmly as she could, 'Okay. That would be . . . it would wonderful. And we'll have fun, won't we? Decorating it? Making it our home?'

They found a large flat in a quiet street off one of the less grand squares near South Kensington. Doing it up turned out to be a series of small battles. Antoine liked everything plain; and preferably in neutral colours. Eva was the exact opposite, but she only resisted his wishes in a mild way.

It became clear, as they decorated and prepared the flat, that they weren't going to be sharing a bedroom. They ordered two beds that were delivered to two separate bedrooms. Since that first time, in Antoine's flat, they'd made love on several occasions, but if Eva were honest, not as often as she'd have wanted. Kisses, caresses, hands held and looks exchanged across a room . . . things that Eva thought would lead to other things, somehow didn't. Or, she corrected herself, didn't very often lead to them. She'd begun to think (and she chided herself for this thought), that when they made love, Antoine was doing it to please her, to make up to her for something. She interrogated herself for hours: what am I doing wrong? Why isn't he keener? Is it me? Should I seduce him more often? How? She had no idea. With other men, she'd never been the one who took the initiative. She thought he ought to want her as much as she wanted him, and he didn't . . . not as far as she could see. She needed to make matters clear between them before they began to live together.

'We've got to talk, Antoine,' she told him. 'We've got things to discuss.' She'd chosen a time she thought was perfect: they'd eaten well and were on the sofa. Eva was sitting up with Antoine's head on her lap.

'I'm too full. Can't discuss anything now.' And then, contradicting himself just as Eva was about to speak. 'What sort of thing do you mean?'

'Sleeping arrangements. Stuff like that.'

Antoine half turned and reaching up, pulled Eva down to him and kissed her on the mouth. Then he lay back again and said: 'Oh, sweetheart. You know I love you, don't you? I just can't . . . I like to sleep on my own. Is that awful of me? I hate the thought of someone—'

'You don't like anyone seeing you when you're less than perfectly turned out. You don't want to be caught snoring. I know. I'm a bit like that myself.'

She didn't add: *Though I'd change in a moment if you said you wanted me to. In an eyeblink . . .* though that was the truth.

'You don't mind, do you? Truly, Eva?'

'No, it's okay. I'll live with it. We can visit each other's bedrooms, can't we?'

'Course we can. All the time.'

That wasn't how it turned out, in the end. At

140

the beginning, when they first started living together, it was true that they made love often enough for Eva not to think there was anything unusual in their relationship. But no one told you what was normal. No one discussed such things frankly and Eva had told herself right from the start that she was the one who loved more. She was the giver and Antoine the taker. What do I have to complain about, Eva used to ask herself as she watched Antoine leaving her bedroom and closing the door behind him. Many women would be only too glad to be left to sleep on their own. No snoring, no funny smells, the whole bed to spread out in. She usually managed to cheer herself up in the end, because Antoine was easy to live with, as long as she didn't make too many demands on him. Eva convinced herself that she was as happy as she could possibly be. He loves me, she told herself. In his own way. As much as he can. Till now, there hasn't been anyone else who's loved me even a little. She would lie on her back staring up at the ceiling, telling herself that everything was okay. Everything was blissful and fine.

'Ma. Ma, you're miles away. I'm going to ask Megan if she'll take you to some of the flats I want you to see while the girls are in school. One day during the week after half term? Or maybe a couple of days. Conor can do the pick-up from school. I would like to see all this settled. I'd go with you but I can't keep taking the day off as I did today.'

'That's fine,' said Eva, feeling pleased at the idea of looking at flats with Megan and also instantly guilty. How disloyal of her, to prefer the idea of being with someone who wasn't her daughter! 'Sorry . . . I was thinking. I'm very happy to go with Megan.'

This, Eva thought is the reverse of being in gaol. She envisaged the days going by, crossed off a calendar one by one, not while waiting to be released but exactly the opposite of that. She imagined the time sliding past, going more and more quickly towards something she dreaded: the last day at Salix House. She played and replayed a scene of them leaving. Everything she owned would be taken from here; sent to a sale room, or an auction or the tall skinny house in London and she'd be left with nothing. She'd step into a car. She could see herself with a couple of small suitcases which, oddly, looked just like the brown leather valise – Mama always used the French word – that she'd brought to England as a little girl. We'll drive down past the salix trees and it'll probably be late spring and the pretty whitish pointed leaves will be trembling on every branch and twig, and we'll go past the eagles on the gatepost for the last time and I'll look back and won't be able to see the house for tears. Every time she thought about that day, and she'd been thinking about it a lot, Eva felt physically ill.

The girls came down in their dressing gowns to say goodnight.

'When can we see the London house?' Dee said.

'We'll all go at half term,' Conor replied. 'Come and give me a kiss, now.'

Bridie went to sit on Rowena's lap. 'Have you got more pictures?'

'I'll show you tomorrow,' Rowena kissed the top of her head. 'They're on my phone which is in my bag and I don't want to start explaining what everything is now. You go up with Megan and get to sleep. It's very late for you.'

'Will we be there in time for Christmas?'

'I doubt it very much,' said Rowena. 'We still have to sell this house. There's only Luke Fielden who seems keen at the moment, but it's still on the market and we're advertising it abroad now too, so there may be other takers. Also, we have to wait till the owners of the London house have found somewhere they like. It might take ages. Though I hope it doesn't drag on for months. It's so wearing.'

Wearing, Eva thought. That's exactly right. That's what I feel: worn. Worn out, too. It's no wonder that the old dreams are coming back. All the old . . . what could she call them? Visions, perhaps. She'd known, ever since she was seven years old, that Angelika came when things were bad: when she was in trouble, or unhappy and when she did come, it wasn't the sight of her so much as the *idea* that she might swim up through the silver at the back of the mirror and be visible, exactly as she used to be long ago: that was what made Eva cold with horror. That was what had led to a life-time of making sure that every mirror she was likely to see was covered up, or else hung in such a way as to make it impossible for her to look into it. When Eva was relaxed and happy, Angelika hid away. She was always there – how could she not be? – but when things were going well Eva knew ways of hiding from her; ways of keeping her at bay.

'If you don't mind,' she said now, standing up, 'I'll skip coffee and go up to my room. I'm a bit tired.'

'But it's early, Granny!' Dee said. 'We're still up. You can't go to bed before we do.'

'I'm not going to sleep yet,' Eva said. 'But I do want to have a nice long bath and perhaps read in bed for a while. Goodnight, everyone.'

The girls came to kiss her and she made her way upstairs. Eva wanted to be by herself. All alone. As alone, she told herself, as you can ever be when you know there's something which won't give up; which will never stop following you. When you know that there is someone who won't forgive you. Why should you be forgiven? What Eva had done was the worst thing and she didn't deserve to have sweet dreams. As she went up the stairs, the voices from the kitchen grew fainter and after she'd closed her bedroom door, she could no longer hear anything except the sound of her own breathing.

CHAPTER 10

Yesterday, I'd gone to fetch the girls from school for half term. There was tons of stuff to bring home: left over Hallowe'en cut-out bats and pumpkins that had been up on the classroom wall, even though Hallowe'en was still to come and would fall during half term. Bridie insisted they must be put up in their room for the actual day even though they were a bit curly at the edges. Dee had all her stories in a big folder. I'd brought along a big carrier bag to put everything into and it was overflowing. Tom Shoreley came into the classroom as we were about to leave.

'Let me help you take that to the car,' he said.

'We can take it,' said Dee. 'I can hold one handle and Bridie can hold the other.'

'Okay, but don't rush. We'll see you out there. I want a word with Megan anyway.'

The girls tottered out carrying the bag and Tom and I followed them. He'd told them not to rush but they seemed to speed up, or else he was hanging back and I slowed my step to keep pace with his.

'Megan, I wanted to ask you . . .' He stopped in the corridor and turned to face me. The girls were at the door that led to the playground and had turned back to look at us. 'Are you coming?'

'Go on out to the playground and wait for us there,' Tom said. I was glad he'd taken charge because I was feeling confused. I didn't know why, but I definitely wanted to catch up with the girls and get out of school as quickly as I could.

'I wanted to ask you out for a meal sometime,' Tom said, looking and sounding casual though he was actually blushing as he spoke. 'The Jewel in the Crown is good if you like Indian. Are you free tomorrow night?'

I don't know how long it was before I answered but I must have gone through all the reasons to say no in my head in a matter of seconds. Mostly they boiled down to one. It was too soon. Was I ready for a date with someone else? Then I said, 'Thanks, that'd be good. I haven't had an Indian meal since I came to work here.'

'Great!' He looked relieved. I could see he was wondering about the logistics of picking me up so I took pity on him. 'Shall I meet you there? You can text me directions. You've got my number, haven't you?'

'Yes, it's on the class contacts list,' he said. Then he laughed. 'I would come and pick you up but—' he nodded briefly in Dee's direction – It might be better to meet there, I agree.'

Dee had sometimes asked me about how I liked

146

Mr Shoreley and did I think he'd be a good boyfriend but I was so convincingly uninterested that she soon got bored.

We'd arrived at the car by now. I opened the boot and the girls put the carrier bag into it. Most of the contents spilled out.

'Never mind,' I said. 'We'll pick it up when we get home. Say goodbye to Mr Shoreley.'

'Bye, Mr Shoreley,' they both called out. I got into my seat and said, 'Bye, Tom,' out of the window. He waved at us as we left. We were only about a minute away from the school when Dee said, 'You called him Tom, Megan. Does that mean you like him?'

'Yes, of course I like him. Why not? Don't you?'

'Not in *that way*,' Dee said.

'What way?' Bridie asked.

'In a boyfriend kind of way.'

'Does Megan like him in a boyfriend kind of way?' Bridie wanted to know.

'Do you, Megan?' Dee wasn't going to leave it alone. I refused to rise to the bait. 'No,' I said. 'Of course I don't. He's your teacher and a very nice man. That's all.'

The girls' questioning subsided after that and they chatted about the coming week the rest of the way home. Did I like him in a boyfriend kind of way? I had no idea. I might have considered him, I suppose, but I'm uncertain about everything. I've become unused to the whole idea of going out. It reminds me of Simon and I try not to think about him. That's hard. Suddenly, when I'm in the middle of something ordinary and boring, I'll remember him and in particular that last ghastly phone call and be filled with a kind of anguish which is three parts a combination of horrified guilt to one part remembered love.

Had I been right to accept Tom's invitation? An Indian meal is an Indian meal but there was a part of me which suspected that a Gobi Aloo Saag could be the beginning of something more intense and I wasn't sure if I was ready for that. But still, I couldn't help feeling pleased and found that I was looking forward to it. I realized that this meant that I was recovering from loving Simon a bit, but even so, I wasn't getting any better at forgetting what I'd done. Simon himself was shrinking, but my guilt seemed to be growing. If I let my mind stray to his phone call, I could almost physically feel a weight of unhappiness settle on me.

Tom was already there at the restaurant when I arrived. I hadn't exactly dressed up for the occasion but thought I ought to wear something a bit smarter than my normal jeans and trainers.

'Gosh, you look nice,' he said as I sat down, and I could see he meant it. Perhaps, I thought, I ought to wear high heels, tights, and a skirt more often.

'Thanks,' I said. I thought of adding: *So do you*, but that would've been a bit odd, seeing that he looked exactly like he always did at school.

I'd forgotten how many preliminaries there are, when you're first getting to know someone. When you're infatuated, besotted, then every little detail of their lives is fascinating, but when you're not, it's a bit dull. We went through the biographical stuff. Tom has a mother and father who live in Farnham. A brother who's a doctor in Glasgow. A sister-in-law who works for Specsavers. Two nieces.

'You're obviously good with children,' I said, dipping a bit of naan bread into the sauce. 'Is that why you became a teacher?'

'I suppose so. I just . . . I don't know. Wandered into it after uni. What about you?'

I pretended to be eating for a little longer than necessary. 'What about me?' I said smiling. I didn't want to sound hostile to Tom, but I really didn't want to talk about myself.

'You haven't always wanted to be a nanny, right?'

'No, it's just for now to help Rowena out. And only till they all go to London. I'd written an article about Eva for *lipstick*. I want to be a journalist. I've always wanted it. A features writer.' As I spoke, it occurred to me that I'd never said those words aloud to anyone. Simon took it for granted and no one else, apart maybe from a careers teacher at school, had ever asked me specifically. I felt sad, suddenly, wondering what I could do to get back to the career I really wanted.

He nodded. 'Did you like working for a fashion mag?'

'Yeah. It was great.'

He didn't say anything but the question hovered

over the table so I helped him out. I said, 'I liked it a lot but I had a fight with my boss. I couldn't stay after that.'

He didn't ask any more and we went on to other things. We talked about the sort of things that people on first dates talk about, mapping out what we agreed and disagreed about. Movies, music, books: we went through almost everything and found that we liked a lot of the same stuff. I tried to work out how I felt about this. If someone at a dating agency could see us, I told myself, they'd think: *These two have so much in common.* I looked across the table at Tom and thought about what it would be like to kiss him. Was he the one to make me forget about Simon? I wasn't sure. We'd got round to talking about the sale of Salix House and the move to London.

'I'm going to take Eva to look at some places next week,' I said. 'I hate the thought of her having to move at her age. She loves that house.'

'It's sad,' Tom said, 'but it must be hard to keep a place like that going. I went there last year, to pick up some things for the Harvest Festival.'

'Someone's interested in it. A property developer. He might turn it into a small hotel.'

'But it could be a nice hotel, couldn't it? And when Eva's gone does it make any difference who's got the place or what they do to it?'

'It does. I don't know why I think that, but I do. I'd like it to be someone's home, I suppose.'

Tom shook his head. 'You'll be going back to

get a job in London, will you? After they've all moved?' He looked a bit crestfallen. I said, 'I don't know what I'll do yet. I'm a bit . . . well, undecided about everything, to be honest.'

'You'll be here for the Nativity Play, won't you? I'm auditioning next week. It's on the third and fourth of December, just before the end of term.'

'I know! Dee and Bridie are so excited. They've told me about it. Are you in charge every year? Is it just you? Or do other teachers muck in as well?'

'It's a joint effort really. A kind of combination of Carol Concert and a play. All the songs in the play are set to the tune of well-known carols and I see to it that no one has too many words to learn.'

'Sounds great. And of course I'll be here. I can't imagine they'll be out of Salix House before Christmas, even if they get an offer tomorrow. And if Dee and Bridie get parts, I'll be the one helping them memorize stuff and going over it.'

'Dee's already lobbying for Mary but just between you and me, I think an angel is more likely. Don't tell her I said so, will you?'

I laughed. 'Your secret is safe with me.'

He was grinning. 'So there's still a bit of time?'

'Time?'

'For you to be living in Salix House.'

'Yes,' I said. It was hard not to smile. It was so obvious that what he'd meant was: *a bit of time for us to see each other*. I was flattered and pleased. The period before Simon was so far away from

151

me, so distant from everything I was now, that I'd forgotten how pleasant it was to be admired. How good it was to have someone sitting opposite me who actually fancied me and who even though he didn't make a great fuss about it, didn't try to hide it.

We walked together to the car park.

'Will you let me pick you up next time?' he said, and in the moment before I answered, he added: 'There will be a next time, won't there? I really would like to see you again, Megan.'

'Yes, of course,' I said. 'I'd like that too.' And as I said it, I found I meant it. I was standing by the door of my car and Tom was standing next to me, waiting to see me off.

'Megan,' he said and there was no hint of a question in his voice. It was trembling slightly and he put a hand on my left arm and turned me to face him. He didn't say a word but just moved his other hand on to my right shoulder and pulled me closer to him. He kissed me then. I'd been expecting it, but still it took me by surprise. At first, there was a second of uncertainty (*How do you do this?*) but then I kissed him back. I'd remembered how it went. My body hadn't forgotten anything. I wanted to shout out with joy. I thought: Simon hasn't succeeded in squashing me entirely. I stepped back a little and said, 'Goodnight, Tom. It was a lovely evening.' Then I got into my car, a bit trembly from the shock of being kissed, and also from the sudden feeling I had that here was someone I liked.

Someone I could like more, perhaps, given time. I waved at him out of the window as I left the car park and I could see him in my rear-view mirror, looking a bit stunned. I felt a little dazed myself.

I smiled as I drove home and asked myself whether it was possible that this evening was the beginning of a return to happiness; a small step along that path. I told myself: *maybe you're getting over Simon. This proves that you are,* but something else occurred to me almost at once: *You're not allowed to be happy.* That was the very next thought in my head: *good things can't happen to you.* A thin, sleety rain had started to fall and I turned on the windscreen wipers.

I heard my phone beeping in my handbag and I knew it was Tom. I checked his message before getting out of the car. *Can you send me your email address? Thanks! Tom x.*

Of course he'd be the sort to punctuate his messages even in a text. I sent him back my address and added my own kiss. It made me smile to think of how he'd interpret that little letter 'x'; how he'd fantasize about what it meant.

When I got into my bedroom, I texted Jay. *Kissed tonite by kids' teacher. Watcha think of that? Xxxx.*

A text arrived in seconds. *Urgent debrief needed. Am Skyping you in five. Jxx.*

I laughed and went to turn on my laptop.

Tom wrote to me on email every day. I didn't know how I felt about that, but I didn't see anything wrong with 'talking' to him. His messages were friendly and casual, with nothing in them that others couldn't have read but last night he asked me out again.

Fox and Hounds about 6? he wrote. *That's walking distance for you. We could eat there and you can have a glass or two of wine if you don't bring your car. I won't bother drinking. It'd be great to see you again. Tom xx.*

I agreed to meet him. Dee stared at me when she saw me. 'You're all dressed up, Megan,' she said. 'Are you going out? We're going to Mandy's house for trick or treating. Daddy's taking us. Granny's made us witches' hats and cloaks.'

'I'm only going down to the Fox and Hounds for a drink and a snack. And I'm not dressed up, either. Trousers and a shirt isn't dressed up.'

'It is if you wear jeans and a T-shirt every day. Who're you going with?'

'Don't be so nosey,' said Bridie, who'd joined in the conversation.

'Can't help it. I *am* nosey. Is it someone secret?'

'No, not really,' I replied. 'It's Mr Shoreley.'

Dee squeaked. 'Are you going to be his girl-friend? You are, aren't you?'

'No,' I said, quite truthfully. 'I'm not. We're going to have a drink and a sandwich. That's it.'

'Will you talk about me?' Bridie asked.

'Doubt it. But don't worry. He's already told me how well you're doing, so there's nothing to worry about, even if we do.'

'Will you tell us? What he says about us?' That was Dee.

'I shouldn't think he'll even mention you.'

I changed the subject after that and they went to do Hallowe'en-type preparations without any further references to boyfriends.

When I was talking to Tom, it was quite easy to forget stuff. I found that I was enjoying myself. At one point during the meal, he went to the Gents and I thought: so far this evening, you've not given Simon, or that telephone conversation, one single thought. That's got to be good. But I'd called them to mind now, hadn't I, so maybe the forgetting bit didn't really count.

'You look as though you're thinking of something sad,' Tom said, sliding back into the bench opposite me.

'No, I'm not,' I said. 'I was just thinking what a nice time I was having.'

'Right! Me too!' He had a way of looking at me as though my answer had really mattered. He never interrupted me when I was speaking and he listened better than anyone I'd ever met.

'You're a good listener,' I said. 'I expect it comes with being a teacher.'

'I dunno,' he grinned at me. 'Most of the time, I'm trying to get the kids to listen to me. But you did look sad.'

'I'm fine.'

'It's that boss you mentioned, isn't it?'

'How do you mean, Tom?'

'You told me you'd left *lipstick* because of a difference with your boss. But it was more than that, wasn't it?'

I was silent for a few moments because he went on: 'Sorry, sorry, it's none of my business,'

'It's okay. I don't mind talking about it,' I said, and didn't know if I was telling the truth. Surely talking about it would make me feel better? Talking about some of it, anyway. 'I had an affair with my boss. He was married. He dumped me. Very boring story.'

He reached out across the table and took my hand. 'I can see that you're still hurt by it. You're not over it, are you?'

'Yes, I am. Truly.'

He smiled. 'You're a liar. Not a terribly good one, either. I'm okay with the truth, if you felt like telling me.'

'Okay, then. Maybe not completely all right but getting there.' I smiled as brightly as I could. 'Can we talk about something else? I've got to be home soon, too. The girls'll have got back from their Hallowe'en party ages ago.'

'No problem,' he said. Before he let go of my hand, he squeezed it. 'Let me get the bill.'

'We're going to split it,' I said and before he could object I added, 'I'll only have meals and things with you if we do.'

Once we were in the car, he said, 'Next time you can come and have a meal at my house. I'm not a bad cook. No worries about the bill then.'

'Okay, that'd be good. I'll bring some wine, if it's not a school night.'

I could easily have walked back to Salix House. We were there within seconds. He didn't drive to the front door but stopped the car at the side of the house.

'Megan,' he said and I knew what was coming. I'd probably known it as I walked down to the Fox and Hounds. I was waiting for it. I'd sort of been waiting for it all evening. Tom put his hand across me and turned me to face him. Then he kissed me. It wasn't like the last time. I'd forgotten what being kissed seriously was like. I didn't think about whether I wanted to respond or what it meant, but somehow my body knew better than I did that it was okay. When we stopped kissing, I had my arms around him. I didn't remember doing that, reaching for him, but I must have done. I felt suddenly shy. I opened the car door.

'Must go, Tom. Thanks for the lift.' I tried to keep my voice casual but I could hear that it sounded a little wobbly.

'I'll email you, Megan.' Keeping hold of one of my hands, he bent to kiss it. 'See you,' he said and he was smiling.

His kiss stayed with me. I might be able to do this, I thought. I might be able to put Simon and everything else behind me. Tom might be able to make me forget what I'd done.

The hall was in darkness. I could hear the television in the drawing room but I couldn't face

Rowena and Conor and I was pretty sure Eva would have gone to her room. As I walked upstairs, I heard someone crying. Dee or Bridie, I thought, and walked quickly towards their room. I opened the door as quietly as I could and peeped in. Both girls were fast asleep, but I could still hear weeping, coming from somewhere quite far away. I stood for a moment on the landing, trying to decide if it was coming from the television. It must have been, I told myself. What else could it possibly be?

CHAPTER 11

There was no point in sulking but sulking was what Eva felt like doing. Rowena had arranged the day and Megan was only doing what she'd been told to do: taking her to look around some flats near the new London house. Things were moving too fast for comfort. Luke Fielden had confirmed that he was seriously thinking of making an offer. Rowena and Conor were pleased and relieved and she realized that she ought to be happy for her daughter and not feeling as though there was something in her throat that wouldn't be swallowed however hard she tried.

'Is anything the matter?' Megan asked and Eva blinked. Was it so obvious?

'I'm sorry,' she said. 'I'm trying to be sensible but the thought of everything moving so quickly . . . the thought of leaving Salix House. I don't know. I'm being difficult. That's what Rowena would say.'

'No, I know how much you love the house. It must be so . . . well.' Megan couldn't look directly at Eva, who was in the passenger seat beside her, but glanced to her left and smiled at her.

'It's nice to have someone who understands,' Eva said. 'Rowena is very keen on this Luke person. What do you think of him?'

'He's okay. I thought he was a bit stuck-up at first but I think that's only his manner. He told me the house would be . . . well, he said he wasn't a vandal.'

'That's something to be grateful for, I suppose,' said Eva. 'I don't so much mind the idea of its becoming a hotel. I rather like it in a way . . . it stops me from being jealous of one family, one set of people living there if I can imagine it simply as a setting for lots of stories unfolding under one roof. That's how I always think of hotels . . . collections of many small dramas happening at the same time.'

'Eva, do you mind if I ask you a question?' Megan said. She looked, Eva thought, embarrassed.

'No, of course not. Anything you like.'

'It's just that I've noticed something. About Salix House. I don't quite know how to say this. Sometimes, in some rooms, there's a kind of atmosphere. I can't really describe it.'

'Nothing's changed as far as I know. I haven't noticed anything different.'

Eva watched Megan closely as she negotiated a roundabout in silence. The short interval gave her time to wonder why she was lying. Of course she'd always been aware of a strangeness in the house, but the last thing in the world she had expected was for Megan to have noticed as well. Isn't it, she thought, all in my mind? And if it isn't, what does that mean? She shivered. Maybe Megan was referring to something entirely different. She was smiling at Eva now, saying, 'Do you feel like stopping for a coffee? There's rather a nice café along here.'

'I'd love to.'

They parked in a side street and made their way to a modest-looking place which Eva would never even have noticed.

'I stopped here on my way back from interviewing you,' Megan said once they'd sat down and ordered cappuccinos and Danish pastries. 'I was so happy. I rang . . . well, it doesn't matter now.'

Eva didn't pursue it. Megan must have rung her boss, the one she'd been in love with. The one who'd sacked her. Part of her wanted to go back to the conversation about the house but she said, 'I oughtn't perhaps to ask you, Megan, but are you feeling better these days? About everything?'

'You mean about Simon?' Megan made a face somewhere between a grimace and a smile and said, 'Well, it's hard to keep on being miserable, I suppose. And have the girls told you about Tom?'

'They have. Anyone would think they'd engineered the whole thing. Are you . . .'

'No, no, it's not like that, honestly. We really are just friends.' She blushed a little as she said that, and Eva didn't press her. She went on, 'Though

I think he'd like it to be . . . well, *more*. But I'm not sure . . .'

'You're not madly in love with him, then?' Eva bit into her pastry and sighed. 'It would be so restful to talk about you and yet I find myself so worried about Salix House and *problems* . . .' she made inverted speech marks with her fingers in the air, 'to do with settling me and making sure I'm provided for, etcetera etcetera. It's constantly on my mind. I'm sick to death of being difficult and yet, I can't seem to face leaving my home.'

'You'll feel better when we've found you somewhere you like. Maybe we'll see it today.'

Eva wrinkled her nose. 'Maybe. I hope so. But what did you mean when you spoke of the changed atmosphere in Salix House?'

Megan stirred the froth on her cappuccino. 'I don't know how to put it, to tell you the truth. Just I've sometimes felt that . . . well, it sounds mad but I've sometimes felt that I'm not alone in rooms where I know I'm by myself.'

Eva looked at her. 'What have you seen exactly?'

'Not seen. Not exactly. Sometimes I think that someone's just left a room I've come into. Sometimes it's cold . . . the downstairs loo is freezing. Well, I try not to go in there. I thought I saw . . .'

'What?'

'I was doing my face the day I brought you the magazine and burst into tears all over you. I saw someone in my make-up mirror.' Megan laughed.

162

'I *thought* I saw someone, of course nobody was actually there. How could they have been?'

Angelika, Eva told herself. *Angelika had been there.* A chill fell on her. *She can't be a figment of my imagination if Megan has seen her.* She said, 'I suppose you must have been feeling very emotional that day. I've long thought that what everyone calls ghosts are simply our guilty feelings made real in some way. They're real to us, in any case. But that can't be right because you haven't got anything to feel guilty about, I'm sure.'

But to Eva's surprise, Megan turned her face away, and began to cry.

'God, I'm sorry,' she said. 'I don't know what . . .'

Eva stared at her for a moment, not sure what to do, not knowing the right thing to say. She opened her handbag and took out a white cotton hankie.

'Here, Megan. Take this. Better than a tissue. Take it. Dry your eyes.'

Megan took the hankie. 'Oh, God, Eva . . . honestly, it's nothing. I'm truly sorry. It's just—'

'Don't speak. Calm down. Take your time. We're not in any hurry. I'll order some more coffee.'

'I'll go and wash my face.'

Megan fled to the Ladies and a nervous-looking waitress approached the table.

'Will the young lady be all right?' she asked.

'She'll be fine,' Eva said. 'Could we have two more cappuccinos, please?'

The woman hurried off and Eva waited. They'd

been talking about guilt. What on earth could Megan have done that a mere mention of it reduced her to tears? Eva had been living for so long with her own burden that she was used to it. The memories were painful but she'd learned how to divert them; how to turn her mind to something else. For many years her work had been a blessing. While she was absorbed in sketching the clothes and then overseeing the translation of the drawing from the paper image to a real garment, everything had been, if not fine, then at least manageable. Since her retirement and then Antoine's death, it had become harder and harder to find distractions. The births of Dee and Bridie had helped. Small children are labour-intensive and Eva, who'd always thought of herself as having been a bad mother, was surprised to find that at one remove, so to speak, everything about childcare she'd previously thought of as mind-numbingly boring was actually not as bad as she remembered.

'Sorry, Eva,' I said. I slid into my seat and part of me was hoping I could just forget about what had just happened but I had to say something. 'I don't know what happened to me. I thought I had it all . . . well. I didn't mean to burst into tears.'

I was trying to smile but I don't know how convincing I was. Eva said, 'You can tell me, you know. If it'll make you feel better.'

'Tell you what?'

'What is worrying you. Why you're feeling guilty.'

It came out before I could stop myself. 'I killed a baby.'

Eva was silent for a bit and I began to wish I'd never said a word. 'I didn't hear you properly. Did you say you'd killed a baby?'

'Yes.'

She said, 'Do you mean . . . forgive me, but do you mean you had an abortion? Is that what you're saying?'

I never thought of that. I realized with horror that I'd let my abortion slip so far to the back of my mind that I'd practically forgotten about it. I couldn't think of what to say at first, and sat in silence, unable to gather my thoughts together properly. I can't, I told myself. I can't tell Eva about it. Never. In the end, I said,

'No. No, I'm sorry. I should've made it clearer. I killed someone else's baby. Not my own.'

'How? How did it happen? You can't have meant to kill it, surely? An awful accident of some kind.' Eva looked as though someone had struck her across the face. 'Oh, my God. A hit-and-run accident.'

I shook my head. 'No, not that. On the night when Simon broke up with me, I rang him up. Much later. He was at home. I shouted at him. His wife, who was pregnant, must have heard some of it. She was in bed next to him. I meant her to hear. I wanted her to know about us, about me and Simon. I was yelling. It made me feel better to think of Simon and his wife having a blazing row after my call. It was awful of me, I know, but . . .'

Eva nodded. She didn't speak and I couldn't bear the silence so I just carried on talking. 'That day, when I brought you the magazine and you found me crying in my car, do you remember? I'd just had a phone call from him. He was completely drunk, but he told me his wife had lost the baby. They must have had a row after that phone call. A dreadful one. It was probably what led to a miscarriage. I know when I'm being rational that it maybe wasn't my fault, but in my heart, that's what it feels like. That I was responsible. So. That's it. I feel . . . I know it sounds melodramatic but I really do feel . . . that I'm a murderer. That this poor little baby's blood is on my hands.'

Eva put her hand out across the table and took mine, 'Oh, Megan!' she said, 'Poor, poor Megan, I'm so sorry. Oh, I know exactly how you must feel but your phone call, the row he had with his wife . . . you don't know that that had anything to do with the miscarriage. Millions of women have dreadful rows in pregnancy without such consequences, and miscarriages happen even to the happiest and most harmonious of couples. I think – I know you feel differently because you're emotionally involved and guilt in any case isn't a thing that you can get rid of by applying logic – but I think that it's a horrible coincidence and no more than that. You'll come to see that in time, I'm sure. You shouldn't blame yourself. You shouldn't. Simon is the one who's guilty of adultery. Guilty of letting down his wife. It's not your fault.'

I couldn't agree with her. I could have stepped back from the relationship and I didn't. I'd brought everything on myself.

I was silent for so long that Eva said, 'Have I said something to hurt you, Megan? I didn't mean to.'

'Oh, God, Eva, no . . . no. No one's ever been as nice to me as you. I feel . . . Well. And perhaps you're right. I should try and think of it like that. But it's hard when I feel that sometimes the baby is watching me. Talking to me. I've heard a baby crying. I feel that he's . . . don't think I'm mad, please, Eva. I think the baby's haunting me.'

Eva put both her hands over mine then, and squeezed them. 'Try not to torment yourself, Megan. And thank you for telling me. I won't say a word to anyone else, I promise.'

'It's good of you to listen. I feel better, just knowing that you know. And I'll think about what you've said. I'll try to believe it.'

'We should go now, Megan, if you're okay to drive. Rowena won't forgive me if we don't look at those places she wants us to see.'

I stood up. I made an effort to smile and tried to bring myself back to what we were meant to be doing. 'We might be about to find the flat of your dreams. Fingers crossed, eh?

We walked to where the car was parked on a

side street. Low clouds filled the sky, threatening rain.

'I don't think this is too bad, is it?' Megan whispered to Eva while the young estate agent made himself as scarce as it was possible to be in such a cramped flat. Poor Megan! She was trying to sound cheerful but Eva herself was dismayed. She was still getting over what they'd already seen. Someone had made an attempt to plant trees, but they were spindly and seemed out of place in a street where most houses kept their wheelie bins in the front garden. This block of flats (an ugly, sixties, box-like structure) had a purpose-built lean-to arrangement at the side of the building where all the bins were housed. Eva tried to imagine herself going out there in all weathers carrying binbags tied up at the top and recoiled from the thought. As they walked into the entrance (dirty concrete-like floor, with a bank of letter-boxes on the wall to the left of the door) her heart sank. I can't live here, she told herself and that was before the estate agent had even opened the door to the flat.

'You have to imagine it with some furniture in it,' Megan continued. Eva nodded as she took in the dun-coloured carpet, the walls which were once cream but were now scattered with rectangles of various sizes, where pictures had hung. In order to take her mind off the squareness of the room, the undersized and badly framed windows which gave way to a view of a scabby bit of lawn edged with weed-filled borders and roses that couldn't have been pruned in the last decade, she thought of other rooms she hadn't much liked. There was Agnes Conway's front room with the red swirly carpet and the brown armchairs sporting crocheted antimacassars. Her first flat, before she'd moved in with Antoine, was in Chelsea. 'World's End, really,' Antoine used to say. 'But you are what makes it Chelsea, darling!' Well, Eva thought, that was true in its way. It had been a horrid flat, and on the third floor, with no lift. The radiators had a mind of their own. The walls were dark red and you felt as though you were in a gothic horror film sometimes but still, she'd made it liveable. Artist friends had painted murals on the walls. She'd filled it with people and food and tables piled high with photographs and fabrics and it was a flat she now remembered with affection though at the time she'd moaned about it constantly.

'Yes,' she said now to Megan. 'That's partly true. If I'd been shown this flat when I was young then maybe I'd have had the energy and the incentive to work on it. Fix it up. Fill it with so many beautiful things that it might have been all right. But as it is,' she smiled, 'I don't have the energy. I don't feel like decorating. I want . . . well, what I really want is to stay in Salix House but if that's not going to be possible, then I want somewhere I can walk into and say: this is lovely.

I don't need to do anything except move my own things into it.'

'I see that,' Megan said. 'I know what you mean. This is a bit . . .'

'Ghastly,' said Eva. 'That's the word you're looking for.'

'You sound quite cheerful, Eva. Doesn't it depress you, seeing places like this?'

Megan was whispering to spare the feelings of the estate agent.

'It does make me feel oddly cheerful,' Eva said. 'I mean, it's so awful that I know Rowena wouldn't make me come and live in it.'

'Well, ladies,' said the estate agent. 'Have you had a good look round?'

For a moment, Eva considered saying something bland and non-committal. Then she changed her mind and decided to put the young man out of his misery.

'I'm afraid this isn't the kind of flat I'm looking for. Not at all. I'm sorry you've had to come and meet us here for nothing. Thanks very much for showing us round.'

'Well,' the young man looked at her in surprise. He was wearing a badge that said his name was Nigel Farron. 'We have a great many other flats on our books. You've only got to say what it is you are looking for and I'm sure I can find you at least half a dozen properties that will be just the thing—'

'Then that will have to be on another day, I'm afraid. We have to go now. We're meeting my

170

daughter for lunch. I'm sure she'll be in touch with your firm very soon.'

Their escape from the flat was very swift indeed. Before poor Nigel could regroup and say another word, Eva and Megan had made their way down in the (inadequate and faintly smelly) lift and out on to the street.

'I've rarely,' said Eva, waving at Nigel Farron as he pulled out in his car with almost indecent speed, 'been happier to be out of a flat in my life.'

'Yes, you're right. Of course you're right. It's like a student flat, really. I suppose I wasn't as shocked as you because lots of my friends in London live in places like this.'

'I know. I know. I'm being fussy. Other people don't have the luxury of such fussiness. They're short of cash, they're at the mercy of the landlords and so on. I will have the means to live in a much nicer place, once Salix House is sold.'

'Rowena says Luke Fielden's interested in it. He really does seem to want to buy it.'

And are you interested in Luke Fielden? Eva wondered, but did not say. The story she'd told in the café was horrifying. Poor thing. It was a lot to have to deal with. Eva could see that Megan was feeling a bit better now, but she knew from long experience how hard it was to get rid of guilt. However much you tried to push it to the furthest corners of your mind, it was still there. Look at me, she told herself. I've lived with it for more than seventy years. Poor Megan! Should I tell her what I did? Eva said nothing. The habit of silence had been too deeply ingrained in her and besides, the fact that someone else has done something terrible – or thinks she has – doesn't alter what you think about your own mistakes.

She said, 'Megan, I've had enough of standing around looking at flats. I told a lie about lunch and now we ought to go and make it true. Let's go and find somewhere nice to eat.'

'Do you have the energy to go and see another one?' Megan asked as they finished up their meal. 'This one is very close by, if you feel up to it.'

'I'm up to it,' Eva said, trying to sound as keen as she could. She was perfectly sure that this one would be no more suitable than the last but if you could lift your mind away from your own predicament: that of facing old age in a place you hated and that was nothing like the home you loved, then there was a kind of gruesome pleasure in seeing just how horrible a home could be. She said as much to Megan, who nodded, so they paid up and walked to the address they'd been given.

'At least there won't be an estate agent to deal with here,' Megan said. 'It's a Ms Clifford, apparently.'

'She'll be older than I am and the flat will smell of dog and there'll be dried-out pot plants everywhere. You'll see.' Eva tried to make light of it, but she could feel herself growing more and more anxious as they approached the front door. The house was Victorian and not very well maintained.

The paint on the front door was faded and scratched. You had to press one of six buttons on a silver intercom panel to get inside. The name *Clifford* didn't inspire confidence. It was written in scribbly pencil on a torn piece of paper which had then been stuck into the available space on the panel.

Eva was on the point of saying: *Let's leave it,* but Megan had already pressed the button and a tinny voice told them to take the lift up to the second floor as the door buzzed open. Eva didn't pay any attention to the lift beyond noting that it smelled revolting.

Ms Clifford turned out to be a blonde, wispy woman with a toddler clamped to her side. The child looked well cared for but was nevertheless whining loudly enough to make speaking difficult. This, Eva reflected, may turn out to be a blessing.

'So sorry about this,' said Ms Clifford. 'And do call me Betty. She's off nursery today. Don't know what can be wrong with her, but you go ahead and look at the place and I'll keep out of your way. That's always the best, isn't it?' She laughed as though she'd made an amusing remark, but Megan was smiling at her and saying yes, yes, looking around alone was always easier. Eva drifted towards the bedroom and let the two young women go on talking.

She didn't need a second opinion. Betty Clifford wasn't the best housekeeper in the world and the state of her bedroom depressed Eva more than she could say. It wasn't a question of money. If you had taste and knew how to clean things, you were well on the way to a perfectly decent house. Taste . . . that was the thing. Who decided what was good and what wasn't? Eva had no idea. She only knew that rayon curtains in a shade that was exactly what Antoine used to call 'mustard if you're feeling kind and shit if you're not', at windows that were far too small for the proportions of the room were not a good look. The paintwork was pink, which made everything worse. The room she'd just left was a combined sitting room/dining room. The kitchen was in an alcove that would be clearly visible if you were, say, watching the television. No. A thousand times no. Eva glanced into the bathroom and shuddered and closed the door firmly on a panorama of drying nappies strung out on a pulley above the bath. She breathed deeply so as not to lose control of herself and faint. In the sitting room, Betty and Megan were chatting. The child was still whining: a thin, droning sound like a disheartened bee.

'Thank you, Betty,' Eva said in the tone she sometimes used in the old days, when she was annoyed with any of her staff. 'I've seen what I need to see. We should be getting along now, Megan.'

'Oh. Right. I s'pose we should,' Megan said and followed Eva out of the flat.

Once they were safely in the car and on their way back to Salix House, Megan said, 'I know, I know. It was dreadful, right?'

'Worse than dreadful. Throat-cuttingly horrible. Oh, this whole thing is a nightmare, Megan. I don't know how it's going to be resolved.'

Eva steeled herself for some cliché, but Megan didn't say a word.

'Thank God you didn't say anything along the lines of: *you'll find the right place eventually*. I think I'd have screamed.'

'I nearly did say that. Glad I didn't now, as it turns out.' She smiled at Eva. 'But you know, you probably will. Find somewhere nice. In the end.'

'If this goes on I'll be dead before I do.'

Megan laughed as though this was a joke. She doesn't realize, Eva thought. Nobody realizes how hard this is for me.

'I'm serious,' she said. 'I sometimes think I'm more attached to my home than most other people because of . . . my history.'

'I know a bit about that,' Megan said, as the car joined what looked to Eva like an endless line of slow-moving traffic. 'I know you had to leave your home when you were very small. That must have been so awful. I find it very hard to imagine it.'

Eva looked down at her knees. 'It was. We had such a lovely home, when I was small. I may be making up most of my memories because I've had years to think about it, and it's quite likely that I'm embroidering or misremembering to suit myself. Things like the dark furniture in my parents' flat. The room I shared with my sister—' Eva's hand flew to her mouth. 'Oh my God.'

'What is it? What's wrong?' The traffic was crawling so slowly now that Megan was able to turn her head and speak directly to Eva. 'You're as white as a sheet. Are you ill?'

Eva shook her head. 'No, but I can't believe—'

'What?'

Eva brought her hands to her face and covered as much of it as she could. Megan was speaking and Eva didn't hear the words, only the sound of her voice, which seemed to come from a long way away. How could that be? She was there, right next to Eva in the car.

'What's wrong? Please, Eva, please tell me.' She paused and then continued as if a thought had just occurred to her. 'I shan't tell a soul about this if you don't want me to. Not a soul. I swear.'

'Oh no, you mustn't tell anyone. Promise me. Promise me that.'

'I do promise. I have promised.' Megan was smiling. 'What's wrong, Eva?'

Eva shook her head. 'I'm sorry. I don't know what got into me. Can we just forget it? Forget I ever spoke about my home. Please?'

'If you like,' Megan said. 'Of course.'

The traffic began to flow more freely and for a few minutes there was silence in the car. How did I do that? she wondered. How could I let that slip after more than seventy years? And why had it come out now, when she was with Megan? She wasn't family. Maybe, she thought, it's precisely because she's not so close that I said it.

176

'Eva?'

'Yes?'

'Are you going to tell me what happened?'

The traffic had thinned. A sleety rain began to fall and Eva stared out of the window at water racing down the pane in diagonal lines.

'If I tell you, you won't say anything to anyone. Not ever, do you swear?'

'I've sworn and promised already, Eva. You can tell me, you know. It's not as though you've committed a crime or anything.'

Eva laughed. 'I have though. You don't know—'

'Then tell me.'

Eva stared at her lap. 'I came to England in 1938 on the *Kindertransport*. I was adopted by Agnes Conway. You know that. Everyone does, I think. What no one knows because I've never breathed a word to anyone is that I didn't set out by myself. My sister was with me. Angelika. I find it hard to say her name because I haven't spoken it for decades. Angelika.'

Eva waited for Megan to exclaim, but she was gazing at the road and said nothing. She went on, not sure how much to tell. 'Angelika didn't come to England. She . . . she was left behind in Germany and then after the War, when Agnes started to look for my parents, they weren't to be found. You can probably guess what happened to them.'

'Why didn't Angelika come with you? What happened?'

'I left her behind. I got on the train to Holland without her and she stayed in Germany and . . .'

'By accident?' Megan turned her head briefly to look at Eva, who didn't answer at once. Then she said, 'I'm not sure. I can't be sure but I think not by accident. I think . . . well, I feel I ought to have told someone. Done something. As it was, she was left behind and I killed her. As good as killed her.'

'But you were only four! Four-year-olds can't be held responsible.'

'But it's not just that. I never told anyone, you see. Not when I was four, nor fourteen, nor twenty-four. I've just wiped Angelika and all memory of her as if she'd never existed. I knew I was guilty of leaving her there. I knew it in some way even then.'

'But that's even younger than Bridie is now! Surely you wouldn't blame Bridie for doing something like that?'

Eva nodded vehemently. 'I would. I certainly would. If Bridie left Dee in a place which she knew was dangerous, then yes, I'd blame her. I might decide not to punish her, but yes, she does know enough to know about danger and leaving her sister alone to face it. And I knew that. I knew we had to look after one another. My mother was always saying: *You've only got each other. Be good to your sister.* Things like that. And that's one kind of crime and another that's even worse is my not having mentioned Angelika's existence. Even if leaving her there was accidental, what do you call neglecting to mention you even had a sister for more than seventy years? Isn't that disgusting? Unnatural?'

'Eva, it was a terrible trauma for you, no wonder you tried to shut it out. And you've mentioned her now to me and nothing bad has happened. Maybe you even feel better. Why don't you just tell Rowena and everyone what happened? I don't think any the worse of you, I'm sure they won't.'

Eva shook her head. 'No. No I can't. I couldn't. Please don't try and make me . . . I'm so . . . I'm so ashamed!' The tears she'd been trying to hold back since she began to talk fell now and she brushed them away with her hands.

'God, Eva, I'm sorry. I shouldn't have said that. Forgive me. Of course you feel dreadful and I'm not going to say a word. If you can't bear the thought of telling anyone then of course you shouldn't.'

Eva nodded. As Megan spoke she'd been looking in her handbag for a tissue, having given her hankie to Megan earlier, and when she'd found it, she took it out and began to wipe her eyes.

'Let's forget that we spoke about this, Megan. All right?' She dabbed at her eyes and then reached into the bag again for her powder compact.

'Fine. I've forgotten already. Let's talk about Betty Clifford's bathroom instead. That'll cheer us up.'

Eva made a sound that was supposed to be a chuckle but she knew that Megan wasn't fooled for a second. I have to trust her. And I do.

Angelika, hidden for seventy years, had finally

risen to the surface. Angelika was always good at concealment. Eva would sometimes come into the room they shared and be unable to find something of hers; a toy, or a favourite doll. Once, Mitzi, her best companion, the doll who shared every secret, the one she always took to bed, disappeared for a week. The whole family looked for Mitzi all over the house. Angelika, Eva thought, told Mama that I'd left her in the café and we went back there the next day but she wasn't there. Of course she wasn't. She reappeared on Eva's bed one night and Mama said, 'Oh, look, here's Mitzi. You should have told me you'd found her! You know how we've been searching.'

Eva hadn't said a word. She stood next to the bed, amazed. I wasn't even four years old, she thought now. How could I have said what I knew: that Angelika must have hidden her out of spite and only brought her back after a very long time? I didn't have the vocabulary to express such thoughts. Thinking about it now made her feel sad and worse: angry on behalf of the small, power-less child that she'd been.

As they drove through the gates of Salix House, the eagles on the gateposts were black against the sky and Eva imagined them spreading their black wings and taking off, following the car, peering down at her with their yellow eyes. She shook her head. Don't be ridiculous, she told herself. They're made of stone. They can't move.

CHAPTER 12

'Granny, Granny!' Dee came running down the steps and threw her arms round Eva as she made her way to the front door. 'I'm an angel. I'm the Archangel. Isn't that wonderful? I'm so, *so*, excited!'

'Wonderful, darling,' said Eva, sounding happier than she had all day long. She'd managed to calm down after her confession to Megan and was beginning to feel that maybe it was possible for everything to return to how it was before she'd let Angelika's name slip. And now here was Dee, who was going to be an angel in the Nativity Play. Eva couldn't help but make a connection. She said, 'Am I allowed to make your costume?'

'I'll ask Mr Shoreley. Maybe they've already got an angel costume. Bridie's a shepherd boy. She gets to carry a lamb. Not a real lamb, but a toy. Freddie's got a really big furry lamb. It's going to be cool. We're having rehearsals every lunchtime and sometimes after school as well.'

Megan said, 'Come on, girls. Let Granny get her coat off. Isn't it nearly supper time?'

They went off together and Eva stood in the hall

and ran her hands through the silk flowers. She could hear the girls laughing in the kitchen. The girls . . . she'd taken them for granted. What would it be like to live in a flat all by herself? Where would the laughter come from then?

'Do you think Megan really likes Mr Shoreley?' Dee asked. Because Megan was going to be out till quite late, Eva had volunteered to take the girls to bed and read them a story before they went to sleep. The three of them were sitting on Bridie's bed, but Dee knew that if she raised an interesting topic of conversation, she bought herself a little more time. Bridie, who was usually half asleep by story time, perked up when she heard the question and said, 'I think she's going to marry Mr Shoreley.'

'Honestly, girls,' Eva said. 'You mustn't gossip. She hardly knows him.'

'Yes she does,' Bridie said. 'She sees him every day at school. And Mr Shoreley is kind and handsome and he really likes Megan. I know he does.'

'Well,' Eva said, 'we're not going to discuss this now because none of us knows what Megan thinks. I think we ought to read our story because it's getting very late.'

'Tell us about your wedding,' Dee said, in a last attempt to delay matters. 'Tell us about Grandpa Antoine.'

They'd never known Antoine except through her stories and Rowena's, which showed two very different sides to the man. Eva always spoke of how famous he was, and what wonderful photographs he took and how glamorous his life had been. Rowena told them about an ideal father, an indulgent man who'd taken her to the cinema, the theatre, out to meet interesting people in London. He'd bought her a kite and taught her to fly it. He'd been a good swimmer and taken her to the pool. He'd bought her pretty things every single time he came home from work: tiny little things, but still, every single time! That impressed Dee and Bridie more than anything because neither of them could imagine their own parents doing such a thing and neither could Eva. It required imagination. It meant that the parent, for at least a small part of the day, had to think about what would please his daughter and then make the effort to get it and remember to keep it safe. These little gifts were never expensive. Sometimes Antoine would bring a few coloured rubber bands from the office, or a little pad from the shop at the station, or a pencil with a pearlized finish to the wood. On other days, he'd find a miniature cake or a cheap necklace. If he'd forgotten during the day, he would grab a tube of Smarties at the station on the way home, even though Eva disapproved of chocolate. She sighed.

'Another time, perhaps. It's getting late now, let's read, girls,' she said. 'I can see Bridie's eyelids drooping.' They settled down on the bed, with Bridie under the duvet.

'She's fallen asleep,' Dee whispered a little later,

interrupting Eva's reading of an old favourite from when Rowena was a child called *Clever Polly and the Stupid Wolf*. 'You can sit on my bed now and chat some more.'

'Well,' said Eva, whispering so as not to wake Bridie. 'We can do that but it's time for you to go to sleep too, you know.'

Dee made grumbling noises, but in the end she lay down in her own bed and said, 'Okay. Will you stay a bit till I fall asleep?'

'A little while, and then I must go down. Night, night.'

She kissed Dee and went to sit on the small armchair near the window. Dee fell asleep almost at once, as Eva had known she would, but she went on sitting there, thinking about Antoine. With hindsight, marrying someone who could never love you as much as you loved them must always be counted a mistake. But I loved him so much, Eva thought. There's a time when you're first in love when you don't see any obstacles as being insurmountable. Like every other bride, Eva on her wedding day had believed that her devotion, their happiness together, would change him. It hadn't, of course it hadn't, but they *had* been happy part of the time, hadn't they?

Eva wondered how that particular calculation would come out. If she made a list of every single year, every month even, of their life together, how many months could she count as happy? I'll never do it, she told herself now. I'm scared of the result.

184

She stood up and went quietly out of the room, closing Dee's door behind her.

When I told Dee that I was going to have lunch with Tom, after the usual *Is he your boyfriend* nonsense, at which I sighed quite convincingly, she said, 'But after lunch. What'll you do the whole afternoon?'

'Depends.'

'On what?'

'The weather, for one. Maybe if it's nice we'll go for a walk.'

Right. We'd go for a delightful walk when the sky looked like corrugated iron and the wind was blowing a near gale. 'Or,' I added, 'we might watch a DVD.'

That seemed to satisfy her. As I outlined the possibilities to Dee, I realized that I'd known all along what we'd be doing. I'd even discussed it with Jay. She'd sent me an email yesterday which said:

FROM: jay2375@gmail.com
TO: meganp84@gmail.com
Subject: OOOH!
This is a Proper Grown-Up Underwear Situation. I don't like saying I told you so but I did tell you so. Listen to me, always. Have fun. Don't let things get too heavy.
Jxx

He'd invited me to his flat, so of course we'd end up in bed. I hadn't put up a fight about kissing him up to this point, and his emails had become increasingly affectionate. The fact was: I liked it when he kissed me. I'd accepted his invitation knowing exactly what was going to happen. I'll make it plain to him, I told myself, that I'm not in love with him. I won't pretend feelings I don't have.

He came to Salix House to pick me up. When we got to the flat he set about making spaghetti bolognese.

'Can I help?' I asked.

'You could pour yourself a glass of wine. I've got everything under control. Sauce is ready. Just a matter of putting the pasta on. You could put the cake on a plate if you like. I haven't got round to that. Afraid it's not homemade. Coffee and walnut.'

'Looks great,' I said. 'Do you want some wine?'

He shook his head.

'You're very good about doing without booze,' I added. 'I could have driven here and had apple juice or something and you could have had a drink.'

'I'm not bothered,' he said. 'I can take it or leave it.'

Over lunch, I drank more than I normally do. This wasn't because I was nervous, though I was, a bit. I was wondering how we'd negotiate the move into the bedroom. I didn't have to be back at Salix House for hours.

To be fair to Tom, he didn't grab me and haul me off the moment I'd scraped the last of the cake off my plate. We sat on the sofa to have our coffee. His flat was exactly what I'd expected. I hadn't seen the bedroom, but the rest of it was pleasant if unspectacular: not too untidy, but full of books, and with things he was marking and bits and bobs from school all over the floor near the bookcase. The kitchen was small but neat. The door to the bedroom was shut.

'Megan,' he whispered, once we were sitting together. He put his arm around me and we began kissing. Part of me wanted to say: *Let's go. Let's go now and get it over with because it's like a barrier between us at the moment. You can't think what to say to get me into bed.* My reactions to the way he was touching me, kissing me, encouraged him.

'Will you . . . can we?' he murmured and before I knew it, we were in the darkened bedroom and on the bed, and he put his arms around me and undid my bra and I went on kissing him and pulled off my jeans and my knickers and I helped him as much as I could. He was making incoherent sounds and nuzzling my neck and I pushed myself against him suddenly like someone slaking a thirst, wanting him, wanting the weight and the warmth of him, the caresses and the tender words. For whole long moments, I was nothing more than a body, responding. I didn't, I couldn't think about anything. Being like this, so close, so tangled up with someone again made me

187

feel as though I'd plunged into a whirlpool, but it was soon over.

'Oh, Megan,' he sighed. 'Darling Megan.'

I stroked his hair but I couldn't bring myself to say: *Darling Tom*, because I knew that what I was feeling wasn't love. Affection, the afterglow of pleasure, the softness in the limbs that happens after sex, yes, all of those, but not love. We lay there for a while, Tom's head on my shoulder. After a bit, I could tell he was asleep. His breathing was deep and steady, like a small engine beside me. The light was on in the living room and it threw deep shadows into the bedroom. I tried to make out details in the half-light but all I could see was some photos in a frame on a chest of drawers. And before I also fell into a doze, I had two thoughts. The first was: *I'm getting over you, Simon, aren't I? Well, aren't I?* And the second, disconcertingly, was, *I wonder if Luke Fielden will come and look at Salix House again?* I could understand the first but I had no idea why Luke Fielden should come into my mind at just that moment.

Eva looked at her watch. Nearly quarter to two in the morning. Something had woken her up . . . probably Megan coming in. She wondered whether to switch on the bedside light and read and decided against it. She'd been asleep and had woken again after a couple of hours: always a recipe for insomnia. She continued to lie in bed and tried to relax. The words of her long-dead adopted mother came suddenly into her head:

'Count backwards from a thousand,' Agnes Conway used to say when Eva was a girl. 'Or count sheep. That does work, you know. It wouldn't be the cliché it is if it didn't work at least some of the time.'

'But it's boring, Agnes,' the young Eva used to protest and the old Eva hadn't changed her opinion. Most of the time, she preferred to let her thoughts run free, wherever they might take her but because of her preoccupation with flats and leaving Salix House and estate agents that was what her mind was trying to return to tonight, and that wasn't restful. A parade of all the squalid rooms she'd seen last week appeared in her head, one after the other. The first flat that she and Megan had looked at had a carpet not unlike the one she remembered from her childhood home with Agnes. Eva turned over on to her back and stared at the ceiling. Most of the time she tried to avoid thinking about her childhood but now, because it made a change from thinking about hideous hovels in which she might live, she found herself remembering Agnes.

Why did she never mention my family? Eva wondered. We went through the War trying to pretend they didn't exist. Perhaps this was the advice given by the vicar, or Dr Crawford, or one of her friends. Eva was twelve years old when the subject came up seriously for the first time.

1946

Eva knew, as soon as she came back from school that day, that something different was about to happen. Agnes was waiting at the kitchen door and even before she'd offered her a drink and a slice of bread and margarine, she said, 'Hello, Eva dear. Would you mind coming into the sitting room for a few minutes? There's something we have to talk about.'

Eva's first thought was: what have I done wrong? She followed Agnes into the little-used room at the front of the house. The two of them generally sat in the warm kitchen, which had a sofa in it, and a table on which to do homework. The fire hadn't been lit for a long time and the sitting room felt chilly and unwelcoming at this time of day as the light was leaving the sky. It must have been autumn, because Eva remembered looking down at her legs and she was wearing woollen socks, darned many times over, and her winter school shoes, which were getting tight. Everything was rationed. There was a great deal of making do and mending in the Conway house and Agnes often said it was Eva's good fortune that she'd been put in the care of someone who'd been taught to darn so well that she could make socks last for years and years. Agnes was also good at undoing old jumpers and knitting them up again in different shapes, but nothing, Eva thought, could alter the fact that the colours were boring and sludgy. As she sat and waited for what Agnes was about to say, she began imagining a jumper knitted to match the autumn leaves: many shades merging into one another, melting into a rich arrangement of orange and brown and gold and with a touch of raspberry red to make the other colours sing. They sat down in the two chairs on either side of the unlit fire. Agnes said, 'We've hardly ever talked before about your family, Eva, and this is a hard thing to say to a child of your age, but I feel that I must.'

'I'm twelve, Mother,' Eva said. 'I'm not a little girl any more.'

'Well, no, I know you aren't, but still. It's hard to say this. When I first took you in, you were very ill. Do you remember? You lay in the bed upstairs and didn't speak for almost a month. You were running a high temperature and cried, sometimes as if your heart was breaking.'

I should help her, Eva thought but instead replied with, 'I don't remember that very well. But you told me what happened. How I came to be in your house. In the bed upstairs.'

'I also told you . . . not then exactly, but later, after. After you started to speak English and when I was sure that you understood, that when the War was over, we'd maybe be able to trace your family. Find out what happened to them.' Eva nodded. Part of her wanted to tell Agnes the truth, but how could she? How could she say: *I never really believed you. I knew I was alone and that everyone I had, everyone who was my family before was gone for ever. I've always felt alone.* Agnes Conway took me in and did her best. It's not her fault she can't ever be my real mother. Eva could see that Agnes was trying to hold back the tears. She was blinking fast and twisting her hands together. She lowered her glance and spoke quietly.

'I've made various enquiries. With the Red Cross and other agencies. It doesn't matter who, really, but I've been in touch with everyone, you may be sure of that. I'm so sorry, dear. I truly am. The thing is—'

'You couldn't trace them. It's all right. I've never expected them to come and find me. Not really.'

'They're dead, Eva. I'm so, so sorry.'

Eva saw tears slowly falling from the corners of Agnes's eyes and she sprang up to comfort her. 'Don't cry, Mother! Please. I never thought they were alive. Really I didn't. Please don't cry.'

'No, of course not. How selfish of me. Fancy my crying when you're the one who should be consoled. Perhaps we should go to church tomorrow and say some prayers for their souls? Do you think we should?'

No, Eva said to herself. The prayers are for you to feel better, not for me. She had never been able to believe in a god, but saying that would make everything more difficult, so in the end, she muttered, 'I don't really mind. If you think that's a good idea.'

'Wouldn't you like a slice of bread and cup of

tea?' Agnes sounded relieved to be talking about normal, everyday things again. She was nervous about any conversation which might lead to strong feelings being expressed.

'No, thank you. I'm all right.'

Agnes smiled, relieved to be reassured. 'I expect you want to be alone, dear. I quite understand.'

Eva reflected on this as she made her way to her bedroom. Alone. That's what I am, really, she told herself, as she sat down on the bed and let her satchel fall to the floor at her feet. Completely alone now. Mama and Papa. She had trained herself never to think about them, but now, she tried as hard as she could to summon all her memories of them. So little. There was hardly anything to grasp, hardly anything to cling to. All she could think about was Angelika.

When Tom brought me home, it was past one o'clock.

'Good morning, darling Megan,' he said and he kissed me before I left the car. We'd slept a bit, during the afternoon and early evening, and also broke off for a bit to eat some revolting takeaway Chinese food but mostly we'd stayed in the bedroom. We'd made love several times and, to be fair to Tom, it got better and better. I felt, when I left, too tired to weigh up my emotions, and now, creeping through the hall, I hoped more than anything that Eva was safely in bed and not rambling round the house. I was sure anyone who saw me would guess at once where I'd been for the past few hours. I wouldn't have much time to recover before Dee and Bridie came to wake me up.

I showered and got into bed, but in spite of being exhausted, I didn't fall asleep at once. I could have Skyped Jay but didn't feel up to an interrogation. How was this going to work? I'd have to call myself Tom's girlfriend now, wouldn't I? If Dee asked me, I'd be unable to deny it. What was wrong with having a nice man like Tom for a boyfriend? The sex was good. Tom was eager and athletic, yet tender too. It ought to have been mindblowing. What was I telling myself? That it wasn't good enough? That there was something missing? I felt suddenly unaccountably sad. Simon. It wasn't the way it used to be with Simon. I'd explained, or tried to explain, to Tom exactly what my feelings for him were. It's a bit hard to do, when the person you're talking to keeps on kissing you and nibbling your neck. At one point I had to push him away and say: 'Listen to me, Tom, it's important,' but he'd just kissed me again and said, 'It's not as important as you think.' I wiped away the tears that had suddenly come into my eyes. Go to sleep, I told myself. You're only weepy because you're so tired. Don't analyse everything so much.

And here, now, I'm no nearer to being asleep, she thought. Eva knew that any insomnia she might suffer from was made much worse by thinking about the past. The times in her life when she'd been happy and fulfilled made her dissatisfied with how empty her life was nowadays. I used, she thought, to be successful, famous, rich and now? Well, she was still comfortable enough, financially speaking, but still, not as rich as she might have been if she'd managed her affairs a little more astutely. Too late to fret about that now, but perhaps leaving her work altogether after the arrangement she'd come to with Antoine wasn't the most sensible thing to do. Now, she was all but forgotten. Articles like Megan's in *lipstick* created an illusion that there were still people out there who cared about her, but if she was well known it was as a kind of historical figure, not as someone who carried any weight today.

Eva sighed. I might as well get up now, she thought, instead of lying around feeling sorry for myself. Outside, it was still dark, but her watch said five o'clock. She must have dozed off, without realizing it. Morning would come soon enough and she knew she could have a nap at some point during the day. While she found her dressing gown and slippers, she had a sudden vision of the woman who'd come to find her that night: the hide-and-seek night. The game they'd played had been Angelika's idea. Do I remember the train, Eva wondered. Not really. She sat down on the end of the bed. She could just about recall Mama's red coat. There was a hat, too. With a veil. She could bring the hat and veil and coat right into her head, as clearly if they had been on the bed beside her. Every detail. But Mama's face had gone and nothing she did, nothing she'd ever been able to do, brought it back. Nothing. She'd tried drawing it, and in every new face she saw, she searched for a resemblance, something she could latch on to and fix. Nothing.

Eva went down the stairs as quietly as she could and walked into the kitchen to make herself a cup of coffee. She looked round, not taking in anything very much, while the kettle boiled, and decided to take her cup up to the dress room and lie on the chaise longue there. In the old days, she used to be in there all the time, looking at old designs, taking dresses out of the cupboard and hanging them from the open doors so that she could be reminded of who she used to be and what she used to do before she grew old.

Eva looked at the available crockery. She liked coffee in a cup with a saucer, but didn't want to risk the long climb to the dress room carrying anything that could spill or break or make a rattling noise. Defeated, she sat down with her drink at the kitchen table. I'll go up when I've finished this, she told herself.

The first thing Eva did whenever she came into the dress room was check that the mirror was properly covered. It was, and she let out a breath she hadn't realized she'd been holding. Draped in what was once a fine white cotton sheet, it stood in its usual place next to the window. She opened the pretty flowered curtains and gazed down at the garden below. Light wasn't exactly flooding the sky, even now, but you could see down past the back lawn and beyond the wooded area behind the house that a trace of something like dawn was struggling over the horizon. She turned to look at the room. The cupboards were shut. The chaise longue looked inviting and as she sat down she realized that she was still a little short of breath after climbing the stairs. How long would it be before she couldn't manage them any longer? She lay back and looked at the high ceiling. All at once, the thought of leaving Salix House, the prospect of having to pack up every one of her possessions, the knowledge that no matter how wonderful any new place might be, she was still going to have to shed an enormous number of her belongings, filled her with dismay. What would go? How much would she be able to keep? What about all these clothes, her entire archive, what about that? Some home would have to be found for them and did she have the energy to start arranging such things? If not she, then who would do it for her? A hideous truth, and something which she'd known all along, seemed to be obvious to her now. Inescapable. Wherever she went, whatever it was like, she would never be as happy as she'd been here. Was that true? Could you say you'd been happy when so much of the time you'd been just the opposite? So many bad things had happened here. She couldn't with any truthfulness say that Salix House had been filled with domestic harmony throughout all the years she'd lived there. Antoine died after leaving the house in a rage which was the result of a hideous quarrel: one Eva would never forget and which still made her turn cold when she thought about it. And Angelika: she was here too, but Eva took it for granted that whatever it was that came floating at her out of mirrors and shiny surfaces would follow her wherever she went. She'd been following her since childhood, so presumably she always would. For a moment, Eva wondered what her life would be like without the shade – somehow she couldn't bring herself to call what she saw a ghost – of her sister.

Tears she'd not even known she was shedding ran down the sides of her cheeks and she sat up, swinging her legs down on to the carpet. She put her hand into her pocket to find the hankie she always kept there and heard Bridie's voice in her head: 'Why don't you like tissues, Granny, like everyone else?'

'Because they get soggy and horrible and you forget them in the pockets of trousers and cardigans and then when the garment goes into the washing machine it turns the tissue into powdery crumby stuff that goes all over your clothes.' By the time Eva had finished listing all the disadvantages of tissues over cotton hankies, Bridie had grown bored and walked away to do something else. Eva mopped at her eyes now with the soft, white cloth. I never used to cry, she thought. From her earliest childhood, from the time when the four-year-old Eva realized that tears were never going to restore anything she'd lost, she'd rarely resorted to weeping. So what's the matter with me now, she wondered, and then remembered yet another of the pat, ready-made answers Agnes Conway seemed to have to every problem: *Being tired always makes you feel weepy.* Perhaps that was true. She stood up and blew her nose with every intention of pulling herself together, but even though she managed to stem the flow of tears, Eva could feel a weight somewhere under her ribcage. That's what it means, she thought. Having a heavy heart. It's not a fanciful way of saying something but the exact truth.

CHAPTER 13

'Are you sure, Conor?' I said. I couldn't believe it. I'd overslept, even though I'd set my alarm. 'I can take the girls and have my breakfast later if you like. I don't mind, honestly.'

'No, that's fine. It's okay. I never drive them any more. It'll be a bit of a treat for me.'

Bridie and Dee certainly thought of it as something special. 'Daddy's taking us!' Dee said, twirling round at the end of the table with a piece of toast and marmalade hanging from her hand. 'Are we going to have a bonfire tonight, Daddy?'

'Of course we are. We'd never miss out on a bonfire, darling. I'll get it all set up while you're at school and we'll light it when you get home. But sit down now, Dee, I want to say something to Megan.'

'Thanks, Conor. It's nice of you to take them. A treat for them too. But only if you're sure.'

'Thing is, there's something else I need you to do, Megan.' He sounded a bit anxious. Rowena had already left for work but it suddenly occurred to me, as I poured milk on to my cereal, that Eva wasn't at the table.

'Is Eva having a lie-in?' I asked.

'Bridie, Dee, go and put on your coats and wait for me in the hall,' he said and the girls ran out of the kitchen, laughing. Dee was still holding her piece of toast and Conor hadn't noticed. He was pushing a hand through his hair and seemed downright worried, now that I'd started to look at him more closely. I said, 'Is everything okay?'

'Well, no. I don't think it is. It's Eva, you see—'

'What's wrong? Is she ill?'

'No, no, nothing's happened. Well, not really happened as such. And she's certainly not ill. Only she stormed out.' He sighed heavily. 'That's the only way to describe it. She almost ran from the table.'

'Was Rowena here then? Did they quarrel or something?'

'No, nothing like that.' He frowned. 'I'm trying to remember exactly what happened. To be honest with you, I've gone over it and over it and I can't think of anything that would have made her leave like that.'

'Did she say anything?'

'Only: *I'm going for a walk now. I'll be back at lunchtime.*'

I took a couple of spoonfuls of cereal while I thought about this. 'What's wrong with that? It's a nice day. Maybe she felt like a walk. She'll be back at lunchtime, she said. Perhaps we shouldn't worry yet?'

What I was thinking was: she's a grown woman. She's allowed to go for a walk if she likes.

'Eva never goes for walks at this time of day. She never has before. And it was more the way she went. She just sort of ran out of the room. I don't suppose . . .'

Conor was looking at me and fidgeting with the car keys.

'Dad! Are you ever coming?' Dee shouted from the hall.

'I am. I'm coming in a second. Just wait a bit and I'll be there.' He turned back to me and said, 'Megan, I'd be so grateful if you could go after her. Go and find her. She's probably only gone down to the village or something. Please. Make it look as though you've just happened to bump into her. I don't want her thinking we're keeping tabs on her. Will you do that?'

'How do you know she's not in the garden?'

'I looked. I went out and looked round the back while the girls were eating. She's not there. She must've gone down the drive, I think. Would you mind?'

'Of course I don't mind. I'll go right away. I'll take my car and drive around. I'm sure I'll find her.'

'Text me when you do, okay? I'll keep an eye out on the way to school in case she went that way, though it's less likely, I think. I'll text you if we happen to see her.'

He hurried away and I pushed my cereal bowl to one side and went to get my coat.

If she hadn't been feeling so cast down, if the whole matter of moving out of Salix House had turned out to be less fraught, then Eva would have found the look on Conor's face at breakfast quite amusing. All she'd said was: 'I'm going out for a walk. I'll be back by lunchtime. I need some fresh air and it's a lovely day', and his mouth dropped open and he'd half risen from his chair, but she'd been too quick for him. She'd pushed her chair away and started to walk quickly out of the kitchen and he'd followed her out into the hall.

'Are you all right, Eva? I could come with you, if you like.'

'I don't need an escort, Conor. I'd rather be on my own if you don't mind.'

'Of course, of course,' he said. He *had* to say that, Eva told herself as she strode much more quickly than she'd intended down the drive. I have to get away and think. She'd never done it in her life: walked out like that. Rowena used to storm out of rooms all the time when she was a teenager. Whenever something annoyed her, off she'd go, slamming the door and leaving a kind of backwash of resentment or fury behind her that Eva could almost see.

I ought to have managed the financial side of

my business better, Eva thought. I ought to have branched out into perfume or scarves or something, instead of running away and burying myself in the country so that now I'm forced to find somewhere small and cramped with no garden to live in till I die.

She walked along, kicking a stone with the toe of her boot from time to time. This was supposed to make her feel better but all it did was add to her worries. Was she wrecking her boots? It wasn't worth it because she wasn't feeling better. The more distance she put between herself and Salix House, the worse she felt.

I found Eva after I'd been driving for about five minutes. She was walking slowly along the side of the road, dressed in flat suede boots and one of her dramatically coloured coats. This one was a dull fuchsia and from behind, with her white hair hidden in the folds of a bitter-green and fuchsia shawl, she looked about twenty. She walked gracefully, like a ballerina or a model, I noticed, but she didn't look as if she was going anywhere. I tooted gently on the horn as I drove up beside her and wound down the window.

'Hello, Eva!' I said.

She stared at me for a moment, as though she didn't recognize me. Luckily, there was a place at the side of the road where I could stop, so I drove up to that, parked and quickly sent Conor a text saying I'd found her. Then I got out. I made my way back to where Eva was standing, looking bewildered.

'What're you doing here, Megan?'

'Well . . .' I didn't know if I should tell her that I'd been looking for her. She noticed my hesitation and said something that might have been 'Pah!' or some other expression of disgust.

'You've come after me, haven't you? He's sent you after me. Oh, my God. I can't even go out now without a bloody search party on my heels. Who was it? Conor? Phyllis? I waited till Rowena had gone before I escaped.'

'What are you escaping from?' I asked. She'd stopped in the road briefly to speak to me but now she was striding along again, faster than before and I quickened my pace to keep up with her.

'Why aren't you taking the girls to school?' She turned her head to look at me.

'Conor wanted to.'

'What lies! Conor wanted you to come and find me. Am I right?'

'Okay, yes. He said you'd run out of the house during breakfast and that you didn't normally go walking at this time of day.'

She nodded. 'I don't. I don't usually only I just . . . I was overcome with . . . I don't know. Something.'

Her voice shook. Was she crying? I didn't feel I could ask. I was just trying to think of what to say next. I was staring at my own feet as we walked along, because I wanted to give her time to recover. She didn't say a word and for a while we walked together along the road. Then she turned up a tree-lined lane and I followed her.

'I've never been up here,' I said. 'It's pretty.'

'In the spring, it is. Everything's a bit wintery now. Not enough green anywhere.'

'I like the bare trees,' I said. 'I don't mind the winter.'

'This is a lovely view,' she said. We were beside a gate that led into a field where some cows were idly chewing at the grass. 'I like cows.'

'Eva, what's wrong? Why did you run away? Why did you say: *escaped*?'

I was taken completely by surprise by what she did next. I'd been expecting all kinds of reactions: *It's none of your business, there's nothing whatsoever wrong, I'm afraid I can't talk about it . . .* anything except what happened. She let out a howl, like a child, or a wounded animal, and then she covered her face with her gloved hands and burst into tears. People say that a lot: *burst into tears*, but I'd never actually seen it happen before. It was as though a tap had been turned inside her head and suddenly, tears were flowing from her eyes, rolling into her mouth, just *pouring* out of her. I didn't know what to do. For a mad second I wanted to laugh, to say: *No, this is wrong Eva. You're the one who cheers me up when I'm weeping.* But I couldn't say that and I had to say something. I didn't stop to consider whether what I was doing was right or not, but I went and put my arms around her and hugged her.

'Don't cry, Eva! What's happened?'

I let her go after a bit and she sniffed and reached into the pocket of her coat and found a hankie and wiped her eyes and blew her nose.

'Oh, God Megan, I'm sorry. I never cry. I don't know why today—'

'It doesn't matter, Eva. Come home now and get warm. We can talk there. You can tell me what happened.'

'Nothing happened. It's nothing new. It's nothing mysterious. I just can't . . . I can't bear the thought of it, that's all.'

'The thought of what?' I asked, though I knew exactly what she was about to say.

'The thought of leaving Salix House,' Eva said as new tears gathered in her eyes.

'I don't want to go back yet,' Eva said. I'd persuaded her to come back to the car. 'Can you drive around a little? I'd rather talk here than at home.'

'No problem.' I knew what she meant about talking in cars and I couldn't stop my mind from going back to the first journey I'd ever taken alone with Simon. How the darkness shut us into a tiny little space where nothing but the two of us existed. I remembered other trips we'd been on together. Other things he'd said to me, simply because he knew that we were cut off from the rest of the world, which seemed to be flying past the windows. I shook my head. *Jesus*, I told myself. *Eva's the one with the problem. Not you.* I deliberately didn't turn my head in her direction but I started driving and pretended to be extra vigilant about the road ahead of us. I knew that she'd be more likely to talk if I said nothing so even though I was dying to prompt her, I kept quiet.

'I know all the arguments for us moving, you see,' she began. 'Rowena is right and there is no way on earth that we can afford to keep Salix House. It's just that the other places we've seen are so horrible that I've lost heart. I don't believe I will find anywhere. Not anywhere I'd really like to live. Nothing that would make up for having to leave Salix House.'

I knew exactly what she meant and as she spoke I began to feel worse and worse on her behalf.

I thought of each room in the house, how beautiful everything was, how full of Eva's taste and character, even in those parts of it which were shabby and could have done with a coat of paint. I couldn't truthfully have said that I'd been happy there, but that was more to do with me than the house.

'I'm not sure,' she said, 'that I understand myself why I'm quite so attached to it. I've been unhappy here too, you know. The memories I have of my time here aren't all good, by any means. I only know that for a long time I didn't have anything. Do you know what that's like? Nothing. Not parents, not a house, not . . . well, nothing. Then I had some things, that were . . . not foisted on me exactly but which weren't really *me*. Not anyone's fault, of course and my adopted mother did her best but still I didn't feel . . . it's hard to explain. I only began to be happy when I started making my clothes. That was a real thing that I could imagine in my head and then make with my own hands and that a woman could put on her body. I knew that this or that arrangement of fabrics would make her beautiful and I'd made it and that satisfied me.'

I nodded and didn't answer. I didn't want her to stop talking. She went on, 'Then I met Antoine and everything changed. Love changes everything. It sounds like the name of a song.'

I laughed. 'It *is* the name of a song!'

'Really? I don't know it. I know very little about today's songs. That's the awful thing. I'm not really part of anything that's going on. I'm . . . well, history, I suppose.'

'Nonsense,' I said. 'Knowing or not knowing an Andrew Lloyd Webber song doesn't matter, Eva. Trust me.'

'I'll take your word for it. But it's not just songs. I can't understand why everything has to be . . . well, perfect. Rowena wants her life to be exactly right. It upsets her that the garden isn't as tidy as it could be. She resents not being able to employ a couple of people to come in and help Phyllis. She'd like the whole of Salix House to be redecorated.

But me, if I could be allowed to live there till the end of my life, I wouldn't care how much of a wreck it was. We could moulder together . . . oh God, what am I saying? I would hate that. I *do* hate it. Rowena is right. We can't afford to keep the poor old place properly so we've got no business living there. Even Phyllis wants to leave it. She's as old as I am and has a sister in Lyme Regis. She deserves to live by the sea if that's what she wants. Rowena's right. It would be like throwing money away to continue in the same way for ever. I'll find somewhere.'

'That's true,' I said and I believed it, but that wasn't the point. I decided to talk to Rowena. It wouldn't hurt to give it a go, for Eva's sake. Perhaps she might consider taking it off the market and putting it on again once they'd found somewhere suitable for her mother. I could suggest it, in any case.

This was, Eva thought, a ridiculous time of the day to be lying down, but she was tired and one of the good things about growing older was that no one batted an eyelid if you said you were taking yourself off to your bed. She hadn't drawn the curtains, proposing to enjoy whatever the winter sunset might produce. Megan had understood her very well, but she hadn't been totally honest. When she was being rational, sensible, grown-up, Eva acknowledged that it wasn't only happy memories that linked her to the house. The unhappy ones;

the terrible things that she'd felt and seen here; the presence of Angelika even when she didn't show herself: all those were like creepers of some kind, binding her to the house, attaching themselves to her skin.

She tried to make her mind blank, to rid herself of thoughts and worries about moving house and everything else as well, but the trouble with closed eyes, with trying to clear your mind, was that other things came into your head to fill the space. As a girl, Eva used to imagine her head as a kind of snow globe. Instead of white, pure flakes falling over everything when you shook it, she had something dark and sooty lying at the very bottom of the glass ball, waiting to drift down over her whole life if she thought about it too hard. This darkness, like a layer of thick black mud, had been with her for as long as she could remember. It sat there quietly and didn't get stirred up very often, but when it happened, her whole being became clouded with sorrow. When she felt better again, it was as though the snow globe was settling into stillness and clarity.

Eva feared that if she fell asleep now one particular nightmare she'd often had as a child would come back to trouble her. As a girl, she used to try and stay awake as long as she could, to defeat the bad dreams, but it never worked because in the end, she always fell asleep.

Think about anything, she told herself, but not the game we played. The game was what she dreamed of, all the time. She closed her eyes. Immediately, she was back there, in the black place between the crates piled up on a German station platform and words were being whispered in her ear. *Cover your eyes. Count to a hundred.* I didn't know how to count to a hundred, she thought. I knew how to count to ten, that was all. I was worried. Worried that I wasn't going to be able to do what she said. What Angelika said. I didn't even know what a hundred was, except that it was part of the game. Eva had kept on counting to ten, over and over again. How many times? She couldn't remember after so many years, but much more than a hundred. She stayed there in the dark and the cold and she didn't move. The voice said nothing else. Eva thought she knew who'd been speaking, who had told her to hide her eyes, but sometimes she believed that the words had come from *her*, out of her own mouth. That *she'd* spoken them. *Cover your eyes. Count to a hundred.*

It was Angelika. Eva had been almost sure of that for most of her life, but now she was far less certain. It could have been me, she decided. It could have been, when you think what happened to each of us. Eva had become so used to the fact that no one except her knew about Angelika that for years at a time she'd managed to smooth over what she'd done and push it out of her mind; obliterate and deny it entirely. What she'd told herself over and over during her lifetime *(I was only four years old)* was true but still she couldn't forgive herself. *You shouldn't have done it. You shouldn't have left her there. Left her to die. You knew England meant being safe. Mama and Papa had told you. It had been drummed into you. Just as Angelika had been told, constantly told:* Look after Eva. You're the big sister. *She would never have disobeyed Mama and Papa. Would she? No, never. So it must have been me. I must have done the bad thing. I left her there. I left her there and she died because I did that.*

Since that night and until just the other day when she'd let slip her name in front of Megan, Eva had managed never to speak of Angelika. It was as though she'd never existed. By the time the transport arrived in England, she'd been beyond speech, traumatized into silence and sickness. All her energies had turned to erasing that memory and she'd done it so well that until quite recently she thought about it only rarely. Because Agnes Conway had known nothing about Angelika, it was easy never to speak of her and Eva had trained herself into a willed forgetfulness. She had tried not to dwell on the past and most of the time she'd succeeded. But now, because she was so worried about leaving this house, because Megan had been so kind to her, things were creeping back into her head which she'd thought were banished for ever. When she came upstairs a few minutes ago, she was sure that Angelika was there, in the mirror, even though Eva wasn't able to see her. Sometimes, it didn't matter how many scarves she threw over the glass, she could still sense her

213

sister's veiled presence. However the story twisted itself up in her dreams, *she had left her there*. Eva had taken the lady's hand and let herself be led on to the train bound for Holland. She'd looked out of the window and seen the station getting smaller and smaller. I knew I was alone, she thought. She hadn't meant to do it, but she'd done it; she was still a murderer and she'd never forgiven herself. You can't ever rid yourself of a thing like that. You can suppress it but it will come out. Somehow. It will float out of the glass and stand in front of you, dressed in brown buckled shoes and a brown coat with a black velvet collar. Your sister.

After Eva and I got back to Salix House, she went to lie down till lunchtime and I went to check my emails. I knew there would be a message there from Tom and there was. *You okay? Can't write much. In staff room. Missed you this morning. Tom x.*

I answered him: *Had to talk to Eva this morning so couldn't come into school but will see you at 3.30. Love, Megan x.*

I thought about the message for a while before I sent it. I was determined not to lie to Tom. I felt that perhaps he was right and life *might* be changing but I didn't know how or if I liked it changing, not yet. As I thought about it, I remembered how we were on Saturday and found myself quite eager to see him. I sent the message and then I went and lay down on the bed and tried to think about Eva. Stop thinking about Tom, I told myself, and work out what you're going to say to Rowena.

Eva stood on the flagged terrace outside the drawing room watching as Conor dealt with the bonfire, the fireworks and managed at the same time to keep the girls under control and out of danger. He was at his best on such occasions. He'd have been a perfect primary school teacher, Eva thought, as she'd thought many times. He was friendly, cheerful, helpful and even quite handsome if you liked the rather hearty, pink-cheeked sort of man who would probably get a bit stout in his old age. Rowena had surprised her when she announced her engagement to a young computer programmer she'd met at a party, but the marriage was happy, as far as she could tell and certainly she couldn't have wished for a better father for her granddaughters.

'Right, now,' he said to Dee, Bridie, Megan and Rowena, who were standing together at a safe distance from the row of bottles with fireworks stuck into their necks that he'd set up earlier in the afternoon. 'You stand back and watch these go up! See how high they go. Ready?' He lit the fuses and the rockets flew up over the garden, leaving sequin-like trails across the night sky. The girls laughed with pleasure. 'More?' Conor asked. 'Yes!' came the answer. 'Yes!' Another fusillade exploded, and then more laughter. The fireworks ran out then, for which Eva was grateful. The first few times were a happy surprise but after a while, when it came to fireworks, she started to calculate the cost of the bright glittering and usually came to the conclusion that sending money burning up into the air was something of a waste. What a killjoy you are, Eva! she told herself. The girls are so happy. Conor and Rowena are happy. Surely that's worth a great deal of money?

'Okay, my darlings . . . and that includes you, Eva,' said Conor, coming up to her and taking her by the arm. 'Let's go down to the kitchen garden and light the bonfire.'

On the way, with the girls skipping ahead of them and Megan not far behind, Conor turned to her and looked at her more solemnly than he normally did.

'Are you feeling more yourself, Eva? After this morning, I mean?' He seemed genuinely concerned. 'I know you're not happy with the moving idea and all but—'

'Don't worry, Conor,' said Eva. The last thing she felt like doing was rehashing her feelings now, after going over everything with Megan. 'Let's catch up with the girls.'

At seven, I found Rowena alone in the kitchen. The girls were watching television with Eva. 'I never mind what it is,' she'd told me soon after I got here. 'I just like sitting on the sofa between the two of them and hugging them if they'll let me. I like seeing how much they're enjoying themselves.'

I didn't know how much time I'd have. Dee might easily get fed up and go looking for other entertainment, though they wouldn't need much feeding after the baked potatoes and bonfire toffee apples we'd all been eating. I said,

'Hi, Rowena, can I talk to you for a sec?'

She looked up, frowning. 'Oh, God, Megan, don't tell me you want to hand in your notice or anything—'

'No, it's nothing like that.'

'Well, that's a relief. What's the problem?'

'Do you need any help chopping up stuff for salad?'

'It's okay. I'm nearly done.'

Phyllis was away so we were having salad. Rowena wasn't much of a cook but Phyllis usually left something in the pantry for us to warm up as well as a pudding in the fridge. Rowena had her back to me, which made it easier to say what I'd prepared.

'I'm a bit worried about Eva,' I began. Rowena whirled round with the knife still in her hand and frowned at me.

'What do you mean? What's the matter with her? I thought she looked fine this morning.'

I told Rowena what had happened after breakfast and also mentioned what Eva had told me. I went on, 'So I wanted to ask you whether it was . . . you know. Definite. I mean, whether it would be possible – at all possible – to delay moving. To stay in Salix House for a bit longer. Take it off the market for a little while.'

'No,' Rowena said. 'It wouldn't.' While I'd been speaking, she'd begun to look more and more angry. She pulled herself together and dropped the knife on the work surface and came to sit down in the chair opposite mine. Then she noticed that there were tomato seeds clinging to her hands and went to the sink to wash them. For a moment, water rushing down the plughole was the only sound in the room, then Rowena spoke.

'Look, I know this sounds unfeeling and I know how persuasive my mother can be, but it's not on. We're moving to London. It's all arranged. I've been looking into schools, we're moving heaven and earth to find Ma a nice place—'

'But she's hated the ones she's seen,' I put in.

'Nevertheless, we'll find somewhere. Somewhere she'll like, I'm sure we will. It's just a matter of looking. And you'll help, won't you, Megan? She trusts you – you could make her look at everything more positively. But we *are* going. Luke Fielden tells me he's on the point of making an offer which is a bit less than what I was looking for, but I might have some other people interested too, soon, I think . . . it's all set up.'

'But your mother's so miserable! She covers it up a lot of the time because she doesn't want to be an inconvenience, but she hates the idea. She wants to stay here.'

'That's exactly what she can't do, I'm afraid.'

I tried again. 'Why not, though? Why can't you at least delay the move? The market might pick up . . . it's dreadful now, isn't it? You might get more money if you waited a bit. You say Luke's offer isn't enough. Even six months would be better than nothing. It's just . . . well, she's marvellous for her age and everything but she *is* old, isn't she? I reckon that ought to be important. Her happiness.'

'Oh, of course it's important,' Rowena said, sounding furious. She apologized at once. 'God, I'm sorry, Megan. I don't know why I'm yelling at you. Only it's so . . . it's so difficult. I know there's truth in what you say and sometimes I feel as if I'm being wicked, making her move and upsetting her and everything, but we have to think of us. Of our children. And of me. I know it sounds selfish but it would be so much easier for all of us if we lived in London.'

I could feel her wavering so I said, 'Except Eva. It wouldn't be better for Eva.'

Rowena was twisting her hands together and staring at the table. Then she sighed.

'I'll talk to Conor, Megan, but I have to tell you, we're determined. But I *will* talk to him again. Okay?'

'Thanks, Rowena. I know I shouldn't be asking you to, but I can't help worrying about Eva.'

She looked at me then, almost as though she were seeing me properly for the first time.

'That's very commendable, Megan, but isn't there something a bit . . . well, you'll most likely be out of a job when we move to London. Are you sure you're not wanting to delay the move for reasons of your own? Forgive me for asking this, but I do have to know how much your own interests are making you—'

I didn't let her finish. I didn't care at that moment whether she fired me on the spot or not. I lost it. I forgot all the boundaries of our relationship and yelled at her anyway.

'How dare you say that? Take it back. I don't care if you believe me or not but I *wasn't* thinking about me, or this job or anything. I just thought it was worth putting Eva's point of view again. Telling her daughter that she's miserable, but I was dead wrong, wasn't I?'

I suppose I would have gone on like this if Rowena hadn't come round to my side of the table and taken me by the shoulders.

'I'm sorry, Megan. You're right. I'm so sorry. I shouldn't have said that. Eva's not the only one with frayed nerves around here. Please forgive me.'

She sounded so imploring that I said, 'Oh, God, Rowena, I'm the one that's sorry. I shouldn't have shouted like that, only I was hurt—'

'I know, I know and you have every right to be hurt. Unforgiveable, what I said. Only you will forgive me, won't you?'

'Of course I will,' I said. I added, 'I'd better go and see what the girls are up to', but I had no intention of doing that. I wanted a chance to be on my own a bit before supper, to calm down. Once a thing has been said, it's out there. I left the room wondering whether there was even the tiniest part of Rowena's remarks which might be true. It didn't make any difference to the fact that I was worried about Eva.

I went to my room. When I first came to Salix House, I used to spend ages in there. I'd never in my life had such a beautiful bedroom and I enjoyed being in it, even now. Recently, though, I'd been much more aware of the mirror. Every time I came in, I approached it anxiously, trying to see as soon as I opened the door whether there was a shadow, a shape lurking in the glass. So far, I hadn't caught sight of anything sinister, but I was nervous of my dressing table, which was, when I thought about it anywhere else in the house or outside the house, completely mad and ridiculous. Somehow, though, when I was here, with the door closed behind me, especially at night, the idea of seeing that face again seemed quite possible. I hadn't covered anything up. I didn't want to admit that I was scared of such a stupid thing, but I did avoid looking into the mirror and there were times when I could have sworn that there was something not quite right about the glass. It looked, in certain lights and from certain angles, as if it were liquid, or pliable. As if it could move and slide and reveal whatever might be hidden within it. *Don't be so daft,* I told myself. Mirrors don't slide and bend and reveal things. They're solid. Hard. You can break them. They can shatter. I shivered. I didn't even like thinking about the glass breaking. More than the seven years of bad luck, I feared that whatever might be trapped behind the surface would come out.

So whenever I came upstairs, I deliberately pushed away such thoughts and immediately went to my laptop and sat looking at the internet with my back to the dressing table. I liked catching up with what was going on in the real world, as I still thought of it. What did that mean? That this place was somehow unreal? I wasn't sure exactly, but it was true that since I'd started working here, I'd had less and less contact with my friends, apart from Jay. I'd spoken to Felix on the phone a couple of times. I texted Tanya occasionally but only when she'd texted me first. Tonight, there was a message from Felix. I always dreaded hearing from anyone at the *lipstick* office, because of Simon's name maybe cropping up, but there wasn't that problem with Felix. He knew he had to avoid the subject.

FROM: FlxPy@liptick.com
TO: meganp84@gmail.com
Subject: Dear Megan . . .
I hope this finds you well, Megan. We all miss you in the office . . . well, I do. I wish you'd write from time to time to tell me what you're doing. Nannying, even for the

divine Eva Conway, is not your *métier*, not really. Do consider coming back to London but if you are determined not to, then at least keep me up to date with your news. Affectionately, Fx

Only Felix would use words like *métier*.

At least writing to Felix would stop me thinking nonsense thoughts about mirrors. I typed him a long message, telling him about the Nativity Play, the bonfire we'd just had and how much I was enjoying life. I even mentioned Tom, though I didn't go into any details. Maybe if he thought I had some kind of boyfriend, he'd be happier about me vegetating in the country, as I was sure he'd put it. I ended up by saying:

'I do intend to come back one of these days, Felix. I'm not always going to be a nanny. Don't worry. Will be filing copy before you can say boo to a goose. Love, Megan.' I closed my laptop and got up and wondered if that was true. The girls were in bed but it would be time for supper soon, and I'd have to go down and chat as though nothing had happened. No one was going to say anything even remotely real and honest. Just as I was about to leave my room, I heard the whooshing noise of a text arriving in my phone. I almost left it. It would be Tom. I went back to read it. *Goodnight, dearest Megan. Can you come round again? Soon. I miss you. Tom x*. I smiled and texted back, *Yes. Soon. Mx*. He did make me feel better about some things and I was glad about that.

'Megan, can I have a word?' Rowena caught me just as I was leaving the sitting room to go to bed. We'd had a perfectly normal evening, even though Eva was a bit quiet and Conor even more deliberately chatty than usual.

'Sure,' I said. She followed me out to the hall and we stood by the table. I could see from the way she looked, from the way she was standing, that I wasn't going to like what she intended to say. I almost told her not to bother but she'd started so I listened.

'I haven't been able to speak to Conor yet about Ma and her situation, and he's off to a conference first thing tomorrow. I'll speak to him when he gets back on Saturday night. I hope you agree that I'm being fair. I mean, in one way, I don't have to discuss it with him at all because I know what he'll say: the same as me, I'm sure. But I did promise you. You'll just have to be a bit patient. Okay?'

'Fine,' I said. 'That's fine. I was just thinking of Eva, that's all.'

'I know, I know,' Rowena smiled. 'And it's an enormous help having you to show her some of the flats. I'll be taking her to one or two tomorrow, but all your driving and so on is much appreciated. And I'm sure Eva prefers going round flats with you than with me.'

I wanted to contradict her but I couldn't. I thought it was true. Whenever we went out together, even if it was to look at horrible places to live, we always had some fun along the way.

'I'm sure she *will* find somewhere nice in the end,' I said, but I didn't know if I believed that completely. One of these days, I promised myself, maybe when we're in the car, driving to yet another flat, I'll ask Eva why she and Rowena aren't close. They're always polite and pleasant to each other but Eva seems readier to talk to me than she does to her own daughter.

CHAPTER 14

'This is really kind of you,' said Luke Fielden, smiling.

'I'm very happy to show you the garden,' she said. 'Rowena works in London as you know, but even if she were here, I'm a much better guide to the outside of Salix House. I made the garden, and so I know everything there is to know about it.'

They walked round the property, starting from the house and going down the drive, past all the salix trees. 'They're not so impressive at this time of year,' Eva said, 'but they're beautiful in the summer. The pale leaves look almost like small feathers.' From the gate, they took a path across the lawns, round the side of the building and on to the terrace.

'In the sun, it's almost warm,' she said. 'But only if we keep moving, I think. Are you going to make an offer for the house, Mr Fielden?'

'I think I am,' said Luke. 'It's beautiful.'

Eva looked at him. He was much taller than she was, but had shortened his stride to accommodate her. He'd been interested, or seemed to be interested, in everything she'd shown him. His eyes were very unusual: amber-coloured, with very long, thick lashes. If I were a young woman, she thought, I'd find him attractive. She didn't approve of matchmaking, but it occurred to her that Megan would do much better with this man than with Tom. What business is it of mine? she told herself. She seems happy now that she and Tom are seeing one another. It had been hard for her to hide what was going on. The girls cottoned on to the fact that she'd been out with him at the weekend and Dee had made up her mind that her teacher and Megan were practically on the verge of marriage. Luke interrupted her thoughts. He said, 'The young woman who showed me round last time . . . Megan, is it?'

'That's right,' said Eva. He knew her name perfectly well, she was sure of it. He went on, 'Will she be coming with you to London when you go?'

'Well, she'll be coming to London, I'm sure, but not with us, I don't think. She's a journalist. She left her job at *lipstick* for personal reasons, but I'm sure she'd be only too happy to get back to that kind of work. Even though she's very good with Dee and Bridie, and they love her.'

'I know the editor of *lipstick*. Well, when I say "know", I come across him here and there from time to time. Rarely, actually, but still. Simon Gradwell. It's a small world.'

Eva looked up at him. 'Don't tell Megan you know him,' she said. 'It wouldn't be a good idea.'

'Right,' said Luke. Eva was prepared to deflect any further questions but he began to ask her about the espaliered peach tree on the south wall and she was relieved not to have to explain.

The kitchen door opened just as they were passing it and Megan came out. 'I saw you both through the window. Aren't you freezing?'

'I am, a bit,' said Eva. 'Maybe you can make us both a cup of tea?'

'Sure. No problem,' she said. They followed her into the warmth of the kitchen. As soon as I've drunk a bit of my tea, Eva thought, as they sat down at the table, I'm going to leave them on their own. This might, she realized, be exactly the kind of matchmaking she normally disapproved of, but on the other hand, what was the harm in it? If Megan was really keen on Tom, nothing would come of it. Anyway, she thought, just because I think he's an attractive man, it doesn't mean she will. She hoped fervently that he'd remember not to mention Simon Gradwell.

'Are you offering for it?' I asked Luke Fielden. Eva had made an excuse about going to her room and had left us to our tea.

'Yes, I think so. I love it. And Eva's shown me the bits of it I didn't see properly last time. It must be spectacular in the spring and summer.'

'She'll find it very hard, moving,' I said and then wished I hadn't. What business was it of mine, after all? I was hardly going to tell him how I'd found her crying about it only a short while ago.

'Well, I can understand that. It must be very difficult when you've lived in a place for so long and invested so much of yourself in it, too.'

I said nothing. He added, 'You know, someone's going to buy this house if I don't. You mustn't blame me for loving it and wanting to acquire it, you know.' His voice was quite gentle and I wondered why I'd ever found him arrogant. But I hadn't said a word, so how had he guessed at my feelings? I said, hastily, 'No, no, of course I don't. It's just—'

'You don't have to explain. I think you're very protective of Eva, aren't you?'

'I just . . . well, I'd like her to be happy, that's all. She's been very kind to me.'

'I'm sure that she'll find somewhere good,' he said. I found it hard to stay angry with him. It *was* ridiculous to blame him for Eva's unhappiness. She seemed to like him. When I'd caught sight of them out of the kitchen window, she'd looked perfectly happy. He was smiling now and his stern face was quite transformed.

'Would you like another slice of cake?'

'No, thanks. I ought to go now. I've taken up far too much of your time already.'

'That's okay. I've got to go and fetch the girls from school soon but I've got a few minutes.'

'No, no, I'm off.' He stood up, so I did as well. 'Shan't hold you up. Thanks so much for this . . .'

He nodded towards the table. 'Goodbye, Megan.' We shook hands. Or at least, it started as a hand-shake but then my hand was enveloped and squeezed in both of his, and when he'd gone I sat down again. I didn't have to go to school quite yet and I was trying to process how I felt. As though something had flipped over in my stomach. I tried to remember details of Luke's face and found myself dwelling on his mouth. Stop it, I told myself. I tried to conjure up an image of Tom, of Tom leaning over me, kissing me, making love to me, but the only thing I could see was Luke's eyes; how there seemed to be some kind of light behind them, shining through them. Thinking about them was unsettling me. I got up and walked quickly out of the house to my car.

'Granny! You're not concentrating. You have to type in the name that you want. In the space here.' Dee pointed to the long rectangle at the top of the screen. Eva peered at the word *Google*, which had struck her at first as a silly, childish name but which she was gradually getting used to. She was at least getting the hang of the mouse and managed to type Rightmove without mishap and click on the correct little symbol . . . icon. That was the right word.

'There!' Eva smiled at Dee. They were in the study. Dee had the proper desk chair and Eva had pulled up a hard chair right next to it and was looking past her granddaughter at the screen of

Conor's old laptop, which she'd inherited when he bought an iPad. Dee liked being in charge of their computer sessions. She (sometimes with help from Bridie) was the teacher and Eva was the pupil and she loved telling Eva about the internet. Dee had first shown her the Rightmove site when Salix House went on the market and Eva liked looking round her own house on the virtual tour. It became a game with the girls: they'd guide the cursor from room to room and the screen would fill with images of her house, looking both familiar and strange: unusually empty, unusually quiet, strangely tidy and clean and somehow not like itself. Now, she needed Rightmove for reasons of her own. The letter that had arrived that morning was in the pocket of her cardigan and she patted it from time to time, to make sure it was still there. Later, when Dee went for her tea, she'd read it again to make sure she hadn't made any mistake about its contents.

'Where do you want to live, Granny?' Dee was asking. 'I'll type it in for you if you tell me how to spell it. And then we have to put in how much you want to pay for it.'

'Goodness,' said Eva, slightly taken aback by the knowledge her young granddaughter seemed to have. She could also see that this looking around at properties might easily become addictive. What was to stop you putting in Mayfair and three million pounds in the right boxes and gawping at properties you couldn't possibly afford? Nothing,

231

really, except the pointlessness of the exercise. Today, however, she had a reason to be looking at the site. A proper reason.

'Dee! Come along,' Megan called from the kitchen. 'Time for your tea. What are you doing?'

'Helping Granny with the computer,' Dee called back. 'But I'm coming in a second.' She turned to Eva. 'I'll come back after if you like.'

'No, darling, that's all right. I can manage now, I'm sure. In any case I've nearly finished.'

Dee ran off. Eva peered at the screen. Tentatively she typed the postcode she'd memorized into the little box. She added a sum of money that she thought might be about right and clicked. A display showing houses of every kind filled the screen. Damn. She should have put 'flat' into the mix, somewhere along the way. She sighed. I'll ask Megan, she thought. She liked being helped by Dee, who took such pride in being grown-up about technical matters, but Megan knew what she was looking for. She would have to do something called *'refining your search'*.

The lettering of the Google page (designed, she thought, to appeal to children, with its bright primary colours and its friendly-looking type-face) appeared on the screen again as she closed the *Rightmove* site. I'm all by myself, she thought. I can try. If anything goes wrong, I'll just close down and go back later, with Megan. Very tenta-tively, she typed in a name: *Lissa Dovedale*. The screen filled with references to Lissa. Well, it wasn't surprising. At the very top of the page was Wikipedia, and Eva felt huge relief. One of the first things she'd ever done on a computer was go to her own entry. And here was one for Lissa.

A famous model in the sixties, Lissa Dovedale's name defined the London fashion world at that time. Together with Jean Shrimpton and Twiggy, her androgynous, leggy look and her long, red, pre-Raphaelite-style hair made her an icon of her day. She is particularly associated with the designer Eva Conway, whose characteristically elegant and understated but exotic designs she wore to perfection.

Eva smiled, remembering how in this very house, when it was nothing more than a shell, with a few broken old desks standing on dusty, cracked floorboards and cobwebs hanging in swags from the light fittings and the banisters, Lissa had posed in the grey and mauve and oyster chiffon of the *Ghost* collection, looking beautiful and as though she were about to fade into the woodwork, like a ghost herself. Very pale lips. Very dark eyes and that hair, the curls like ribbons of copper unscrolling over Lissa's bony shoulders.

In 1970, she retired from the fashion world to marry property billionaire, Herman Abernathy, after a much-publicized romance. Her husband, who was more than twenty years her senior, died in 1990. Even though she has stayed away from the limelight, Lissa Dovedale is prominent in the USA as a sponsor of several important arts foundations, all over the world.

In the seventies, Eva reflected, we didn't know the meaning of 'much-publicized'. A few articles in the paper and that was it, more or less. She imagined what would have gone on today. Twitter and Facebook and the hacking of phones by the papers . . . they'd have had a wonderful time dissecting the story of Lissa and Herman, who was short and not particularly good-looking and moreover, thoroughly married. People drew their own conclusions at the time and would have done so even more now. Lissa was represented as a gold-digger and a home-wrecker and today she'd have been torn limb from limb. As it was, she went to America and wasn't heard of again till Abernathy died, leaving her a very rich woman indeed, but also (and this came as a surprise to many people) bereft at the loss of a husband she loved more deeply than anyone could have im-agined. We love, Eva thought, the most unlikely people and for the most ridiculous of reasons but if your story doesn't fit a template laid down in fiction and the media, then it was not always to be believed. Me and Antoine Bragonard, she thought. Not many people had understood that, either, and now with the benefit of hindsight, Eva wasn't altogether sure she could make sense of it herself. I ought to have tried, she thought. I ought to have explained it much earlier and better to Rowena, then our whole relationship might have been different.

Suddenly, she felt exhausted. Enough for one

day, she thought. I know as much as I need to know. She closed the laptop, got up from the desk and went to sit on the sofa. The velvet and satin cushions were piled up behind her. She leaned against them and took the letter out of her cardigan pocket.

The house was quiet. Dee and Bridie must have finished eating and gone upstairs with Megan. Rowena wasn't due home for some time and Conor was busy getting ready for his conference. Why shouldn't I phone now? What's stopping me? Nothing, Eva decided. I'm just going to do it. I'm going to pick up the phone as though forty years and more haven't gone by since we met, and speak to Lissa. She left her nest of soft cushions and went back to the desk, where she picked up the receiver and began to key in the numbers.

'What do you reckon?' Tom said. He and Megan were sitting in the school hall, watching a Nativity Play rehearsal. The teacher in charge, Mrs Plumtree, was marshalling the ranks of angels, shepherds, kings and Mary and Joseph in a final tableau.

'That's right. Tall ones at the back, please. Melissa, come to the front at once. Dee, you'll be on Mary's right and I want someone about Dee's height . . . that's right, you, James . . . on Joseph's left.'

Megan said, 'I'm just glad I don't have to organize it, that's all. I don't envy Mrs P. Nor you, come to that.'

'I love it. I have to make a real effort to teach the kids something that isn't to do with the play. We've got our words to learn now.'

'Makes it easier that they don't also have to learn tunes.'

'That was my idea!' Tom beamed and Megan couldn't help smiling. 'Clever or what?'

'Not bad.' Tom had made up new words for the children, but he'd used existing carol tunes which made the process simpler for everyone. 'I know your updated version of "Angels From the Realms of Glory" by heart.'

'Megan?'

'Yes?'

We were whispering. I kind of knew what was coming before he spoke.

'What're you doing tonight? Can you come over . . . I'll cook for you again?'

I knew what that meant. It was clearly going to be our language, our code for having sex. And I wanted to. Did I want to? We had been together once only . . . was it going to be different this time? Better? Worse? Did I want this thing between me and Tom to become a relationship? I had to find out, one way or another. I said, 'Fine. Only this time I'll drive over to you. I'll be the one who doesn't have wine, okay?'

'Okay,' he said. 'I wish you could stay over.'

'Better not,' I said. 'The girls . . .' I added.

'Sure. Of course,' he said. 'Maybe we could go away for a weekend sometime.'

'Maybe,' I said. I wasn't sure what I thought about that.

'Whatever are you doing, Ma? I saw the dining-room light on and wondered who could possibly be in here at this time of night.'

'Not so late, is it? Only about nine o'clock. I'm starting on Dee's angel wings.' Eva smiled at her daughter. The table was covered with a thick blanket on which she'd spread a couple of yards of stiff white gauzy fabric.

'Do you mind working so hard for a child's costume?' Rowena came to sit at the table, taking the chair opposite Eva.

'Not hard at all. It's fun. It gives me something to do and something to think about which isn't just . . . I enjoy it. I'm not doing feathers. Angels always have feathers, don't they? I'm going to do something different.'

'Well, it'll be lovely, I'm sure, Ma. Only I came to talk about something else. I'm sorry to bring it up like this, but we should discuss the flats you've seen so far. Are you quite sure they're all awful?'

'Quite sure.' A thought occurred to Eva. 'Has Megan been talking to you?'

'She has, actually, but this is nothing to do with Megan. I'm anxious for you to find somewhere you'll be happy to move to.'

Megan has spoken to Rowena, Eva thought. She said, 'So. Tell me what she said. Go on. I want to know what the two of you have been saying.'

'Only that you're very unhappy about leaving Salix House. She said you were quite miserable about it.'

Eva laughed. 'Well, that surely can't be news to you, can it? I haven't disguised my feelings, Rowena.'

'But you know we've got to go, don't you? It's going to be quite impossible to keep this place up.'

Eva bent her head to the fabric spread out in front of her and concentrated on drawing thin lines on it with a fine felt-tipped pen. Rowena had used the same tone in her voice ever since she was a tiny child as soon as she sensed a disagreement in the offing. Eva sighed. My fault, this relationship, she thought. From the very first day I knew I was pregnant, I wasn't entirely happy about it. The rest, everything that's happened between me and Rowena, probably follows from that.

1970

Eva had tried to avoid thinking about the sickness, the swollen breasts, the heavy legs for weeks. I can't be pregnant, she kept on telling herself, but the nights when she and Antoine made love were so infrequent that she could remember clearly when the last one was, nearly two months ago. Eva had almost decided to tell him the news, was casting about for how to do it, when he said, 'You're pregnant, aren't you?', and Eva nearly dropped the casserole she was bringing to the table. She'd spent half the afternoon making a chicken chasseur and didn't answer the question immediately, but asked one of her own.

'Spuds?' She held the serving-spoon as though it were a conductor's baton.

'Don't pretend you didn't hear, Eva. I asked you a question. Are you pregnant?'

'I'm giving you some spuds. And some green beans.'

'I don't care what you give me. I'm taking your evasion as a "yes". You're pregnant, Eva. When did you find out?'

She forced herself to eat a mouthful of food before she answered. 'I've known for a bit. I was going to tell you. Honestly. How did you know? Am I fat yet?'

They stared at one another across the table. Eva put her cutlery down on the plate. Antoine hadn't even picked his up.

'How did you know?'

'You've been sick in the mornings. I've heard you. And you've been looking pale and tired.'

'Really? Pale and tired?' Eva sighed. She closed her eyes. At first, when ghastly nausea woke her every day and she'd spent ages every morning hunched over the lavatory bowl, she'd tried to explain it away, but in the end, she could no longer go on lying to herself. She'd missed two periods. You didn't have to be a doctor to work out what was happening. She'd forgotten to put in her Dutch cap (was it forgetting? Did I want

239

to get pregnant? Deep down?) and now she was expecting a child. She didn't even think of the *thing*, whatever it was that was making her feel so horrible, as a baby. She couldn't, not yet. Whatever her unconscious was doing, in her real life a baby was the last thing she could bring herself to imagine.

'I was going to tell you, Antoine. Truly I was. I told myself I'd confess next time we . . .' She meant: next time he came to her bed. She didn't know in advance when this would happen. He'd sometimes take it into his head to sleep in her room, and Eva spent the time between one occasion and the next in a state of longing. Every few weeks, Antoine would find himself aroused by something she'd said or done and then they made love and for a brief time, Eva was able to pretend that all was well between them. She told herself on these occasions that yes, he loved her as much or almost as much as she loved him. She'd learned how to gather her desires into a moment of blissful release that she knew would have to last her until whenever it was he turned to her again.

Now she said, 'We'd better eat, or it'll get cold.'

Antoine smiled at her. 'Let's get married, then. I don't want my child not to have a father.'

'It's got a father,' Eva said, 'whether we get married or not.'

'You know what I mean. A proper, married father. A traditional dad.'

That proves it, Eva told herself. He wants to marry me. He loves me. He does.

On the day that they'd come back from the hospital to the house with their baby daughter, Antoine had driven and Eva sat in the back of the car with Rowena in a portable carrycot. As they got out of the car and walked up the steps and into Salix House, Eva tasted in her mouth, felt in her speeded-up heartbeat, a sense of utter panic and horror. She handed the carrycot to Antoine as soon as they were inside. She could just see Rowena's little face peeping out of a hood formed from the folds of a pink, cotton blanket. Her eyes were closed. Tight shut. Her mouth was like a small pink bud. Eva felt cold terror grip her heart.

'I'm going to the loo,' she muttered and ran upstairs, Antoine shouting after her: 'Is something wrong? Eva?'

She couldn't answer. She didn't answer for two days. She locked herself into the bathroom and refused to come out. This, she thought as she sat on the edge of the bath, is almost the worst thing I ever did in my life. It's the second worst thing.

During those two days, trays were left outside the door and Eva would wait till she knew whoever had brought them had gone back downstairs to open the door and get them. From time to time, Antoine came and pleaded through the keyhole but Eva didn't want to hear what he said. She could feel herself spiralling down to a mental collapse and that was part of the reason she came out in the end. What everyone thought, what Eva encouraged them to think, was that she'd recovered and accepted that she had to look after her own child, however hard she found the task. That was half true, but it wasn't the only reason she'd unlocked the bathroom door. Part of it was seeing Angelika, not being able to hide from her. Eva had tried to cover the mirror but it was huge and attached to one wall and because she was still weak and sore from the birth she hadn't had the strength to rig up an arrangement that would cover the glass completely. Her sister was almost always there whenever she looked up and in the end Eva couldn't bear it. She'd come out.

No one suggested that she'd hidden because she didn't love little Rowena, but that was what was tearing her apart while she sat on a pile of towels on the floor. The received wisdom was: mothers who love their children properly love them at once. Immediately. Completely. And because she hadn't done that, Eva felt herself to be inadequate, lacking in some feeling others had access to and she didn't. But I *do* love her, she thought, staring down at the tiled floor. That thought, those feelings, didn't seem to help much.

While Eva was locked away, Antoine found Phyllis and from then on she hadn't ever been completely alone with her own daughter. She'd never had to manage anything by herself. Eva's 'crisis', as it was called, was a one-off and the doctors put it down to post-natal depression. Day succeeded day and Rowena grew up and Eva went on loving her but she never felt close, never felt that the two of them enjoyed the kind of relationship a mother and daughter were meant to have.

Eva went back to work as soon as she possibly could. Her whole life depended on it. Other people also looked to her for their livelihoods, and she didn't feel it was right to let them down. Mainly, though, she was working to save her sanity.

Antoine was, as usual, at the bottom of her unhappiness. She began to notice, shortly after Rowena was born, that he stayed away from the house at night, more and more often. Sometimes the phone would ring when he was at home and if Eva picked it up, what she heard was silence on the end of the line. This happened too often for it to be a wrong number each time. Then there was chat, overheard at work. She'd catch the tail end of someone's sneaky giggle and hear phrases like 'typical Bragonard'. She asked the model who'd said that what it meant, directly to her face. The poor girl blushed and muttered something about being 'You know, French', but she was lying and Eva knew it. It was obvious what the problem was. Antoine had found someone else. Another woman. That must be it. Because I'm so fat after the birth. Because I work so hard and because I'm so ratty. He doesn't love me any more. Eva made up her mind to ask him about it, to his face. Whatever else he was, Antoine was not a liar. If she wanted to know the truth, she knew that she could. For a long time, she hesitated. The weeks and the months passed. Sometimes Eva thought that they could go on for ever in this state but that was nonsense. She had to find out. One night, after a particularly delicious supper, when they were sitting together in the study with the lamps lit and the curtains drawn, Eva said, 'Antoine, I have to ask you a question.'

'A question? Sure. Go ahead.' He took a sip from the brandy he'd poured himself.

'Have you . . . that is, do you . . . I mean, is there someone else? Another woman?'

'Another woman? No, of course not. Why'd you say such a thing?' He frowned and his face darkened. Eva hated that angry look of his so much that she now made a habit of trying to please him. But she had to know. Not knowing was slowly wrecking her peace of mind. She took a deep breath.

'You're away a lot. More than ever. You're absent-minded when you *are* here. Not with Rowena, but with me. I feel as if I'm not there sometimes . . . I mean, for you. Not there as far as you're concerned. Also, there are the telephone calls. Someone keeps hanging up on me. So . . . I wondered. It's the obvious thing to think.'

Antoine said nothing for a moment or two but sat and stared at his hands. Eva felt as though her whole being was suspended, as if she weren't breathing. She wanted to scream: *Speak! Say something. Anything. Say anything.*

'It's not a woman,' he said at last. 'It's a man. I prefer men. There. Do you know how many years I've been wanting to tell you that? Since the beginning. Since I first met you.'

'Why didn't you, then?' Eva felt as though someone had scooped her body quite empty and left it echoing and hollow. Her head began to swim and she closed her eyes. 'Why didn't you tell me? There were so many chances to do that . . .'

'I thought you knew when we met. Didn't you? Be honest? I'm sure you did, at some level.'

Eva said nothing for a moment. Was it true? She'd stopped wondering why sex with Antoine was somehow unsatisfactory. She'd tried not to think about it too much. It *had* crossed her mind to wonder whether Antoine was homosexual, but there was nothing camp about him and she hadn't heard any gossip. Was that because she'd deliberately ignored things for all this time? She asked, in as steady a voice as she could muster:

'But us . . . we've . . . the two of us . . . are you . . . I mean, don't you like women as well?' It was a feeble question but she needed to know.

'I wouldn't say I'm bisexual. Of course I enjoy our times together, Eva. You know I do, but that's because it's you. And I love you . . . in every other way, I love you. You know that, don't you? You're my best friend in the whole world. I mean it, Eva. Say you're not angry. Say you forgive me. Please say it.'

'Of course I forgive you,' Eva said, wondering whether she did or not. She had to. If she didn't, then he'd leave. He'd go and live with his lover, and that was something Eva knew she couldn't bear. She added, 'There's nothing to forgive. You can't help what you feel. It makes no difference to how I feel about you.'

She was lying, and realized it even as the words came out of her mouth. Despair washed over her and she had to make an effort not to cry. She felt as though someone had knocked her hard in the stomach. It crossed her mind to wonder whether Antoine had deliberately chosen her as a kind of alibi. When they'd first started living together, homosexual acts were punishable by law. If the world knew he lived with a woman, that made him safe, almost impregnable. How could he be homo-sexual if Eva Conway loved him? If they shared a house? They were photographed at parties, film premières, rock concerts, and fashion shows. I was, I am, a good cover for him, Eva thought and then felt guilty for it.

There were a million questions she wanted to ask and couldn't. Is there someone you're in love with? Do I know him? She would have said she knew which of the men of their acquaintance were homo-sexual but evidently she didn't. Or maybe this man wasn't someone she knew, but a man Antoine had met on his own.

Eva stood up and went over to the window. She pulled back the curtains a little and looked out at the dark garden. A terrifying question formed itself in her head and she had to ask it, before he said another word.

'Can you promise you won't leave me, Antoine? Will you stay with me? With Rowena?'

That, she knew, was a deciding factor. Antoine adored his daughter. He was the one who had moved his studio to the house so that he could be with her more often.

'Of course I want to stay, Eva, but you can see the problem. Now that you know . . .'

How could she actually say the words she knew he wanted to hear? *Yes, fine, have all the lovers you want as long as you keep up the pretence of being my husband? As long as you stay here with me?* She knew she should probably kick him out, but then they'd have to divorce and he'd never leave her Salix House. He'd created it as much as she had. He loved it as much as she did. They'd have to sell it. And, worse than anything, the most damning thing of all was the realization that she still loved him. No, she wasn't going to kick him out. 'No,' she said. 'Stay. Please stay . . . I . . . we . . . I don't want to live apart from you.'

Now she thought: perhaps I was wrong. Maybe I ought to have asked him to leave. Would he have let her buy him out of his share of Salix House? But I loved him and he *did* love me, even if his love was worse than useless because he didn't mean the same thing by it as I did. Eva often wondered whether she could have borne infidelity better if it had been other women. As it was, she'd had to get used to the men. And until that last dreadful night which still returned to her in dreams, she'd managed to do that.

Eva picked up the scissors and began to cut around the lines she'd drawn on the stiffened gauze. I should never, she thought, have given up my work. I shouldn't have let him destroy my career. There had been, she saw now, no need for it. She should have divorced him at once, even at the cost of losing Salix House. Always, always it came back to those two things: she loved Antoine and she loved Salix House.

1972

'Phyllis? Where are you, Phyllis?' Eva called out as she took off her coat and flung it on to a chair in the hall. 'Antoine?'

She went to the kitchen. Antoine was there, over-seeing Rowena's supper. The child was sitting at her high chair, eating some unspeakable mush with every appearance of relish. 'Hello, Rowena darling, Mummy's home!' She went to kiss her daughter who waved a spoon dangerously close to Eva's blouse. 'Careful, sweetheart!' she said as she kissed the top of Rowena's head.

'You're late today,' Antoine said. He was in a

bad mood. Eva knew this at once – she would have known it even if he hadn't spoken. She knew by the way he looked at her, the way he stood, the way he breathed, almost, what kind of a state he was in. Today had clearly not gone well and Eva took a deep breath. Did she have the energy to cope with this? Would he be okay to put Rowena to bed?

'I've had a nightmare of a day,' she said, trying to keep her voice light. 'On the phone all day long to Italy about that silk . . . remember I told you about the silk? And I'm still not sure if it's going to arrive on time. I despair. I'm making some tea. Would you like a cup?'

Antoine pretended to be absorbed in Rowena's doings and looked up only after he'd wiped her face carefully. 'No, no tea for me. I'm going to run Rowena's bath. Unless of course you'd like to?'

'God, no, not after the day I've had. I'm finished. I'll come up and kiss her goodnight.'

'Right,' said Antoine, lifting Rowena out of the high chair. A whole universe of resentment was contained in the way he said that single word.

'Where's Phyllis? Why are you doing this now? I thought you had work to do in your darkroom.'

'I did. I haven't done it. Phyllis is in her room. Migraine. So I had to step in.'

'Angel! How lucky that you were here.'

'I'm always here. Nearly always.'

Eva could see the words *unlike some people I could*

mention hovering above her husband's head as clearly as if they'd been outlined in neon. He left the room holding Rowena's hand.

When Eva went up to kiss her daughter good-night, the child was already asleep. She felt, for no good reason, as though Antoine and Rowena were deliberately plotting against her.

'We need to talk, Eva,' Antoine whispered as they left the room. 'Come to the study.'

They went downstairs together, not speaking. When they got there, Antoine sat down behind the desk in the seat which Eva thought of (though she'd never mentioned this) as hers. She went to the sofa, but felt too tense to lean back. She perched there awkwardly, dreading what was coming.

'I can't go on like this,' Antoine began.

'Like what?'

'Do you love Rowena at all?'

A pulse began to beat in Eva's head. Didn't Antoine realize how much she hated him being angry with her?

'Of course I do. Whatever are you talking about?'

'I'm talking about the fact that you couldn't give a damn whether you see her or not. You don't care if you come back from London after she's in bed. Don't care if you never put her to bed. Just . . . you don't give a shit about her.'

Eva sprang to her feet. 'How can you say a thing like that? She's my daughter. I love her more than anything in the world.'

'Then why the fuck can't you show it?'

'Please don't swear at me, Antoine. You know I hate that . . .'

To herself she said: *Don't cry. Don't on any account cry.*

Antoine sighed. 'Okay. Okay, I won't swear but I can't go on like this. I'm responsible for all the childcare round here.'

'But . . .' Eva said, 'that's why we have Phyllis, isn't it? That's what her job is, looking after Rowena.' She made an effort speak gently, doing her best to sound sympathetic; not to be seen to be making light of what was worrying Antoine.

'And cleaning this enormous house and cooking our meals. Doing all kinds of things that you'd do if you were ever home for more than five minutes.'

Eva turned her back on Antoine and moved over to the bookcase. He went on, 'So this is what I'm suggesting. Come and sit down and listen to me.'

Reluctantly, Eva went back to sit on the sofa. I'm like a school child in the Head's study, she thought. How can that be? This is my house as much as his. More . . . a nasty, unworthy, horrible thought came into her head: *It's mostly my money that pays for everything. I'm the one earning the real money in this household.*

'Why couldn't you be here? Every day. Whenever Rowena needs you. If you can't do that, I'll have to think of some other way of organizing the household. Phyllis can't do housework and cooking and childcare. Stephen could come and help me. He could even move in, if that was more convenient?'

Stephen was Antoine's latest lover. He'd lasted some months and Antoine was besotted with him. Almost every time Eva came into the house, or so it seemed, her husband was giggling on the phone to this man and always, always cut the call short when she appeared. 'Only Stephen,' he'd say and then: 'I can call him back later.'

'I see what you're doing, Antoine. A form of blackmail. You're saying: *Give up your job or I'll move my lover into our house*. Isn't that right?'

'Just about, yes. I think that is what I'm saying. I'm just tired of being the one who does everything. Who's always on duty. Not that I don't adore Rowena, you know I do, but I have a career of my own and besides, it's not on, the way you just shove off any responsibility for her happiness to other people. I think it's time you grew up and did something for your own child.'

Eva said nothing. She wanted to answer but could find no words for anything she wanted to say. Didn't she do something? Was what Antoine was saying true? How could she admit how important her work was to her? How much she loved it? Antoine saw her hesitation and added, 'I know how much your work means to you, and of course there's the money to consider, but even if you gave up designing tomorrow you've saved enough and invested wisely enough for years to make sure you'll have everything you might need. We own this house outright, don't forget. And I have work to do as well, you know.'

'I do know. Of course I do. I'll think about it,' Eva said, making a move towards the door. Staying at home with Rowena and Phyllis. Every day. Knowing that Antoine was with someone else. Stephen. *But he's threatening to bring Stephen here to Salix House.* She would know that while she was absent he wouldn't be alone. Her space, her rooms, her furniture would become tainted. If I'm here, she had told herself, I can look after the house. Phyllis will help me with Rowena. Maybe I can learn to be a good mother to her. Antoine said, 'Hang on, there's something else. I didn't want to say this, Eva, but I think I should.' He hesitated.

'Well? Are you going to tell me?'

'Remember I'm speaking as someone who's always loved your work. Loved it. The fact is, Eva, you're past your best. The last two collections haven't exactly been . . . earth-shattering, have they? The focus is on younger designers, isn't it? You know it is, if you're honest with yourself. You might think about the benefit of quitting while you're ahead, so to speak.'

Eva shuddered, even now at a distance of more than forty years, at how hurt, how *soiled* Antoine had made her feel that night. Retrospectively, she felt more fury than anything else and more at herself than at Antoine for the bloody spineless fool she'd been. She'd thought there was no alternative, but maybe she ought to have moved out, on her own and left Salix House and Antoine and Rowena and flown to Paris to start over again. *Something.*

For a while after she'd closed the design studio there had been articles in the fashion magazines mourning her departure, but as Antoine kept on telling her, things move quickly and before you know where you are, you were no longer what was wanted. No longer part of what was going on.

'Ma? When you've finished cutting that . . . are you listening to me?'

'Of course, of course. I do know. I realize. You can't stay here in Salix House just to please me. I will find somewhere, I'm sure, but you can't expect me to be happy about it.'

'But why do you have to tell Megan these things? Why don't you tell me? She's not your daughter, I am!'

Rowena might be in her forties but the tone of her voice took Eva right back to when she was a teenager. It wasn't exactly a whine but it was a thread of discontent, of complaint, quite audible to anyone. For a second she thought of answering frivolously: *Are you seriously jealous of Megan, Rowena?* But she said only, 'Megan just happened to catch me at a low moment, that's all. Conor sent her to find me when I went out to walk my bad mood off. I'm not trying to hide anything from you.'

Rowena nodded. 'Glad to hear it.' She stood up. 'We'll find some other places to look at, don't worry.'

'That's fine. Dee's wings are the only thing on

my mind now, so you can stop fretting about me. I shall go up in a moment when I've done this bit.'

'Goodnight, then,' Rowena said and walked round the table to bend down and kiss Eva on the cheek.

'Goodnight, darling.' Eva turned to kiss her back, but Rowena had already straightened up and was on her way out of the room.

She *is* jealous of Megan, Eva told herself. She remembered how much it mattered to Rowena that Antoine loved her the very best. 'Better than Ma?' she used to ask when she was tiny and he always answered, 'Best in the whole wide world. I love you all there is.' Which, she now reflected, he never said to me. As soon as Rowena was born the baby became the centre of his life, but even before that and certainly afterwards, there was a whole series of men who were more important to him than Eva was. There wasn't much she could do about that, having come into the marriage knowing from the beginning that it was less than what it should be and learning later how much of a compromise and a deception it was.

The angel wings were lying on the blanket. All she needed to do now was sew on the ribbons. Finding them wouldn't be a problem. There was a shop in Amersham she could go to. She couldn't borrow Conor's car tomorrow as he was using it and Rowena hated lending hers. She sighed. She would have to ask Megan to give her a lift, even though she disliked having to do it: disliked having to depend on other people. Never mind. She would make a determined effort to think about pleasanter things.

How lovely it had been, talking to Lissa earlier! Now, thinking about their long conversation made Eva feel happy. They'd arranged to meet for lunch in London later in November. Also, she had a plan. Dee had shown her how to find her way more skilfully around the Rightmove website, and earlier in the day, as soon as she'd finished talking to Lissa, she'd gone back to the computer and almost at once had found somewhere that looked possible. She'd come across it by accident, almost, and could hardly believe what she'd read. She wrote the estate agent's number in her notebook. Tomorrow, she'd ring them up and make an appointment to see the place on the same day she was seeing Lissa – two birds with one stone. Who said she had to live next door, practically, to Rowena? There were other parts of London that might be much nicer for any number of reasons.

I lay in Tom's bed staring up at the ceiling. The green numbers on the digital clock on the bedside table said 22:30. I could get up and go home now. Tom was lying on his back with his eyes closed. He'd been dozing but I knew he was awake now because he'd put out a hand and was stroking my thigh.

'Darling Megan,' he murmured. 'That was . . .'

'Mmm,' I said. I didn't want him to say anything. I couldn't say I hadn't enjoyed it, but something was missing. The whole time Tom was asleep, I'd been trying to work out my emotions. Were my memories of Simon getting in the way, somehow? Or not Simon himself, but what I felt about his baby? That hadn't gone away. I came to the conclusion that I didn't deserve to be happy. I hadn't felt as if I deserved to be happy since the abortion. The memories of that time were always there, even though they had been pushed to the back of my mind, especially after I met Simon. For a while I thought I was over it, that I'd forgiven myself, but I hadn't. I thought getting to know Tom would be a help. But even while we were making love, I was on my guard: watching out for the pictures in my head to return: blood, a small curled-up creature that was both a baby and not a baby. Everything was there, and I would never be free of the guilt.

CHAPTER 15

'You look happy,' Eva said. 'Has something good happened? Let me guess. The Fosters have found a place to move to.'

Rowena had come into the study with the kind of smile on her face that makes anyone looking at it have to ask a question.

'No they haven't, more's the pity, but it doesn't really matter. This news is better than that.' Rowena sat down on the sofa, flinging aside cushions as she did so. Eva was at the desk, sorting through the ribbons she and Megan had bought that morning. Metres and metres of glossy satin ribbon in white and silver and gold; more metres of lurex-threaded white and tinselly gold and even some of very palest grey were spread out in front of her. Megan was on a chair beside the desk, putting the elastic bands on the rolled-up bundles to keep them tidy.

'The estate agent phoned me at work. I didn't want to phone you with the news, but to tell you myself. Luke Fielden's upped the money. He's offering the full asking price now. That's five thousand more than before. Wants me to take the house off the market, which of course I agreed to at once. Isn't that wonderful? I must ring Luke after supper. Tell him how delighted we are.'

Eva tried to smile sincerely, though she felt as though someone had just passed sentence on her. 'Wonderful,' she said and then added: 'You must be so relieved.'

'God, I am. I can't tell you what a huge weight that is off my mind. Now all we need is to get somewhere super for you to live and for the Fosters to find something that suits them so that we can buy their house and then we'll be laughing.'

Eva noticed that Megan had stopped bundling up the ribbons and was sitting very still. She glanced sideways at her. 'Is something the matter, Megan?' she asked.

'Oh, gosh, Megan,' Rowena said quickly. 'I completely forgot to tell you. But I did speak to Conor and just as I'd expected, he agreed with me. I do hope you're not too upset?'

'No, no I'm fine. Thanks, Rowena.'

Rowena watched Megan leave the room. 'What's up with her?' she asked.

'Is something up? I hadn't noticed really.'

Eva put all the ribbons into a plastic bag. Rowena said, 'We must look out for more places for you to see, mustn't we?'

'I suppose so,' Eva said. 'I've been looking at various things myself on the internet.'

'Have you? Really? How did you get into that?'

'Dee showed me. I like it. I've been finding some interesting things.'

'What sort of things?'

'I look people up on Wikipedia. I Google things.'

'Such as?'

'Do you remember Lissa Dovedale?'

'Well, I know who she was, of course. That model Dad liked taking photos of. The one in the *Ghost* collection, right?'

'That's the one. Well, she wrote to me the other day.'

'Really? What's she doing nowadays? What did she say?'

Eva paused. 'Oh, you know . . . stuff. But she's in London for a bit. I'm going to have lunch with her on Saturday.'

'Lovely! It'll be a treat for you. I wonder what she looks like after all these years.'

'According to Google Images, very much as she used to, but with added wrinkles. Also, she doesn't dye her hair. Salt and pepper with more salt than pepper. And cropped short too. Very chic.'

Eva smiled. Lissa Dovedale's letter was the best thing that had happened to her since the moving business started, but she wasn't going to tell Rowena about that for the moment. There'd be time enough after she'd met Lissa and they'd worked out more of the details. There may also, she reflected, be something to tell Rowena after she'd been round 22 Frobisher Court.

'Is Megan not eating with us tonight?' Eva asked.

'No, she isn't. I spoke to her when I got home

and she said she's eating with Tom Shoreley. He came to pick her up, too, which thrilled Dee and Bridie.'

'They shouldn't get too excited,' Eva said. 'I know she's seeing a lot of him but I'm sure it's nothing serious. Megan would have told me.'

She frowned. She'd wanted to make her announcement to everyone and now she'd have to go over everything again when she next saw Megan. But that doesn't matter, she told herself. It's such good news that I won't mind repeating it. 'You're looking very smart, Ma,' Rowena said. 'Any special reason? You don't often change for dinner.'

'Oh, I just felt like it this evening,' Eva said. 'I've got something to tell you both.' That wasn't quite the truth. She'd decided to dress up as a way of making herself powerful. She'd chosen the clothes specifically to create an impression of someone to be reckoned with. Her silver-and-jade necklace looked good, she thought, against the dark green of her silk blouse and she'd added silver earrings and put her hair up with more than usual care. Feeble old lady was the look she had tried to avoid. With no more than the cursory glance in the mirror that she'd allowed herself, she was pretty confident that she looked as good as she was capable of looking.

'Sounds a bit ominous,' said Conor, helping himself to more roasted vegetables.

'Not at all,' said Eva. 'It's good news for a change.' She put down her knife and fork and dabbed at the corner of her mouth with the napkin. 'I told you, didn't I, that Lissa Dovedale had written to me?'

Rowena nodded and Conor looked bemused. Eva went on, 'She's a widow nowadays. Her husband was a wealthy American property developer. Did I tell you?'

'Doesn't matter, Ma. Go on.'

'Well, Lissa is opening a Museum of Modern Fashion. In Chalk Farm. She's bought an old Victorian house which is now in the process of being converted. She wants to buy a good few of my dresses to display there. In the Museum. I'd have, she told me, a room given over to my designs. Imagine: *the Eva Conway Room*.'

'Oh, my God,' said Rowena. 'That is the most marvellous news. You must be so thrilled. How lovely of Lissa to remember you after all this time.'

Eva smiled and decided not to dwell on the fact that her daughter's remark could be interpreted as meaning: *Not many other people* would *remember you*. Don't be uncharitable, she told herself. Rowena didn't intend it as a put-down, she was almost sure.

'Yes, it is. It's marvellous. When I meet her, she's going to show me how far they've got with the building. And we'll firm up arrangements. She'll have to come here and choose what she wants to take.'

'There's going to be some money involved, isn't there?' Conor said.

'Yes, of course, though we still have to discuss

how much each dress is worth. I believe Lissa has an independent consultant who advises her on such matters.'

'I can give you a hand there too, Ma. Make sure you're getting a good price.'

'Thanks, Rowena,' Eva said, trying to sound gracious. 'Lissa said she knew of other people who might be willing to buy anything she doesn't need.' She couldn't help feeling a pang of regret at the thought of her dresses in other cupboards, with other owners. She tried to imagine a time when all she'd have left from everything she'd created was a bunch of memories. Don't be silly, she chided herself. There are files and drawers full of drawings and photographs. Or would Lissa want to buy those too?

'Well,' said Conor. 'You're going to be coming into a fair amount of money, I'd have thought. That'll be useful when you're thinking about where to live, won't it?'

Eva nodded. Rowena had been dishing out the plum crumble and was coming back from the fridge with a small jug of cream. Now she said, 'I hadn't thought of that. But it's true. We can be a bit more ambitious now about what we look at.'

'That's another thing I wanted to tell you,' Eva said, helping herself to cream. 'I've made an appointment to look at somewhere. The day I go and meet Lissa. I'll go straight from our lunch.'

'Really? Oh, Ma, tell us about it. I'll come with you if you like.'

'No need. Not for the first viewing. Lissa said she'll come with me and if it's nice, there'll be time enough for you to see it and give it your stamp of approval.' She thought: I don't need your approval. I don't need anyone's approval.

'Okay. Only tell us a bit about it. Where is it?'

'Chalk Farm.'

Rowena paused with her spoon half way to her mouth. She put it down in the dish and leaned towards Eva. 'Chalk Farm? That's not exactly on our doorstep. Why ever are you looking there? It's also a very expensive area.'

'Well, it'll be very near the Museum. I shall be able to visit my dresses.'

'But what about visiting us? How'll you manage that?'

'I'll take a bus. Or the Underground. I can get a Freedom Pass.'

'Oh, for goodness' sake, Ma!'

'What are you exclaiming about? I love buses and I don't even mind the Tube. And there are taxis, aren't there?'

'But they're so expensive!'

Eva smiled. 'You said it yourself. I'll have a lot more disposable income after the sale of my archive. Enough to buy me lots and lots of taxi rides once I'm incapable of driving.'

'You're being frivolous, Ma! You know what I mean. You should be near us. It makes so much more sense. What if you fall ill? What if we need you to babysit the girls sometimes? How will they come and visit you, if you're the other side of London? Can't you find somewhere closer than Chalk Farm?'

'Shall we postpone the argument about this till after I've seen the flat in question? We may be arguing to no purpose whatsoever.'

Rowena ate the rest of her plum crumble in silence. Then she said, 'I suppose you're right. There's no point meeting trouble halfway. But I can't say I'm happy about this. The Museum thing'll be brilliant, I can see, but—'

Eva stood up. 'Don't worry about it, Rowena. I'm sure all will be well in the end. I'm going up to my room now. I want to make an early start tomorrow. I'm going to go through the dresses and see what's what. Goodnight, both of you.'

'Goodnight, Ma.'

'Goodnight, Eva.'

As she left the room, Eva began to imagine the kind of conversation Conor and Rowena would have now that she was no longer there. She smiled at the thought. There's nothing they can really say, she thought. If I've got the money, I can do exactly what I like.

Frobisher Court took Eva by surprise, even though she'd seen it on the Rightmove website and had taken the virtual tour of one of the flats. It was a converted Victorian house, set back from the road. A cast-iron gate (opened by Jason, the estate agent who was showing them round) was set into a high hedge.

'A bit unusual, for this part of London,' Lissa said. 'I suspect the firm that converted the house must have bought these bushes ready-grown. Isn't it great that you can do that?'

'I'm so glad you had time to come and look at it with me.' Eva put her arm through Lissa's. The young, very beautiful model she remembered had turned into one of those ultra-thin, super-chic women you saw in the front row of fashion shows and in photographs at the back of *Harper's Bazaar*. Eva had stopped calculating how much Lissa's outfit was worth after she'd noticed the Anya Hindmarch bag which she knew, thanks to *Vogue*, cost more than two thousand pounds. The face was unchanged but much older.

'I'm like a prune.' Lissa had laughed as she took something from the plate in front of her which held what passed for her lunch. Eva had chosen soup and a roll, followed by a Danish pastry and coffee with cream, but Lissa's choice seemed to consist of nothing but leaves and seeds. 'I blame the Texas sun,' she added, taking a sip from her lime-flower tisane.

Over lunch, Lissa had spoken of her plans for Eva's dresses.

'I'll buy some for the Museum, of course, but I think you should hold an auction for all the others. People would be falling over themselves to come. I can arrange it, Eva. I know so many people in the auction business. We can do it together. It'd be fun.'

Eva smiled, 'Honestly, Lissa, to listen to you, you'd think there was nothing even a bit sad about losing the dresses.'

'There isn't.' Lissa sounded so definite that she almost managed to convince Eva. 'What good are they doing in your cupboards, in the dark? Wouldn't you like to think of women wearing them, looking beautiful, being happy, showing off what you've made?'

'If you put it like that,' Eva said, 'I can't think of a thing to say against it.'

'Good! I'm always right, you know.' She took the last sip of her drink and added, 'Okay! That flat. I can't wait to see it. I adore looking round flats, houses, you name it.'

'You are just the right person to come with me. I wanted to see it with someone like you who knows what's what before getting Rowena to look at it. It seems too good to be true.'

'And it's so close to where the Museum's going to be. You could walk down and visit your dresses. I am so excited, Eva! It'll be marvellous when we open.'

Eva nodded. What Lissa had described to her did indeed sound good. They'd met before lunch at a hollowed-out shell of the house which was in the process of being converted into the Museum.

'I thought you'd like to see where your lovely creations will be living,' said Lissa, moving through empty rooms where workmen were busy knocking down walls, building complicated platforms. 'To get at the ceilings,' said Lissa. 'I don't do the details of this, darling. I have a great architect who's in charge of it and he says – it's hard to believe it – this will all be done by the end of next summer. Amazing. I'll show you the sketches over lunch. I wanted you to see the street, the whole thing.'

Eva had loved the street. Sometimes, in London, it was possible to find places like this, away from the main stream of city life, which seemed to have remained untouched for more than a century. Tall, white, stucco-fronted houses and pretty ash trees growing along the pavement gave the impression of a quieter time, in spite of the cars parked in the road. The house which was destined to become the Museum was on a corner and there were already three men at work there, landscaping the space into a garden.

'I'll put in a magnolia tree,' said Lissa. 'And maybe a Japanese maple as well, with those scarlet leaves in the fall. Something beautiful in any case.'

'It's wonderful,' Eva said, 'and it's going to be even better when everything's finished, of course.'

'Let's go and eat and I'll show you the sketches of what it'll look like inside.'

Now, Jason was speaking to Eva and she returned to what she was supposed to be doing: looking at Frobisher Court. 'You'll see,' he said, 'how secure it is. No one gets in without the code. And do notice the communal gardens. At the front, and also round the back. All residents have access to the space but because there are only six flats in the complex, you don't ever feel crowded. No children of course, except as occasional visitors coming to see the residents. And a warden, so that you're always sure of someone on the spot to help with anything you need.'

Until, Eva thought, you get too infirm and ancient and unable even to make yourself a cup of tea or an omelette, and then it's the care home and the plastic chairs in a row in front of the television. She shuddered. But there's no reason to think so negatively, she told herself, as they all walked together into the building. Lissa, she noticed, was exclaiming over every fresh feature Jason drew to their attention.

'Oh, Eva, it's blissful!' she said, almost before they'd opened the door. I can't concentrate with her squealing, Eva thought, and I could do without Jason as well. She whispered to Lissa: 'Can you get him to go round with you? I want to see the place by myself and not listen to the whole sales thing. Pretend you're interested, darling. I'd be so grateful.'

CHAPTER 16

'Your heart's not in this, is it?' Tom said.
'What do you mean?' We were in his flat, quite early in the morning and it struck me as mad to be lying in bed only an hour or so after I'd got up. I'd told him we could spend the day together and the sun for once was shining outside. Normal people would be out and about doing ordinary stuff. We saw one another so little, according to Tom, that we had to make the most of every minute and that meant that the first thing we did was go to bed, almost as soon as I'd crossed the threshold. It wasn't that I didn't enjoy making love to Tom. I did, and of course he could tell that I did, so that made what he'd just said even harder to understand. He was leaning on his elbow, staring down at me. He said, 'You were somewhere else.'

I couldn't deny it. He was speaking gently, kindly. He didn't seem to be pissed off with me.

'I'm not a fool. This Simon character – you're not over him. Not properly. Feels to me like you've been trying too hard to forget him and well . . . I don't fancy being a sort of comfort blanket for you. Sorry.'

Comfort blanket. I was about to say something denying this, but he was right. I *had* been using him to cheer myself up. It hadn't occurred to me before but we'd never spoken about anything important. I'd never told him about my childhood, apart from recounting a selection of 'stupid things I did when I was a teenager' stories. I hadn't gone into detail about Simon and I wouldn't have dreamed of telling Tom about dead babies or rooms at Salix House that I thought might be haunted.

'I could love you,' he carried on, 'but I can't see that there's much point in it. I don't want to go on with this kind of . . . The way we feel about one another, I mean. The way you feel about me. Or don't feel about me.'

I nodded, not trusting myself to speak. In the end I said, 'But I do like you so much, Tom. We can still be friends, can't we?'

'Yes. Of course we can. But we'd better stop all this . . .' He waved a hand over the bed. 'Though I'll miss you. You know that, Megan, right?'

'We can still see each other, can't we? Have a drink every so often?'

'I guess. It won't be the same, but it's better than nothing.' He got up and started dressing. 'Actually, there's rather a lot I've got to do today, what with the Nativity Play, so perhaps . . .'

I could take a hint. 'Okay, no problem. I've got stuff to do too. I ought to run an errand for Eva. She needs supplies for her sewing and I might have to take her up to town or something. She's busy doing the costumes for *The Boy Friend*. See you soon, okay?'

It was a lie. I knew Eva had gone to London to meet her friend Lissa but I needed to be on my own. I just wanted to be out of there. Part of me hurt a little. I'd come to rely on Tom, devoted, in the background. Even though I'd arrived at his house this morning meaning to pull back a bit from getting too involved. He held the door for me as I left and said, 'Bye, Megan. Sorry it hasn't worked out. See you soon.' And he kissed me on both cheeks.

Even though I'd been thinking about dumping him, Tom had beaten me to it. He didn't seem exactly heartbroken either, I told myself. It's never pleasant to be given the push, but I was relieved in a way. We could still be friends, and I decided that I'd do everything I could to be nice to him, within strict limits. He's a nice man, I told myself. He deserves to find someone who loves him, and I can't. I looked at my watch. It was half past eleven and the weekend. I could drive home and go for a walk. The girls were out with Conor and Rowena visiting some friends and they weren't due back till after five o'clock. The weather was perfect: sunshine and frosty air and pale blue skies. I'd go and have lunch in the Fox and Hounds. I would go the long way round, through the fields at the back of Salix House. I reckoned it was less than two miles. Walking would give me time to think.

I'd been striding along for about twenty minutes when I heard someone calling my name. I turned, thinking that perhaps Tom had come after me. I peered at a figure waving at me. The sun was in my eyes so I couldn't see clearly but it looked like Luke Fielden. As he approached, he said, 'Hello, Megan. How nice to run into you like this!'

'How could you see who I was from so far away?'

'I recognized your walk,' he said. 'I'm on my way to the Fox and Hounds for lunch.'

'Oh,' I said, wondering if I should admit that was where I was going too. 'Do join me,' he said. 'I'd love some company. They do very nice Ploughman's.'

'Thanks,' I said and added, 'I was going there too. There's no one at the house and it's such a lovely day that I wanted to get out.'

'Right,' he said and we walked along in silence for a minute or two. Then he said: 'Have you heard that my latest offer on the house has been accepted?'

'Well . . .' I didn't know how to continue. I was thinking of Eva and how unhappy she would be at this news. Luke said, 'You don't have to be polite. I know how you feel about Mrs Conway leaving the house. I can see it'll be hard for her, but there's no way they can keep the house. That's what Rowena's said. And I'm sure Eva'll find a place she likes in the end. I certainly hope so. I'd hate to be seen as the one driving her out of the home she loves. But like I said: if I don't buy it, someone else will.'

'I know,' I said. 'You're right of course.' I smiled at him. He was dressed in jeans and a Barbour jacket and had a scarf round his neck that looked like cashmere. Not wearing a suit made him more approachable. More normal. He didn't seem a bit arrogant.

'If you buy the house and the family moves to London,' I said, 'I can start looking for work as a journalist again.'

'Yes, Eva told me that you worked at *lipstick*. You came to interview her, she said.'

'That's right. I'm not a nanny, even though Dee and Bridie are lovely and it's not as bad a job as I feared it might be. Also I love Salix House and yes, I do feel sorry for Eva but of course you're right.' I wanted to add that if anyone was going to buy it I was glad it would be him, but before I could, we reached the pub and he said, 'Let me buy you a drink and a Ploughman's.' I thanked him and went to sit at a small table to wait. I realized as I watched him crossing the pub with our drinks that I knew very little about him. I said so, as soon as he sat down.

'Well, there's nothing to know really. I'm thirty-seven years old. I work too hard. I'm going to buy Salix House. I've a sister called Marion who lives in Belstone. It's one of the reasons I've been so keen to buy something in this area—'

I don't know why I said what I said next. Maybe it was because he mentioned Salix House.

'D'you believe in ghosts?' I asked him suddenly

and then paused because he didn't answer at once. I added, 'I'm sorry. Don't answer if you don't want to. It's a bit of a mad question.'

Luke looked straight at me, unsmiling. 'It depends what you mean by ghosts,' he said at last, and he was speaking very quietly so that I had to lean forward a little to hear him. 'I do still see them, or at least I think I'm seeing them. That's my wife and son. Who are –,' he looked down, taking a long time to get a sip of his beer – 'dead. I'm a widower.'

'Oh my God,' I said, feeling sick with mortification. 'I'm so sorry. I had no idea. That must be . . . how awful.'

'I don't mind talking about it. It's been four years. My wife and baby son were killed. Really, Megan, there's no need to apologize.'

There was nothing to say. I made a sound in my throat like a kind of groan and flailed about for words. I blinked back tears and couldn't find anything to say that didn't sound flat and inappropriate.

Luke went on: 'They died in a car crash on the way back from the supermarket. Ridiculous sort of crash, out of nowhere. No adverse weather conditions, no bad roads, nothing strange or exotic. Just a common-or-garden fatal accident. She was going too fast . . . a bit too fast and someone else was going much too fast. There you go. Bad luck. Alison, Mattie and the other driver dead at the scene. Mattie should have been with me. He was often with me when Alison went

275

shopping. He loved going in the trolleys and that day, he'd made such a fuss when we tried to suggest that he stayed at home. Alison was in a rush and she was shopping for a dinner party and didn't want him distracting her. But in the end . . . well, I should've put my foot down and insisted he stayed with me. I didn't insist. Part of me was happy, can you believe that? Relieved that I could do some work from home for a bit and didn't have to be saddled with Saturday morning childcare. Jesus.'

Luke put one hand over his mouth and closed his eyes briefly. 'And sometimes I think I've seen them. I'll see a toddler, wearing the same kind of clothes, or a woman who walks just like Alison. On the street, in the shops. It's not them, and I know it's not but there's a second when whoever it is looks enough like them to trick me. Just for a heartbeat. It's happening less and less as time goes on. At the beginning . . . well. They were everywhere in the house. So I got rid of the house and bought a flat that was the exact opposite of what our home had been like.' He smiled. 'My flat is very modern and functional and minimalist. It's hard to be minimalist when a kid's around.' He sounded like his normal self again and he began to talk about his upstairs neighbours who were from Switzerland and gave fondue parties every month. Then food came, and even though the talk had left the subject of his dead wife and child, I hardly noticed what I was swallowing.

'It's good, isn't it?' he asked.

'Yes, it is,' I said but the truth was I wouldn't have cared one jot if it had been a burger and chips at McDonald's. I was too busy readjusting my view of him. I'd thought of him as a bit stand-offish, but maybe he was simply unhappy. How long did it take to get over a bereavement like that? I wanted to ask him other questions but didn't feel I knew him well enough. He said, speaking gently, 'We *can* go on talking, you know. I didn't mean to put a cloud over the day.'

'No, it's fine, really. It's just . . .' I wanted to say: *It's so sad,* but stopped myself in time. That would have been both stupid and obvious. I drank some of my cider.

He said, 'Let's talk about you. Are you actively looking for a job?'

'No, I'm not. But I ought to start if the Fitzpatricks are going to move. I left London . . . well.' I don't know why I said what I said next but maybe it was because I was starting to like him. I said, 'I sort of had to come here. I couldn't stay in London. Couldn't stay at *lipstick.* I had an affair with my boss. Simon was his name. Simon Gradwell. What happened was my fault. I knew from the start he was married. I didn't . . . It was mad. And wrong of both of us, and I should have put a stop to it, I suppose. But I *did* love him. I thought, for a while, that he'd leave his wife but he didn't. His wife became pregnant and he chose her. I can understand it.'

I must have sounded less cheerful than I was trying to be because Luke put out a hand and covered my hand and squeezed it. Then he took his hand away and said: 'Don't blame yourself, Megan. It's a horrible thing to happen. Particularly bad that you felt you had to leave your job, but you'll get over it and I'm sure it won't be long before you find another job.'

'Things are pretty dire in newspapers and magazines,' I said. 'I'm not sure many jobs are coming up.'

'Look,' Luke said, 'Eva told me I shouldn't say anything about this. She's very protective of you and didn't want you to be hurt, but you've brought up Simon Gradwell's name and I feel it would be dishonest if I didn't tell you at once that I know him a bit. Not at all well, but I run into him sometimes. I saw him just the other day. I was in the hospitality tent at a rugby match. He was with his wife, who was very obviously pregnant. Oh God, Eva will be angry with me now. I hope you aren't—'

'What? What did you say?'

'Megan? What's wrong? You've gone quite white, Megan. What's the matter?'

'I'm sorry. I'm sorry. I must have misheard you.' I took a deep breath and closed my eyes. I counted to ten and then opened them again to see Luke staring at me anxiously. He must have made a mistake. I said, 'Did you say Gail Gradwell was with Simon? And pregnant?'

'Yes. I spoke to both of them for a bit. There were crowds of people about but I remember thinking the whole occasion must have been tiring for her.'

'Luke, I'm sorry. This has been so nice and thanks for telling me that you know Simon. That was good of you. But I've got to go now. Everyone will be back at Salix House soon and I've got so much to do before they get home. Thanks for the lunch. I've had such a good time.' I could hear myself babbling.

'Let me come with you. You look—'

'No, no really.'

'Then another time. Will you let me take you to dinner? If give you my card will you phone me? Just to say you're okay?'

My head was filled with fog. I heard the word *dinner* and couldn't think why it was being said and why to me. I wanted, I needed, only to leave the pub. To get out of there. To be on my own. I felt as if I was holding back a flood and I knew that if I started to speak, I'd lose control entirely. So I nodded and he gave me a card which I put into the pocket of my coat. And then I left the pub and went back into the fields I'd come through with Luke and started running as fast as I could, as though there was some hope of outrunning my thoughts.

Lissa went off with Jason in one direction and Eva was free to look at the flat on her own. She stood in the small hallway and gazed around her. I feel comfortable, she thought. She liked the colour of the walls: a pale, oyster grey on which any picture would look good. She liked the height of the ceiling. She liked the space. Every room was airy and well proportioned and while Eva realized that of course it was bound to look a bit more cluttered when her furniture was in, the whole flat gave an impression of both space and light. The sitting-room/dining-room window opened on to the communal garden and beyond that she could see a child's swing in the garden of an adjoining house. A small girl in a blue jacket was playing on the swing and because every leaf had fallen from the trees, Eva could see her quite clearly. The double-glazed windows shut out the traffic sounds from the main road, which was just round the corner.

She heard Lissa and Jason laughing as she moved from one room to another. The kitchen was small but perfect. The bedroom had fitted cupboards and more room in them than she'd expected, but still, she told herself, I'll have to get rid of so much. For a moment this thought depressed her, but then she caught sight of the en-suite bathroom, through an archway, and this distracted her. She wandered into it, admiring the simplicity of the fittings and the intelligent layout. A mirror was fixed into the wall above the sink and seeing it (though what else did she expect in a bathroom?) made her turn away, rather too quickly and she sat down on the edge of the bath feeling a little dizzy. That'll have to be covered, she thought. Perhaps I could hang an embroidered cloth of some kind over it. I'll have to put hooks into the wall but it could be very striking, if I get the right fabric. She managed to leave the bathroom without so much as glancing in the mirror again.

Once Jason had shown them everything in the flat and walked them round the garden, he left Eva and Lissa together at the gate.

'I'll be in touch very soon,' Eva said. 'I'd like to come and see it again with my daughter.'

'Don't leave it too long,' Jason smiled. 'They're going very quickly, you know. In spite of the recession.'

'Are you going to take it?' Lissa asked when he'd driven away. 'I do hope so. It is a most gorgeous place and think of it, there are five other flats full of probably the most wonderful people for you to be friends with.'

'You don't change, Lissa. You always were ridiculously optimistic. What if the other flat owners are crashing bores or even worse?'

'They won't be! I promise you they won't.'

Eva smiled. She was already imagining herself in those rooms. She was seeing the flat as a possibility. With the sale of her dresses, and the proceeds of the auction, she had enough in her personal savings to be able to afford it. I don't have to keep my money, she thought. I can spend it. When she died, the flat could be sold and that money passed on, but meanwhile, there was no reason for it to sit in a bank somewhere. For the first time since Rowena had told her that Salix House was to be sold, she felt something like anticipation. The dread – it had been like a physical weight on her for a long time – had suddenly gone. She could hardly wait to tell Rowena. And Megan, too, was sure to be happy for her.

After Lissa had said goodbye and waved her off in her taxi, Eva took out her phone. Why not, she thought? What am I waiting for? I know this is right. She punched in Jason's number and when he answered, she said, 'This is Eva Conway. I'd like to make an offer for 22 Frobisher Court.'

When the phone call ended, she put her phone back in her handbag and felt happier than she had for a very long time.

By the time I reached Salix House, I was out of breath. I'd stopped running after about ten minutes and had walked the rest of the way in a daze, feeling as if I'd been punched in the face. I was too shocked to cry. Round and round in my head went a carousel of horrible thoughts. I'd tried over the last few weeks to put Simon's phone call out of my head but it was there now and I went over it again and again, asking myself why he'd done it. What possible reason did he have for lying to me like that? For making me believe I'd been responsible for the death of his child? The answer was obvious. He'd wanted to hurt me and he'd succeeded. He'd made sure that whatever else happened to me for as long as I lived, one thing would be there in my heart for ever. My head felt as though a buzzing insect had taken up residence behind my eyes. Be rational, I told myself. Be sensible. How can this possibly be bad? Look what's happened. Look what you've discovered. You haven't killed anyone after all. What was I supposed to be feeling? Happiness? Relief at being let off the hook? I was blameless, so why wasn't I rejoicing? What was the matter with me? Because far from rejoicing, I could feel myself filling up with a kind of black self-loathing and fury and above all, anguish at the way the entire history of our time together now had to be rewritten. It was false from beginning to end, everything about it. Simon never had any intention of leaving his wife, and far from loving me, there must have been a sort of hatred there which allowed him to condemn me to a whole lifetime of thinking I was wicked.

I wanted to ring him up, to send him a screaming email, to threaten him, to expose him. I didn't. Instead, when I got to Salix House, I went into my bedroom and lay on the bed and started to cry. I wept till I didn't have a single tear left inside me. The girls and Rowena wouldn't be back for a while but I didn't want Eva to find me. I had no idea when she'd be home. I decided to go for a drive. I didn't care where. I needed to think.

'Does anyone know where Megan is?' Eva asked Dee.

'She was sitting in her car when we got home,' Dee answered. 'Bridie went over and asked her if she was coming inside but Megan looked funny. And she hasn't come inside yet. She's probably still in the car, I expect. Shall I go and find her?'

'No, I'm sure everything's fine,' Eva asked. 'It's nearly your suppertime so I'll go and talk to her. Maybe she just wanted a bit of time on her own to think. You can turn on the television if you like.'

She picked up the jacket she'd put on the back of a chair and put it on again. On her way to the door, Eva wondered what could possibly have upset Megan so badly that she didn't even want to come inside. Could she have had some kind of a fight with Tom? Hadn't she been seeing him today?

Eva stood on the porch till her eyes grew accustomed to the darkness. The air smelled of bonfires and dead leaves. She turned up her collar against the cold. There was Megan's car, parked alongside Conor's, a little bit crookedly. She couldn't really see into the vehicle but thought that perhaps that might be Megan's head she could make out, leaning on the steering wheel. Eva approached the car boldly. There was no point in trying to disguise her footsteps on the gravel. She knocked on the window and peered in. Megan's face loomed suddenly white, almost under her hand as she rapped on the glass.

'Megan? Open up, dear. Whatever is wrong?'

For a moment, Megan seemed to hesitate then

the car door suddenly opened and Megan's voice, as ragged and hoarse as though she'd been screaming for days, said, 'Oh, God, Eva. Get in. I can't bear to see anyone at the moment but I suppose . . .'

'Megan! Megan, dearest child. What is wrong with you? What has happened? Tell me.'

'I can't even cry, Eva. Bet you don't believe that, but this is too awful even to cry about. I don't know what to feel. I have no idea what to do or even if I *should* do anything.'

'Tell me.'

Megan took a deep breath. 'Okay. Yes.' She paused. 'I met Luke Fielden today when I was out for a walk and he told me something . . .'

'Let me guess. He told you he knew Simon Gradwell. I did warn him not to . . .'

'Well, yes, he told me that, but I'm not upset about that. I wouldn't have cared about that. It's what else he said. He told me that he'd seen them at lunch recently and he could see that Gail was pregnant.'

Can I be hearing her properly, Eva asked herself. This baby Gail was carrying had to be the one Megan thought she'd killed. The one he'd mentioned in that terrible phone call, on the day Megan came to Salix House with the magazine. Megan couldn't possibly think of herself as a murderer now. The dead weight of guilt that had been round her neck the whole time Eva had known her was surely lifted now, wasn't it? She looked at Megan for signs of something resembling relief and could see only misery and the haggard face of despair.

'You're not saying anything, Eva. Can't you understand how this makes me feel?'

'I'd have thought you'd be relieved. You didn't hurt Simon at all. Nor his wife. His baby will be born and all is fine.'

'But don't you understand? It's far worse like this. It means I obviously never meant anything to him. Everything I thought we had, every word he ever said to me was a lie. He didn't have to do what he did, ring me up and suggest that it was my fault Gail had lost her baby. He knew I'd feel terrible about what I'd done for the rest of my life and he was okay with letting me go on suffering. I feel as if I was nothing to him and less than nothing. I thought there couldn't be anything worse than what I'd done, but it's worse to be the one that things are done to. Worse to be the victim.'

'You can't possibly think that!' Eva burst out, unable to stop herself from interrupting. What was Megan saying? 'Didn't you tell me he was drunk? He can't be held responsible for what he says at such a time.'

'But there was the next morning, wasn't there? And all the mornings after that. He could have rung again. Apologized. What am I supposed to think, then? He meant to hurt me. That was the only reason he rang up and why he was happy for me to go on believing a lie. I don't feel better, I feel much worse.'

'If that's really what you feel, then I don't understand you. Your whole attitude baffles me and I don't know what to say to you. I'm going inside now.'

She could hear the coldness in her own voice. She couldn't help it. Suddenly, unaccountably, she wanted Megan far away. What she was saying, her attitude to this latest discovery, set Eva's whole being on edge, as though someone were scraping fingernails across a blackboard. She could feel a lurch in her stomach and a kind of dizziness came over her, as though she'd started down a path that led to something dreadful, to something she didn't want to look at or contemplate but that suddenly she was being forced to confront.

'I think,' she said, taking a deep breath to steady herself, 'that it might be a good idea for you to go away by yourself for a few days. Think matters over. You're not in a fit state to look after the girls.'

'Me? How can you possibly say that? *You're* the one who's being completely weird, Eva! What's the matter with you? I've never seen you like this before. I've told you how I feel and you're just . . . you're not like yourself. You've been unsympathetic and unkind and now you're basically telling me to leave.'

'All I said was: I think it would be a good idea for you to get some distance from Salix House for a few days. For your own good. I'm going inside now. You should go up and pack your things.'

'Eva! You can't mean it. Are you saying I've got to go?'

'I am. You must go. You must go now. Until you've calmed down.'

'But what about the girls? It's the Nativity Play soon. They've got rehearsals. Who's going to ferry them around? What's Rowena going to say?'

'I don't care what Rowena says. We managed for a good long time to get the girls to school before you came. Conor'll just have to help out for a while, won't he?'

'Please get out of this car, Eva. Go on.' Megan was shouting now, tears standing in her eyes. 'Get out. *Now*. I'm not going to bother to pack. Please ask Phyllis to put some things in a case for me. My laptop. I want that but I don't care about the rest of the stuff. Tom'll come and pick it up tomorrow. Go on, get out.'

Megan's face was bone-white but she had stopped crying and part of Eva wanted to put out a hand and touch her, and say *No, I don't mean any of it. Stay. I'm sorry*, but it seemed as though she'd started down what felt like a slope and didn't know how to climb back to where she'd been before. Something had frozen in her. What Megan had said: *It's worse to be the one that things are done to; it's worse to be the victim*, kept going round and round in her head till Eva felt sick with thinking about it. Also, looking at Megan frightened her and she couldn't work out why. *I need her to be* out of Salix House, Eva thought, and then maybe I'll be able to think straight. As things stood, she was confused and frightened and angry with Megan and wanted her gone. Everything else she'd been thinking about had shrunk into such insignificance that she struggled to remember what it was. The flat at Frobisher Court, the Museum, Lissa . . . all of it no more than bits and pieces seen through a telescope: very small and very far away.

Perhaps I oughtn't to have driven, but it was the only thing that made me feel a little more like a normal person. I'd already spent half the day going nowhere and then coming back and I was tired but I had to leave at once. Eva had sent me away. I couldn't work out what was supposed to happen next. I drove and drove without really noticing where I was going. I just wanted the motion and the silence and nothing but the noise of the engine and my own breathing around me. Where was I meant to spend the night? Where was the nearest hotel? Could I phone Tom? After what had happened this morning? It was hard to believe that was only a few hours ago. It felt like a lifetime. I didn't know what I was going to do. All I knew was: something had happened to Eva. She'd totally lost it. Even though I was still torn up about Simon's baby and the way he'd treated me, this was what was taking up the space in my head. I felt worse about what Eva had said than I could possibly account for. If what she was doing was sacking me, she didn't have the right. Rowena had employed me and was paying my wages. The girls . . . what would she tell Dee and Bridie? How could I leave them without a word? I was going to cry. I tried to think of something else. Where was I? I had no idea but I could see a service station coming up ahead of me and turned into the car park. I'd be sensible. I'd have a drink and something to eat and think about what I was going to do next.

The café was drab. The coffee tasted of nothing and was grey and not brown. The bun I picked out from a selection quietly going stale under a transparent plastic hood was sweet and that was about all you could say for it. I asked the cashier where I was. She looked at me as if I was mad. 'On the M40, just outside Oxford.'

'Right, thanks,' I said.

I sat at a corner table and ate my bun. I looked out at the procession of lights whizzing past on the road outside and wondered for a moment about those thousands and thousands of people, preoccupied with their own worries, their own lives, their own small successes, sealed off from one another in fast-moving metal boxes. Then I looked at my watch. I felt as if I'd been on the road for ever but it was only half past six, but it was so dark outside and felt like the middle of the night. I wanted to phone Tom, but how pathetic was that? The only person I felt like talking to was Jay, but before that I needed to find somewhere to go tonight. Felix would have been friendly and helpful but I didn't feel I could just phone him out of the blue and suggest bedding down in his spare room. Also, I didn't feel up to explaining everything.

I felt around in my coat pocket for Luke Fielden's card. What if I rang him instead? He'd looked anxious when I dashed out of the pub. Perhaps he was worried about me. I turned this thought around in my head and somehow couldn't imagine it. It was much more likely that he'd said to himself: *She's lost it. Best not to interfere.* If he was bothered, he could phone Salix House. Maybe he had. Maybe he'd spoken to Eva. What would she have told him? I could ring and put him right. Tell him my side of things. I put the little rectangle away but more carefully this time, next to my credit cards in my purse. I wasn't going to phone him. I didn't know him nearly well enough to land him with my whole life history. I'd feel ridiculous confessing something like that in the light of what he'd told me about his wife and son. But he *had* said he wanted to see me again. For a moment, something like a gleam of happiness flashed into my head, in among all the horrible things. Luke was probably only being polite.

My thoughts went back to Eva. She was the person I expected to help me through this. Almost the worst part of this whole situation, I told myself, is that I've lost Eva. I'd thought we were close. I'd thought she trusted me and liked me. Who had she told her big secret to, after all? She'd kept

291

quiet about something for seventy-odd years and then she'd chosen me. She must feel . . . she must have felt, at least, something for me. And the more I thought about my feelings for her, the more I realized how much she meant to me. What was I going to say to Tom? I'd punched in the numbers before I'd had time to think.

'It's me, Tom . . .' I began.

'Oh! Hi, Megan.' He fell silent then, and no wonder. 'Are you okay?'

'Well. No. Not exactly. I'm sorry, Tom. I've got no right phoning you for help only I didn't know where else to go.'

'Where are you?' he asked, sounding worried. 'What's happened?'

I couldn't answer. I was busy biting back my tears, and trying to find a tissue in my bag in case I started crying anyway.

'I'm in a café,' I said at last.

'Right,' he said, and then, 'tell me what's up.'

'Okay . . . well . . .'

'Are you crying, Megan?'

'No. I was before but I'm better now.'

'Megan, I need you to tell me what's wrong. And where you are so that I can come and fetch you.'

'You can't come and fetch me. I'm practically in Oxford. I can come to you, Tom, if you'll have me, only the thing is—'

'Oxford? How did you get there? Why?'

'I'll explain everything when I get to yours. I suppose it'll take me about an hour.'

'Jesus, Megan, tell me something. I'll be worrying otherwise. Are you fit to drive?'

'I haven't been drinking, if that's what you mean. I'm fine to drive. I'll fill you in later but the bottom line is I've been sacked from my job. I think . . .'

'You *think*?'

'I was sacked last time I looked. But that was Eva and it's Rowena who's my employer so I'm not quite sure. Question is, even if I'm not sacked, do I really want to go back to somewhere I'm not wanted?'

I could hear Tom taking this in on the other end. 'Okay, we can talk this through when you get here. I'll get some food ready for when you arrive. Please drive carefully.'

'See you, Tom. And thanks so much,' I said. When I ended the call, I felt bad about taking advantage of him again. I hadn't said anything about staying the night. I'd have to sleep on the sofa. Should I ring him back and warn him? I decided to leave it till I saw him. I left the dregs of my grey coffee and went to find my car.

'You *what*?' Rowena leaned forward across the table. 'I can't believe what I'm hearing. How could you do such a thing? What on earth could Megan have done for you to behave in such an unbelievably high-handed fashion? What gives you the right to tell Megan what she must and mustn't do? I'm her employer, for God's sake.' She flung the fork she'd been brandishing like a weapon down on to

293

her plate. 'And your timing is perfect. Nativity Play coming up next week, me as busy as I've ever been, the house stuff going on as well and we still haven't found a place for you to live . . . Oh, I give up, honestly.'

'What's the matter, Mummy? Why are you shouting?' Dee said. She came into the kitchen with Bridie trailing behind her. They were in their nightclothes. 'Why did Phyllis give us our bath tonight? Where's Megan? Who's going to put us to bed?'

'Darlings, I'm so sorry . . . I'll put you to bed in a minute. Megan's gone out for the evening.'

'Without saying goodbye to us?' Bridie frowned.

'I've sent Megan away for a few days,' Eva said. 'She needs a bit of time on her own. She's had some news which has made her a bit unhappy and she is getting over it.'

'That's horrible of you, Granny!' Dee said. 'I wanted to tell her about . . . I just want her to come back. When's she coming back?'

'Yes,' Bridie added. 'I want her to come back as well.'

'Don't talk to your granny like that, Dee,' Rowena said sharply. 'Go upstairs now while we finish talking and I'll come and put you to bed in a minute.'

'Sorry, Granny,' said Dee. 'But will Megan come back?'

'If I've got anything to do with it, she will,' said Rowena. 'Go along now.'

As soon as Dee and Bridie were out of the room, Rowena rounded on Eva again.

'See what you've done now? I simply can't understand why, either. Don't bother thinking of a reason because frankly, nothing you say is going to make any difference. I'm going to put the girls to bed.'

Rowena stood up and marched out of the room, slamming the door behind her. Eva continued to sit at the table. Her daughter, Eva thought, would no doubt be back to yell at her some more once she'd finished with Dee and Bridie. I don't have to sit here and go through that, she told herself. She stood up, went to get herself some biscuits and cheese. Then she made herself a cup of tea. She wasn't in the least hungry. She'd take some fruit to her room once she'd eaten what was on her plate. As she ate, she reminded herself that Rowena was given to slamming doors. Eva shuddered. She hadn't had a fight with Rowena for years. After the row on the evening of Antoine's funeral, they'd both avoided it.

1982

It had been a terribly difficult day, but the funeral was over now and Eva was sitting at her desk in the study stroking Kitty, a ginger-and-white giant of a cat, who was curled up on top of a pile of letters of condolence. The room was filled with the sound of purring.

'I don't know how you can sit there and just stroke the bloody cat!' Rowena said, coming into the room with such force that the door crashed into the wall behind it. Kitty jumped off the desk, startled by the noise.

'Well, I can't stroke her now, can I? You might consider poor Kitty before you go slamming about.'

'I don't care about Kitty. Or you, for that matter. I just can't bear to see you sitting there so smug and complacent. It's your fault.' She was screaming as she came up close to Eva and stood in front of her, red in the face. Eva said, 'Rowena, calm down please. I'm not smug and complacent. How dare you?'

'You are! Why aren't you crying? I thought you loved him but you didn't, not really. Not like me. And I heard you. You thought I'd gone up to bed but I hadn't. I heard you, practically kicking him out. You were shrieking at him and he ran away. It's all your fault. If you hadn't made him go, he'd still be alive. How can you live with yourself? You killed him. You're a killer. A murderer. *Murderer.*'

Eva stared at Rowena and listened to each word as it was spoken. Yelled. She felt every one of them falling on her, one blow after another. She took a deep breath, determined to say nothing, repeating over and over to herself: *It's the stress. She's just hysterical with grief. She's only twelve. Take no notice. She doesn't mean it. You're her mother. Comfort her. Say something that'll make her feel better.*

But what? Eva looked over at Rowena, who had thrown herself down on the sofa and turned to sob into the cushions. I'll let her cry herself out, Eva decided. Then I'll speak. Suggest we go and eat. Or just give her a cup of tea or something. She looked around the room, as though teacups and saucers would magically appear. Then Rowena whirled round. She started quite quietly, so that for a moment, just for a moment, Eva thought the worst was over.

'I think you treated him rottenly. I wouldn't be a bit surprised if you had lovers. He kept going away all the time, didn't he? I know he said it was work but I bet it was something else. He couldn't bear you . . . couldn't bear your lack of interest. Your other men.'

'My other men?' Eva thought: am I hearing this right? Did she say 'other men'? For some reason, this struck her as funny. Terrible, heart-breaking but funny. She'd begun to laugh and this had enraged Rowena even more.

'You see? You just don't care. You killed Dad. He loved me. You don't. You can't or you'd have thought about what you were doing. Now you've lost him for ever and it serves you bloody well right.'

Eva decided to ignore Rowena's last words. 'I'll tell you something, darling,' she began and speaking, she realized, was like vomiting. The words she'd kept pushed down, pressed into silence for almost twelve years were rising from her

297

stomach and whatever they were and whatever effect they might have when they were spoken became irrelevant as the flood of sound came into her mouth and spilled out. 'Don't talk to me about other men. Ever since we married, he was the one. The one who didn't love me. The one who went to other men. Yes, that's right. *Men.* I'm surprised you haven't guessed. I fooled myself for years, but I loved him so much that I didn't care. Or I told myself I didn't care and I still loved him whatever he did to me. However many lovers he went off with. He always came back to me. To us. But you don't know, Rowena. You have no idea what it's like to live for so long with a man who doesn't, who won't . . . He had his lovers and occasionally, once or twice a year, he'd come to my bed and that was it. Do you understand? The night he died . . . well. That was the end. The end of the marriage for him, not for me. He wanted to leave. Do you understand now? *He* wanted to leave *me* and he would have left you too, however much he loved you. He told me that night. He wanted to go. Go and live with Pietro. You've just seen Pietro at the funeral. Who did you think he was? Your father's latest lover, that's who. Antoine stormed out of the house in a rage and he'd been drinking. His car hit a tree and he was killed. There's nothing more to say than that.'

Rowena stared down at the floor. She didn't speak, not a word. She got up from the sofa and left the room. Eva was out of breath from the effort of saying so much. She should have paused; perhaps not told her yet, but there would have had to be a time, when what Antoine was and what that had meant for her would have to be explained. Never mind, she told herself. She'll get over it. Perhaps she'll even forgive me and understand one day how it was; that I wasn't to blame for Antoine's death.

Rowena woke up the next morning to all intents and purposes exactly as she always was: a bit distant to her mother, as though she were more interested in everything else, formally polite and quite pleasant for most of the time but not close. Never close.

CHAPTER 17

'Okay,' said Tom. 'This is what's going to happen. I've cleared a space for you in my cupboard and chest-of-drawers so you can put your stuff there while you're staying here. You can have my bedroom. The sofa converts into a bed, so I'll stay there. After we've eaten, I'm going to pop over to Salix House. I've spoken to Mrs Fitzpatrick and she'll have a suitcase ready for me with a few clothes, and your laptop. She sounded gutted, I must say. She said to tell you that you'll be back there soon.'

Tom was being nice. He was always nice.

'It's really kind of you, Tom, but you must stay in your room. I'll have the sofa.'

'We'll argue tomorrow. Tonight you're having the big bed. You look knackered and you need a good night's sleep more than I do. I'm not discussing it.'

I wanted to say: why can't I go back to Salix House now? Why has she packed for me? What's she told the girls? And what has Eva said to Rowena? What'll I do if Eva still doesn't want me there? Even if she does, do I want to go back? I've got to. I want to see the Nativity Play. I don't want to leave the girls, not yet. The bottom line was I had no other work to go to and nowhere to live. My flat was sublet and if I wanted it back, I'd have to give notice to the agent. The idea of all that hassle made me dizzy. I said, 'Thanks, Tom. I don't know what I'd do without you.'

'No worries,' Tom said and left me alone while he went into kitchen. 'I'm making risotto. It's very comforting food. It's nearly ready.'

'You're being really nice to me. After this morning and everything.'

'We're friends, right?' Tom said.

'But why, Granny? Why did she have to go away, even for a few days?' Dee was sitting on the end of Eva's bed. Eva was already under the covers. If she'd been left to her own devices, she'd have buried her face in the pillow and kept it there, whether she fell asleep or not, but Dee had decided to knock on the door.

'Aren't you meant to be in bed by now, darling?' said Eva. Usually, she loved these sessions when the girls came and sat with her and told her what was going on at school, chattering away and sometimes allowing her to read them a story or sing them a song. Once, sitting like that, she'd found herself singing in German, a song she hadn't realized she'd remembered. The girls had been quick to remark on it.

'I know songs in lots of different languages,' Eva

had said, quickly. 'Would you like to hear one in French?'

The moment had passed and Eva never sang in German again, but for that short time, she'd been taken back to something she'd forgotten, seeing it as though it were a scene in a theatre, as though she were a spectator, high up above the stage: she and Angelika, tucked up in their beds, in the bedroom they shared. Mama was sitting on her bed and singing. Eva could hear the words. If she closed her eyes she could smell her mother's fragrance; she couldn't remember the name of it and anyway she'd never smelled it again, though in the old days she used to go round perfume departments sniffing at bottles in an effort to track it down.

'I'm sure it'll be all right in the end, darling,' Eva said but Dee wasn't satisfied with that.

'It won't be all right unless Megan comes back. Will you speak to her and make her come back? What if she misses the Nativity Play? I want her to come.'

Just at that moment, Rowena put her head round the door.

'There you are, Dee. Come on. It's very late.'

Dee jumped off the bed. 'Who's going to take us to school tomorrow?' she asked her mother.

'We'll see,' said Rowena. 'Now say goodnight to Granny and come to your room. I've got a lot to do this evening.'

'Goodnight, Granny. Please ring Megan up and tell her to come back.'

'Goodnight, darling. Sleep well,' Eva said.

Rowena and Dee left her door open on their way out. For a moment, Eva considered calling Rowena back to shut it, but she didn't feel like shouting and in any case, they were probably in the girls' bedroom by now. She got out of bed and went across the carpet in her bare feet to shut it herself, ashamed at feeling so annoyed about such a trivial thing. *But I was warm and comfortable and now I've been disturbed*, she thought, and for no reason she could understand, tears came to her eyes. There was a sour taste in her mouth and suddenly, everything she loved about her own room was somehow skewed, off-centre, as though something wasn't right in her physical world. Her stomach felt as though she'd swallowed a stone: heavy and almost painful. Her throat was dry. Also, she kept on wanting to cry, blinking away tears from time to time. She looked at the bed and knew that if she got back into it, she would pull the duvet up round her head and start to wail like a child. I won't do that, she told herself. If she stayed out of bed, if she remained upright, there would be less chance of letting everything go.

Megan. The thing with Megan had turned her upside down. Eva didn't really know why she'd sent her away. She thought: I know I shouldn't have done that to Megan but I can't call it back now and I can't confess to having been so stupid. *Of course you can*, said a voice in her head. Eva stood near her dressing table and wondered if she ought to do it now: go after Rowena. Say something like: '*I've been a fool. It's the stress of house moving,*' and all would be well. Rowena would ring Megan. Or she, Eva, could drive round to Tom's flat and apologize to Megan, face to face. She sat down on the stool in front of the veiled mirror. I can't, she thought. I can't bear to have her here. Eva cast about for good reasons for why she should feel like this towards Megan and found none. *Why* had she shouted at her? Why had she banished from the house the one person who really seemed to understand her? It was almost as though she'd been infected with something, some illness, some madness. Am I going crazy? she wondered. It wasn't impossible. Every day there was a story in the papers or on the radio about dementia in old people. Perhaps this was an unusual form of Alzheimer's. If she wanted Megan gone, was it was because she was afraid of her? Afraid of something about her? Mad, mad thoughts you're having, Eva told herself. You're a stupid old woman and you're going to pieces.

'*It's worse to be the one that things are done to. Worse to be the victim,*' Megan had said and ever since she'd spoken them those words had been in Eva's head, like the refrain of a song that wouldn't leave you but twisted round and round till it almost drove you mad. *Victim. The one things are done to. Worse to be the victim. Worse.* Eva stared at her scarves, falling over the surface of the mirror. How could that be? Surely someone who acted badly, committed a crime, perpetrated an atrocity . . . surely *they* had to be the bad one? Victims are innocent. She was sitting at the dressing table in near darkness. The table lamp on her bedside table was the only light on in the room but that was turned in the direction of her pillow and away from where she was sitting. She twisted round to look at it and saw that part of her bed was illuminated, but most of the rest of what she could see was shadows and more shadows; she saw no colours anywhere, only black over every surface. Her own heartbeats . . . Eva could not only feel them but hear them too. Yes, she thought, it must be my heart, pounding like that in my ears. It occurred to Eva that perhaps she really *was* ill. I should get into bed, she told herself.

Instead, she did something she'd never done before. With both hands, she gathered up the scarves that covered the mirror and pulled every one of them away. They fell to the floor and lay twisted there together like a coil of silk and chiffon snakes.

'Angelika?' Eva said, quietly, fearfully. In all the years since she'd first seen a girl's wavering outline in the small mirror in Agnes Conway's house, she'd been hiding from her sister. Until she'd spoken of Angelika to Megan, Eva had worked hard to wipe her mind clear of distressing memories, and almost everything she remembered about Angelika was worse than distressing.

But now, suddenly, out of the blackness that

seemed to have spread from her surroundings and into her head, she wanted, *needed* to see her. Eva stared at the glass. That's me, she thought. That old woman with white hair.

Her own face in the mirror swam in front of her as she stared, the outlines wavering, the features sliding about on the glass. She closed her eyes.

'Please come, Angelika,' she said and shivered as she heard her own voice sounding too loud even though she'd spoken almost in a whisper.

'*Guck ins Spiegel*,' a voice spoke somewhere in her head. Was that . . . could it be? Speaking in German. Asking her to look in the mirror . . .

'*Bist du, Angelika? Bist du wirklich? Sprichst du zu mir?*' Eva could scarcely form the unfamiliar German words, which seemed to stumble on her lips as she stared into the mirror, searching for her sister. *Is that you, Angelika? Really you? Are you speaking to me?* Oh, God, she thought. I can't bear it. Is this how it will be now, with her voice in my head? Her words in German whispering in my ear? How will I stop her? I should have let her stay covered up for ever.

'You can't speak to me,' Eva spoke in English. 'Don't say another word, Angelika. Don't talk to me. I don't want to hear you.'

The voice brought everything back. She gazed at her own face, as it faded and trembled and then disappeared from the glass entirely and Eva found herself once again pulled down into the dark surface of the mirror. She had moved from the self she was now to the small child she was then, four years old and on a train, the memories unspooling like a film before her eyes.

1938

They were speeding through the darkness. Eva knew where they were going. Mama had told them: 'You'll be safe in England and soon, soon, we'll be there too. And meanwhile, Angelika, you must look after your little sister.'

'But I'm not little. I can look after myself too! And Angelika. Why don't I have to look after her?'

'Because you're four and I'm eight!' Angelika sounded triumphant, gloating. She always had that note in her voice when she won a game, or got something for herself that Eva wanted. 'You have to listen to me. Mama said so.'

Eva didn't bother to argue. At first, as the train was leaving the station, she looked at Mama, waving from the platform. Then her figure grew smaller and smaller and after a few moments she wasn't there any longer and all Eva could see if she looked out of the windows were the dark sides of houses and no people anywhere. No Mama. That was when Eva realized that they were really, properly on their own, she and Angelika, in a crowd of other children with strange grown-ups in charge of them. They wouldn't be going home, but to England, a place that Eva didn't know how to imagine. She started to cry, and Angelika was kind to her and gave her a hankie which she used to mop up her tears. Then she fell into a half-sleep, still in some way aware of the rhythm of the train wheels on the track, and the occasional screeching of the whistle.

They stopped somewhere in the middle of the night and the children were herded off the train and on to a platform.

'They're giving us something to eat and drink, look,' said Angelika, and Eva saw a few women moving among the children, with trays of cocoa and slices of bread.

When they'd finished eating, Angelika took Eva by the hand.

'Where are we going?' Eva asked.

'Not very far. I want to look at this train.'

Eva didn't want to go, but she didn't want to stay with the others if Angelika wasn't going to be with her, so she followed her sister.

'I'm scared, Angelika.'

'Baby! It's only a train.'

While Eva and Angelika were looking at the train (which seemed very boring to Eva) some men came up to them.

'Are you girls looking for someone? Are you taking the train to Berlin? Where are your parents?'

'No, we're . . .' Angelika started to answer, and then she grabbed Eva's hand and they ran away to their own platform.

'Were they bad men?' Eva wanted to know.

'No. I don't know.'

'If they aren't bad, why did you run away?'

'Doesn't matter, does it? Come on, I want to explore a little.'

'But what if our train goes?' Eva looked to check it was still there where they'd left it. It was, and the other children were milling about. Some had found benches to sit on and were eating their rations and drinking their cups of cocoa very slowly.

'Come over here,' Angelika said, leading Eva into a dark, high-ceilinged place which was like nowhere Eva had ever been before. Wooden crates were piled up into a kind of mountain in the corner and were spread about everywhere: some quite small but some so big that she couldn't see over them. The floor was grey and cold and hard.

'I'm not going to England,' Angelika said. 'I don't want to go and I'm not going.'

'But we have to. Mama said. She's coming to find us, she and Papa. She said so.'

'I don't care,' said Angelika and then she smiled at Eva. 'Let's play hide-and-seek. Do you want to play? It'll be good here. Look, there are lots and lots of places to hide.'

Angelika never wanted to play with her little sister. Eva was so excited at the invitation that she stopped thinking about what they'd just been talking about, stopped thinking about going home or going to England and said, 'Yes! I want to play with you. Can I hide first?'

'No, I'm hiding first. I'm hiding first or I'm not playing.'

'All right. What must I do?'

'Cover your eyes and count to one hundred. Close your eyes and then cover them with your hands. Do you understand?'

Eva nodded. Only when her eyes were closed and also hidden under her hands did she realize that she couldn't count to one hundred. She could count to ten and knew some of the numbers up to twenty but not all. What should she do?

'Angelika!' she called but her sister was gone. Eva waited and waited for what felt to her like a long time – and then she opened her eyes again. Surely by now Angelika would have found a good hiding place? She hated it here. She was frightened and cold and wished more fervently than she'd ever wished for anything that Angelika would change her mind and come out from wherever she was and say: *We're going back on the train now. I've had enough of hiding.* Eva was scared but also happy because, after all, Angelika had suggested a game. Angelika, who always told her to go away and play somewhere else, had asked her to join in.

When she came out from behind the wooden crate, Eva looked around and didn't know where to begin. She was paralysed by a dread of what might be behind the crates, ready to jump out and get her. *But Angelika might be behind them too*, she told herself. *I've got to go and find her and I don't want to. I can't. I can't go in there.* The impossibility of everything was too much for Eva and she began to cry and to shout out for her sister: 'Angelika! Come out. I don't want to play. Come out now. I'm scared.'

Eva called out over and over again and no one emerged from the darkness. Then a woman came running towards her.

'What's the matter, child? Who are you? What's your name?'

'I'm Eva Bergmann. It's on my label. I've lost my sister. She's Angelika Bergmann. We were playing—'

'What have you done with your label? I can't see any label.'

Eva looked down and the cardboard ticket with her name on it had disappeared.

'I don't know where it is. My mama pinned it on . . . here. I can't . . . I don't . . .'

'Well,' said the woman, sighing with irritation, 'come along now. Can't be helped, though it is careless of you to lose it, you know.'

Eva felt more miserable than ever. She'd been so proud of the label. Mama had printed her name in black letters and when they'd left the house, she'd called her and Angelika 'my pretty parcels'. She was posting them, she said, all the way to England and how could parcels get any-where if they didn't have a label attached to them? Would she now not be able to go to England on the train? Eva sobbed and kept on crying for Angelika, hoping that even now she'd come out from wherever she was, reveal herself and everything would go back to being like it was before they'd started playing.

'Stop that noise at once, child,' said the woman, dragging Eva by the hand towards the platform. 'Who is Angelika?'

'My sister. She's supposed . . .' Words failed Eva and she stopped. Angelika was supposed to be looking after her. Mama had said so. Angelika had promised. 'Oh, well,' said the woman. 'She'll be on the train already. Come along. No time to waste. We're off in a few minutes. I'm sure you'll find her once we get on. Where else could she be?'

Perhaps the lady was right. Eva believed that grown-ups were almost always right. Maybe Angelika was there, waiting on the train. As they walked along the corridor towards their carriage, Eva became more and more certain that yes, everything would be just as it should be, with everyone in their right place and ready for the rest of the journey.

Angelika wasn't in the carriage.

'She's not here, and this is her seat,' Eva said.

'Let's wait for the train to start and then we'll look in all the other carriages. She's probably gone into one of the others. They're very alike, aren't they? You wait here till we leave the station and I'll come back and find you and we'll look together. Yes?'

Eva nodded. How could she say no? She pushed her way to the open window and stared out at the black platform. And there, suddenly, was Angelika. She was standing quite close to the train, with her back to it. Eva recognized her brown coat, her plaited hair like two red-gold ropes hanging down, her velvet collar, her white socks and black shoes.

'Angelika!' she shrieked and her sister turned round. Eva couldn't think of anything to say so she repeated the name. 'Angelika!'

'Stop shouting at me,' Angelika called back. 'Goodbye, Eva. I'm going home. Without you. Mama and Papa will be so pleased to see me. I know they will. I'm going on that train to Berlin.' She pointed at the train they'd looked at before. 'They didn't really want me to leave them. I know that.'

'But me,' Eva shouted. 'What about me? Take me, take me too, Angelika! Please. Please wait.'

But Angelika was already walking away. Eva watched her getting on to the other train. The wrong train. The one going to Berlin and to Mama and Papa. She didn't look back once. She didn't wave. Angelika went up the steps of the Berlin train and was lost from sight just as Eva's train began to pull out of the station and Eva shrieked so loudly that the children in the carriage with her started shouting at her to stop, to keep quiet, to calm down.

'My sister! My sister! She's leaving me,' Eva yelled. 'She's going home and leaving me behind.'

'She won't get to England if she's not on this train. She's silly.'

Eva didn't stop shrieking and crying. In the end, one of the older children went to fetch the woman who was in charge of them and this person slapped Eva across the face. 'To stop your hysterics, child. Stop crying and calm down. You'll have to in the end, you know.'

Eva stopped crying and decided not to make another sound. All through the night, as the train made its way to the Dutch coast, she sat in the dark with the other children sleeping around her. By the time she arrived in England, she'd worked it out. Mama and Papa had probably agreed on everything with Angelika. It was like the story about Hansel and Gretel, except that in the story, the two children were together. But Mama and Papa, Eva decided, must have asked Angelika to lose Eva, to take her into a dark place and leave her there and then run back to Berlin, back to their lovely flat. Back to them. They didn't care about her. Angelika didn't care. She didn't love her. Mama and Papa didn't love her. She was completely alone. She had no idea where she was going. She sat in the dark and felt the chill and the silence fill her and envelop her until there was nothing but sadness left in the whole world. By the time they reached England, something in Eva had frozen solid.

As they travelled, the wheels of the train made a rhythm in her head. *Angelika's gone. Angelika's left me. Angelika's gone.* By the time she reached England, Eva had stopped speaking. She had understood the full horror of what had happened and she couldn't bear it. The knowledge that her sister had abandoned her meant Angelika didn't love her. Not one little bit, and that wasn't something Eva could live with. If the truth was so dreadful that she couldn't even think about it, then the truth had to be altered. Eva changed the whole story, turned it on its head.

Eva, no longer four years old, but nearly eighty, found herself in tears in front of the mirror. She blinked and sat back a little so that her own face was no longer reflected in the glass. What she saw now was rippling silver and, dimly, part of the darkened room behind her. But the voice was there again, in her head and Eva shivered. *'Willst du mir verzeihen?'* Her sister was asking to be forgiven. Suddenly it occurred to Eva that maybe, during the whole of the last seventy years and more, while she'd been terrified of catching a glimpse of Angelika; while she'd been fearful of the fury of her sister's ghostly presence, there had been no reason for her terror. The dim shadow, which she'd caught sight of from time to time, from which she'd been hiding all her life was wanting only to be forgiven. Hatred of Angelika, dread of what might still be there in the glass filled Eva for a moment so that she almost flung the scarves back over the mirror and ran from the room. But instead she peered into it more closely. A hand. She saw a hand with its palm facing the room and reaching out, as though someone were trying to swim up from the unimaginable depths of the past towards her, towards her real hand. Eva could scarcely form the words but she put out her own hand and placed the palm directly over the flickering image she could just make out. She closed her eyes before she spoke.

'I forgive you, Angelika. Of course I forgive you,' she said. She said it in German. *'Ich vergebe dir. Selbstverständlich vergebe ich dir.'* Her hand felt only the unyielding cold of the glass and she wanted to snatch it away but she forced herself to keep it there. She opened her eyes. Their hands were touching, Eva's and Angelika's, across decades, across death and sorrow and guilt there was her sister; exactly as she'd been the last time Eva had seen her: brown coat, plaited red hair, very white socks. Eva could see her plainly, as if there were another room on the other side of the glass and Angelika was there, in that place.

She's not real, Eva thought. I'm imagining her. Nevertheless, she sat quite still, holding her warm hand to Angelika's cold one. She had no idea of how long she'd been there on the dressing-table stool, swallowed up by memories of the past. Perhaps it was no more than a few seconds. Angelika's image was fading.

'Don't go,' Eva called to her, but it was too late. The pale hand that seemed to Eva to be reaching out to touch her own: that went last of all but bit by bit every vestige of Angelika faded away. Eva held her face close up to the mirror and could see every line and wrinkle that time had left on her skin. Of her sister there wasn't a trace and Eva knew as surely as she knew anything, that she would never see her again. *I've forgiven her*, she thought. *There's no reason for her to come back.*

Eva stood up and returned to her bed. There was something about the quality of the silence in her room that was different, almost as though some humming, like a boiler or a central heating system, had been turned off. *Now that Angelika's gone*, Eva thought, *something like a whole other world or dimension has disappeared.* The ghost, the presence, whatever it had been, and that had probably been no more than her own imagination, wasn't there any longer and the quietness it left behind was comfortable and comforting. Eva couldn't remember when she'd been more exhausted but still she couldn't sleep. Stop thinking about Angelika, she told herself. You're not the bad person. You're free. You didn't abandon your sister. She abandoned you. And then she sat up in bed, thinking of Megan. Now, *now* she understood exactly what the poor girl had meant. Tomorrow, she vowed. Tomorrow I'll put that right if I can. If it's not too late.

CHAPTER 18

When I woke up, I felt as though I hadn't slept at all, but I must have done because my bedclothes were on the floor and I was hanging half out of the bed. Tom was already up; dressed and showered and sitting at the table under the window, marking some books. He'd even folded the sofa back into its normal shape. He hadn't needed to drive to Salix House to pick up my stuff. Rowena had brought a case round last night, even before I'd finished not eating the risotto Tom had made so lovingly. Tom had gone to the door as I ran into the bedroom. Now, I got out of bed and put on the dressing gown that Rowena had packed in my case. I went into the sitting room.

'Hello!' Tom said. 'You look a bit rough.'

'Oh, ta. How to make someone feel good about themselves. You should write the book.' I smiled to show him I was joking and how okay I was. He'd been kind last night. He'd said goodnight to me quite early and shut the bedroom door. I'd lain in his bed and stared into the darkness for hours.

'You don't look that bad, actually. But you didn't

have to wake up so soon, though. No Dee and Bridie to take to school.'

That made me feel like crying again. He said, 'I'm off there in a mo. Nativity Play next week means it's all go from now on, I'm afraid. I might be a bit late back. You going to be okay? There's plenty of food in the fridge.'

'I'll wait for you to eat. I'll make us dinner tonight. It'll give me something to do.'

'Oh? That's nice. No need. We could go out if you like.'

'No, I'm happy to cook. It's . . . I haven't done any cooking for ages. I'd like to really. As a way of thanking you. You've been so kind to me.'

Tom stood up and smiled at me. I smiled back, rather feebly. He said, 'Gotta go. See you later. Phone me at once if—'

'If what? You're teaching.'

'Doesn't matter. Phone if you need me.'

'I'm fine. Really. Thanks.'

He was getting his stuff together to take to school, but when he stood up to go and get his coat, I felt a rush of affection for him. I put my arms around him and hugged him. He kissed the top of my head. Then he went off downstairs, carrying a plastic box loaded with exercise books and a few props and with a shepherd's crook tucked under one arm. I offered to help him but he said, 'No, you're okay. If I give you anything it upsets the balance. I'll see you tonight, okay?'

I watched him getting into his car. Once he'd

left, I sat down with a cup of coffee and the rest of the day, when I thought about it, seemed like a desert that I had to cross. Perhaps I'd clean the whole flat as a way of thanking Tom. Or perhaps I'd just sit here and not get dressed and start crying again. Don't be so bloody spineless, I told myself. Go and get dressed and get some food in and some really nice wine for tonight. Tom will help you drown your sorrows. I toyed for a moment with the idea of making him some brownies as well as cooking the tea. Baking was soothing and there weren't many situations that brownies didn't improve. The only problem was I felt paralysed because I couldn't do the two things I really wanted to: go back to Salix House and phone Luke.

I kept on seeing his face in my mind's eye. I thought of the utter bleakness he must feel: the hours and days and years of knowing that he'd never see his little boy or his wife ever again. How had he managed to gather himself together after that and function in an ordinary way? I had a dreadful flash of what the accident must have been like: a child's small body smashed and enmeshed in metal and a woman's hair caught up in a tangle of bent steel. I felt ill when I thought about it. What a hideous irony: Luke trying to cheer *me* up. I remembered how it felt when he touched my hand to comfort me. I thought of the worry in his strange, lit-up eyes when I rushed away. I should phone him. He'd asked me to. Or text? Or I could email him. There was an address on the card. Maybe I *would* email him, but I wanted to hear his voice. For a few seconds I sat with my phone in my hand and nearly dialled the number. Then I realized that I'd just be apologizing for running away. I couldn't tell him the whole story. Not on the phone.

I was wondering what to do when a loud buzzing noise startled me: Tom's doorbell. I looked out of the window to see who it was, and there was Eva, looking nothing like her normal self, but with her hair wound carelessly on top of her head and stuck with a tortoiseshell pin and wearing what looked very much like Rowena's Barbour jacket, the one that normally hung just inside the kitchen door. I didn't bother pressing the buzzer, but ran downstairs myself, to let her in.

'Eva!' I said. 'What's wrong? Are you okay? You look . . .' Why was I saying this? Why wasn't I furious with her? Why, in fact did I open the door to her at all, after she'd thrown me out?

'I know, I know. I came in a hurry. I just dressed without thinking.'

'Come in now. Come and have a cup of coffee.'

I stood aside to let her go first but she took my hand and squeezed it. 'Thank you,' she said, sounding shaky, and not like herself. 'I'm glad you opened the door. I thought maybe you wouldn't want to see me. Talk to me.'

I didn't answer, but led her into Tom's sitting room. 'Sit down, Eva. I'll go and put the kettle on. Tea or coffee?'

'Tea, please.'

I should have known. Eva was deeply suspicious of any coffee she hadn't overseen herself.

Tom had half a packet of Hobnobs which I put out on a plate. I poured the tea.

'Thank you,' Eva said, picking up her mug (Tom didn't do cups and saucers) and taking a small sip. 'I had to see you. I have to ask you to forgive me for what I did to you.'

I didn't say anything. Eva went on. 'I'm sorry. I shouldn't have sent you away. I see that now and I apologize. Please come back. The girls miss you. I miss you. Please.'

'Eva, of course I will. And of course I'll forgive you. Don't look so sad.'

I felt like getting up and hugging her and dancing round the room, but her unhappiness, the way she was sitting as if a weight of misery was on her shoulders, prevented me from leaping about.

'Why not? I *am* sad. I hurt you and I never meant to. Unforgiveable. I didn't understand what you were saying.'

'What do you mean?'

'You said: *It's worse to be the victim* and that made me . . . I don't know . . . furious. I didn't want to think such a thing. I didn't know why the thought of what you said had that effect on me. Now I see. I've had . . . well. Can I tell you what I saw last night?'

I nodded and Eva began to tell me, from the beginning, everything that happened when she and her sister left Germany, more than seventy years ago. While she was speaking, I didn't say a word. She only picked up her mug when the story was over.

'I've told you now,' she said. 'Told you everything.' She looked down at the carpet. Some of her hair had escaped from the knot and curled down to her shoulders. She picked it up and anchored it back again with the pin. 'I hadn't understood what you meant, you see,' she said. 'Now I do. When I was small, I couldn't bear the thought that Angelika didn't love me. Couldn't admit to myself that, yes, I was so unimportant to her that she was prepared to abandon me to anything that might have turned up. She didn't know whether I'd be safe or not and she didn't care. She didn't care for me. It was easier for me to become the one who left her. I could deal with that more easily.'

'But,' I said. 'How come *I* saw Angelika? Because I did, you know. She was there in Salix House.'

Eva shrugged. 'I don't know. I can't explain it. Maybe because you were so kind to me, because you understood me so well, you tuned in to what I was seeing? Or that we both shared a feeling that we were guilty of something. Oh, God, I don't know. I don't understand about such matters.'

She waved her hand in the air and for a moment she was no longer the sad, old woman who'd been living almost her whole life in an agony of guilt, but back to being the positive, imperious, Eva

Conway: the dress designer, the creator of Salix House.

'I don't understand them and I don't care about them. Angelika is gone. She has left me, finally. She's not there any longer. You know what it's like when a machine is on, somewhere? Say a washing machine in another room? You're aware of the noise, on some level, even if you're not in the same room?'

I nodded.

'Well,' she went on, 'that's what I told myself last night. It was exactly as though some humming, some vibration, had stopped. Gone from my head. Now there's nothing but *silence*. Peace. And I wish, I so wish that you'd come back. It's not just the girls who miss you, you know.'

'Really?' I asked. 'You won't mind? You'd want me to come back?'

'Of course. Naturally. I should have made that clearer. Dee and Bridie'll be so happy when I tell them that you're coming. You will come, won't you? You want to? Then come now, with me. You haven't got much to pack.'

'I can't now, Eva. Later. I've promised Tom I'd make supper for us both, as a thank you for putting me up last night. I can't get to Salix House before ten, I don't think. So I won't see the girls till tomorrow morning but you'll tell them why I can't come tonight, won't you?'

'Of course!'

'And there's something else I want to say. I

shouted at you for not understanding my point of view yesterday, about how I felt when I found out that Simon's baby was alive, but I've been thinking about what you said as well and I think I'm going to be able to be happy, after all, that the baby is okay. That has to be good, right? Even if what I said about Simon and me and our history is true, it's okay to be pleased that the baby's still there, isn't it?'

'Oh, of course it is! That's what I was trying to tell you. That's what I couldn't understand your not grasping. You are free of Simon and his wretched family for ever. I'm going home now to tell the girls the good news of your return. They'll be very happy. If I say you're with Tom, that'll make them even happier. They're very keen on the idea of you and him, you know. They want to be bridesmaids.'

I laughed. 'No chance of that, I'm afraid.'

'No chance?'

'None whatsoever. I'm sorry. There it is.'

Eva stood up. 'I must go. I can't say I'm surprised.'

Should I tell her about having lunch with Luke Fielden? I decided not to. I just hugged her and said, 'Thanks so much for coming round, Eva. I feel okay now.'

I watched her go down the stairs and went back into the flat. Did I really feel okay? I'd said so to Eva but was it true? Standing there in Tom's messy sitting room it felt as though I might be. I tested myself by trying to think about Simon and the pain I felt wasn't like a fresh knife wound any longer: more like a dull bruise somewhere, fading all the time. 'Fuck you, Simon,' I said aloud and it sounded good. 'I don't give a shit about you any longer. You're history.' That sounded so good and chat-show-like that I said it again. 'You're history.' I smiled and went to find some carrier bags for my shopping expedition. Next thing you know, I told myself, you'll be singing 'I Will Survive'.

I felt as though I could breathe again. What I'd told Eva about Simon's baby was true. Perhaps I could let myself off that particular hook. Getting over what I'd done to my own baby might take a while longer, but that was something that I'd lived with so long that it was part of who I was. At the moment, I was thinking about Tom. I'd have to explain to him why I was going back to Salix House so suddenly. I didn't think he'd mind much. He'd probably be relieved. In any case, I picked up my handbag and went down to my car. For the next few hours, I was going to think about nothing but nice food. I'd Skype Dad in New Zealand tonight, and he'd be able to see that I was feeling better. I'd been feeling a bit guilty lately, having to make up stories for why I was looking, as he put it, 'not quite the thing'. And I'd talk to Jay tonight, too. Late at night when there was time for a good natter. I had too much to tell her for one email. I wasn't even going to think about Luke Fielden. I wanted to relish my new good mood, my pleasure at being able to go back to my job, and see Dee and Bridie again. I would email him later on and apologize for running out of the pub.

'But why in God's name didn't you tell me?' Rowena grabbed handfuls of her hair with both her hands. She was, Eva thought, literally tearing her hair out. Or almost. Certainly holding it and pulling it in a way that signalled desperation. 'Didn't you think it was going to be of interest to me to know that you'd found somewhere you like? And did I hear you properly? You've made an *offer* on it, after seeing it only once? And without consulting me? I do not believe it. Honestly, you're not safe out on your own sometimes.' Rowena's phone began to ring and she picked it up from the table. 'I've got to take this, I'm afraid,' she said, walking out of the room. 'But I'm coming straight back.'

And she did. Eva had hardly had time to think about what she was going to say before Rowena was sitting down and looking earnestly at her. 'Okay, that's dealt with,' she said. 'Ma?'

Eva took a deep breath and made sure she was smiling as she spoke, so that Rowena would see that she didn't want any kind of fight. She said, 'I made an offer as soon as I left Frobisher Court. I didn't want to find that the flat had gone while

327

I dithered. Nothing is set in stone. It's an offer, that's all. I'm perfectly safe on my own as you know. And please don't be angry with me for not telling you. I wasn't trying to hide anything, only that evening, when I came back there was that business with Megan and you were furious with me and I was upset. I wasn't myself and I simply wasn't thinking about the flat. I'm sorry. But I *have* got one piece of good news, anyway. Megan's coming back. Later on tonight.'

'Really? How did you manage that? Oh, I'm so relieved. And the girls will be too. What happened?'

'I went and found her at Tom Shoreley's flat and I apologized.'

'Really? That's amazing!'

Eva knew what she meant. According to Rowena, her mother took the well-known advice about never apologizing and never explaining to ridiculous extremes. She let it pass and said nothing. Rowena then started asking about the flat.

'Where is Frobisher Court? I'll need to come and see it.'

No, you won't, Eva thought. *It's none of your business*. Then she felt bad about giving room in her head to such unkind thoughts about Rowena, who, after all, only wanted to make sure that her mother wasn't making a dreadful mistake.

'It's in Chalk Farm,' she said, 'near Lissa's Costume Museum. The one I told you about.'

'That's miles away from where we're going to be.

You might have thought of that.' Rowena sounded at the same time so petulant and so exasperated that Eva wished you could say: *Take that tone out of your voice* to someone over forty.

'I did think of that and I decided that the problem wasn't one we couldn't get over. There *is* transport in London. Taxis, and free tubes and buses for me. I've said this before to you and you pooh-poohed it then but it's true.'

'I can't discuss it now,' Rowena said. 'I'm going to see to the girls' baths.'

'They were thrilled that Megan was coming back,' Eva said. 'That's surely something to be happy about.'

'It is. I'm very happy about it. But I can still wish your flat was nearer to the house we're buying. Never mind!'

My phone rang while I was in the supermarket. For a moment I considered letting it go to voice-mail but then I worried that it might be Eva.

'Hello?'

'It's Luke. Luke Fielden.'

'Right! Right!' God, what a stupid thing to say. And say twice, what's more. I tried again. 'It's very nice to hear from you.'

'I was worried about you. You seemed . . . you were very distressed when you left the pub and I wondered—'

'Oh God, I'm sorry. I meant to phone you and say I was okay. I am okay. I mean, thanks so much for ringing and wondering.' How, I asked myself, did he find my number? As though I'd asked the question aloud, he said, 'I rang Eva and asked her for your number. I didn't tell her why I wanted to phone you, of course, but she gave me your number. Hope that's okay?'

Suddenly, I wanted to see him again. I wanted that much more than was reasonable. I said, 'Fine! I'm glad you rang, really. I should have got in touch with you. Thank you for the lunch, by the way.

'We'll do it again when I get back. Or dinner perhaps. I'm in Germany, but I'll be in touch when I return, okay?'

I nodded and then realized that he couldn't see me. 'Okay!' I said. 'That'd be lovely.'

'Right! Goodbye, Megan. Take care.'

'Bye,' I said and the call was over. I stared at the phone. There was the number. I could ring him back. I could say: *I can explain about running off*. He hadn't asked me why I'd done that. Was that kind of him, or did it mean he didn't care? Never mind, he said he'd ring when he came back. I hadn't asked when that was. I went around picking up what I needed for making supper and most of the time I was in a kind of dream, thinking about my chocolate brownies.

Conor came into the study and looked around.

'Isn't Rowena here, Eva?' he said.

'She's just gone up to do the girls' baths.'

He sank down into the sofa and pushed the hair back off his forehead. 'What a bloody awful day!' he said, and Eva tried not to smile. Really, this room was like a confessional chamber for moaners, she thought. What on earth could have happened to make the generally cheerful and phlegmatic Conor sound so upset? She said, 'Is anything wrong, Conor? Anything you can tell me?'

'You could say. Take a look at that.' He stood up again and gave Eva a sheet of paper. 'That came in today's post. I need a huge gin and tonic. How I'm going to break it to Rowena I really don't know.'

Eva stopped listening to him as she read. She hated legal letters and this was from Rowena and Conor's solicitor. She read it and then read it again.

'Does this mean what I think it means?' she asked.

''Fraid so. The Fosters seem to be unable to get a mortgage so they've taken their house off the market and we can no longer buy it.'

'Oh, God!' Eva's hands flew to her mouth. Rowena was going to be in despair. She closed her eyes. I don't want to be here when she hears that news, Eva thought. Rowena and Conor were back where they'd started, as though the last two months hadn't happened. How strangely things turn out. She, who used to be the only person in Salix House who didn't want to sell it and move, was now both actively looking forward to leaving it and also in a position to do so. It's funny, Eva thought. I don't want to stay in Salix House any longer. I haven't been content here for a long time.

The first few years of her marriage had been happy, or partially happy but after that, what was there? Nothing but a kind of desert filled with childcare which Eva hated, more and more distance between herself and Antoine and no contact with the world of her work. Time had passed and turned her from Eva Conway, dress designer, into a person whom no one really needed. Rowena's daughters had been like lights in the general darkness of her landscape. She loved them and was happy to be living with them, but they were getting older now and more and more, they'd be off, gone to follow their own interests and she'd be nothing but a granny to visit from time to time. The days of Dee and Bridie jumping on to her bed in the early mornings were almost over.

Maybe she should have left as soon as she'd made the house over to Rowena and Conor. Perhaps it was only Angelika who'd been keeping her here. Eva had been so convinced of her own badness long ago that staying in the house while Angelika was still present was a way of demonstrating goodness; of proving that she wouldn't leave her sister for a second time. Now that Angelika's shadow was lifted, it was as though Salix House, too, had lost its hold over Eva. Was it possible that what bound her to the house wasn't happiness but its opposite? She thought now: that's the way I coped with it. The guilt from her childhood, her marriage with all its attendant frustrations and miseries and the horror of Rowena's first few days of life had coalesced in her mind to form a network of inter-locking memories and feelings which filled the whole of her horizon at Salix House and which she'd managed to convince herself meant that she loved the place and couldn't leave it. Angelika's ghost had now given her permission to leave.

'But,' said Tom, 'I don't believe in ghosts.'

I'd told him the whole story over dinner. He listened carefully, not interrupting except to exclaim at the tastiness of the chicken casserole I'd made. The brownies were waiting near the oven and I knew those were good because I'd had one almost as soon as they were ready.

'I don't either. Or I didn't. But there was some-thing odd about a couple of rooms in Salix House and I did see what I told you, in my mirror. I wasn't making it up. At that point, Eva hadn't said a word to me. How could I have just dreamed it up by myself?'

'Dunno,' Tom said. 'I reckon you're confusing stuff. Eva might have mentioned it and you've forgotten.'

'Nah, I wouldn't have forgotten anything like that. And I felt that coldness in the downstairs loo even before I started working there.'

'So, have you got an explanation?'

'I tuned in to what Eva was feeling. Her guilt.'

'What on earth had Eva got to be guilty about?'

I was silent. I couldn't tell Tom what Eva had confided in me.

'I mean her sorrow. At the loss of her family in Germany, and her husband. I think she might feel a bit guilty about his death . . . I told you how I felt about Simon's baby, didn't I?'

He nodded. 'So let me get this right: you felt guilty and so did she and you kind of picked up on her guilt.'

'Exactly.'

'Anyway . . .' Tom said and I could tell from the way he said it, stretching out the syllables, that he wanted to change the subject. He was bored and I didn't think I could really blame him for that. I understood as little as he did when it came to explaining the strange things I'd seen and felt at Salix House. Eva had said they'd gone: all the bad vibes that somehow we'd both been picking up on. I hadn't felt it myself but I knew in my bones that she must be right. I said, 'I'm sorry. We've been talking about me ever since you came home. How was school? How's the play coming?'

'It's great!' he beamed. 'I'm very happy with it. Dee is really good and she clearly enjoys performing. And those wings! They're amazing.'

'Eva did everything herself, you know.'

'I know. Megan?'

'Yes?'

'I'm sorry . . . about everything,' he said. 'I'm sorry we . . . that is, I am gutted that it didn't work out between us. You know that.'

I nodded. 'I don't regret anything,' I said. 'I've loved the time I've spent with you. Don't think I haven't. It's just . . .'

'I know.'

'I think you deserve proper love, that's all.'

'Let's hope I find it then,' he said. 'And let's stay friends, okay?'

'Of course we will.' We clinked glasses and drank and helped ourselves to a brownie each. 'I'm not thinking of love at the moment.'

That was true. I could hardly count wanting to speak to Luke, wanting to see him again as anything serious. He might be in a relationship, for all I knew. He was concerned about me, and that was nice of him but it didn't necessarily mean that he felt anything romantic. Don't get your hopes up, Megan, I told myself. Don't count chickens, or cross bridges or *anything* yet. But when I thought of him, remembered how it felt to have his hand cover mine, to have the light of his amazing eyes turned on me, goosebumps rose on my arms.

'Okay,' Tom said. 'I'll do the dishes. You made the meal and it was absolutely fantastic.'

'I don't know what I'd have done without you last night. You're the kindest man I know. I mean that.'

'Megan?' Tom was standing at the sink and he turned round to look at me.

'Yes?'

'You want to get back to Salix House, don't you?'

'There's no rush. I was going to dry up for you.'

'No, that's okay. You go now. I'm going to work when I've done the dishes.'

'I'll see you tomorrow at school, won't I?'

'Sure. See you then. I bet you're dying to see Eva and the girls.'

'Well, I am rather. And I have to Skype my dad. Bye, then,' I said and went to the hall to pick up the case Rowena had brought round.

'Bye!'

I left the flat and as I went down the stairs, I couldn't help but feel the lift in my spirits. I started the car and began to drive towards Salix House.

CHAPTER 19

'I should have done this years ago,' Eva said, looking at Rowena across the small table in the Italian bistro they'd found. 'I've never invited you to have lunch with me. It's mad.'

'Well,' said Rowena. 'Not *that* mad. We live in the same house. We have lunch together at home. It's fun to have a day out, though.'

Eva nodded. It had been fun. And Rowena was wrong. Even though they did live together, they scarcely ever talked properly. Partly it was the normal busyness of the house that got in the way, but Eva knew that she sometimes avoided being on her own with her daughter and was glad if the girls or Conor were there too. But now Rowena had put her foot down and decided that she must see Frobisher Court as soon as possible. The way she put it was characteristic of her. 'If I can't see us settled yet, at least it will be a weight off my mind to know you're okay. And maybe we can find another place nearer Chalk Farm.'

They'd taken a train to London. On the journey, Eva was nervous, wondering what objections Rowena would find, what she'd say about the flat, what persuasive powers she was going to use to make Eva change her mind. She was so relieved when Rowena declared Frobisher Court a treasure, that she immediately suggested lunch in the restaurant she'd noticed from the window of the taxi.

'Are you very upset about losing the house?' she asked when they'd discussed the merits of Eva's flat in great detail. 'I'm sure you'll find another. One that's meant for you.'

'I thought this one was meant for us but there you go.' Rowena smiled ruefully and took Eva's chocolate from the side of her coffee cup. 'You don't want this, do you?'

Eva shook her head. 'There's something I want to say to you, Rowena.'

'Oh God, what have I done now?'

'Nothing. It's not you. It's nothing to do with you. It's simply that,' She paused and took a deep breath. 'I think we ought to order another coffee each. This is likely to take some time.'

'You're very pale, Ma. Are you okay? I'll get the coffees.' Rowena nodded her head in the direction of a passing waiter and ordered. Then she turned to Eva, who sighed and sat up a little straighter.

'I should have spoken about this to you years and years ago. I would have felt better about many things if I'd done so, but I didn't, and now, more than seventy years after it happened, I have to tell you the truth about how I came to England. You have to hear the whole truth.'

'Okay,' Rowena said. She looked completely mystified. 'I'm ready. Go on.'

'I had a sister,' Eva began. 'Her name was Angelika. She was four years older than me.'

'Granny, can I have some more glitter? On my hair?' Dee was sitting at a mirror in the room that had been put aside to be the girls' dressing-room. It was a classroom that had been transformed by the introduction of a long mirror turned on its side and propped up on a line of desks. There weren't any bulbs studding the glass but in every other way the place had become a junior version of the backstage space at many fashion shows Eva had supervised. The smell of powder and hairspray was heavy in the air; there were costumes hanging up on rails, and more magnificent than Mary and Joseph's robes, outshining even the glittery outfits of the three Kings, Dee's wings hung on a special padded hanger which Eva herself had brought in.

'Can I put them on now, Granny? It's nearly time.'

'In a minute. I'm going over to see to Bridie.'

She walked to the other side of the classroom where Megan was helping Bridie to get into her checked tea towel headdress. The lamb she was going to be holding on stage was lying on the floor of the classroom and Eva picked it up and gave it to Bridie.

'Are you all right, Megan?' she said.

'Hmm,' said Megan.

'You look a bit tired.'

'I didn't sleep very well. But I'm okay. Can't wait for the show, Bridie. Are you excited?'

Bridie nodded. 'What happens if I make a mistake?' she asked.

'Nothing,' Eva said. 'Nothing will happen. But you won't make any mistakes. Just hang on to your lamb and you'll be fine. You remember the songs, don't you?'

'Yes,' said Bridie.

Eva dropped a kiss on top of Bridie's head and said, 'Then you'll be all right, don't worry. Megan and I are going to sit down near the front. We want a really good view. Good luck, darling.'

She and Megan walked over to Dee. 'Good luck, Dee darling,' said Eva.

'Break a leg,' said Megan. 'That's what the real actors say.'

'That's silly,' Dee giggled. Eva had to blink because her granddaughter looked so beautiful. She left the cast to the attentions of various teachers, including Tom, who'd been busy sorting out a props problem and had only now come into the classroom.

'Megan! Mrs Conway!' he grinned. 'We're nearly ready. I wanted to thank you for the wonderful wings you made. They're marvellous, truly.'

'You can keep them for the school after this is over. I won't want them back.'

'That's really kind of you but Dee'll want them, won't she?'

'I'll ask her. If she doesn't, you can keep them.'

'Thank you!'

Eva walked out of the classroom quickly, just in case Megan had something to say to Tom, but she'd only walked a couple of steps into the corridor when Megan caught up with her. They went into the hall together. The chairs were lined up in rows and the curtains were drawn on the stage and Eva could see Rowena and Conor already in their seats.

'Was that awkward for you, with Tom?' Eva asked.

'No, he's fine.'

'You look happier than I've seen you looking for a long time, Megan. I'm so pleased.'

'Well, it's good to be back at Salix House and your news has made me really happy. I can't wait to see Frobisher Court. Rowena loved it.'

'You'll see it very soon, I promise. I just wish the London house hadn't fallen through.'

'There they are,' Megan said, pointing to Rowena and Conor. 'Let's go and sit down.'

I knew the Nativity Play by heart. Dee and Bridie had been singing the carols for weeks, and they'd made me sit and watch them rehearse at home. I'd been into school a few times and seen them going through their paces there and I thought that I knew how it would all be. But then the music started and Dee and the other angels came out to the front of the stage and began to sing and I felt tears coming to my eyes. The wings Eva had made were like nothing, surely, that had ever been seen on a primary school stage. Curls of ribbon: shiny, matte, glittery, textured, all sewn on to stiff white canvas made a kind of chain-mail effect that caught the light. Everyone gasped when Dee first came on. She looked wonderful, with her hair caught up in more ribbons and piled up high on her head. The cast did what they were meant to do. Bridie was the smallest shepherd and she and her lamb made everyone laugh and she remembered every word of every carol. I could hear her voice above everyone else's, but then I suppose I was listening out for her especially.

I glanced at Rowena and Conor, both completely absorbed by the action on stage. Eva seemed to be concentrating too, and I felt suddenly elated. Luke wanted to see me again. That made me happy every time I thought about it. Eva had told me about her lunch with Rowena. She'd told her everything: every single thing she'd told me and a lot more besides and although she didn't put it like that, I knew that the two of them were closer than they'd ever been and that Eva felt good about that. Her eyes had misted up when she was telling me about it. She said, 'I could have loved my daughter properly much earlier, if I'd had more sense. If I'd tried to explain things to her. If I'd confessed long ago. But it's happened now and that makes me happy. I don't mind leaving Salix House now. Not at all. The last memories I'll have of it will be good ones.'

I didn't know what I felt about the fact that the

sale of Salix House was now on hold. Part of me was relieved that I didn't immediately have to write to the agent managing my flat and ask him to give notice to the tenants who were living in it. Also, although I loved Dee and Bridie, I wasn't really a nanny and I didn't want to do that for ever. I was longing to start writing articles again. I couldn't wait to apply for jobs. Since Luke's phone call, I'd felt not only more and more as if I wanted to do things, but also as if perhaps the things I wanted to do were a possibility: not entirely out of my reach. As I sat in the dark and listened to the voices of the children singing the familiar tunes, hope filled me: the kind of hope that had been missing from my life for a long time.

As the Kings went through their gift-giving routine, I became aware of someone opening and closing the hall door very quietly. Tom, probably, I thought. I glanced over at the door, but it was too dark to see properly.

I'd left my handbag in the car and my phone was in my jacket pocket. During the singing of 'Hark the Herald Angels' it vibrated silently against my side. A text. I took the phone out and tried to be as unobtrusive as possible. I read the message.

Am here. See you when it's over. Luke.

Luke. Luke was away. How could he be here? I turned round and saw a dark shape outlined against the back of the hall, near the door. I hardly noticed the rest of the play. I sang 'O Come, All Ye Faithful' with the rest when it ended, but all the time I was conscious of Luke standing there, waiting for me.

When the lights went on again in the hall as the curtain came down, I turned round at once and saw him leaving. I was on the end of a row. I said to Eva, 'Sorry, Eva, I must dash out before you. I'll see you later.' She smiled at me and almost pushed me out of my seat. 'Go,' she said. 'Go quickly. Before everyone starts moving.'

When I stepped out into the corridor I could see him standing a little way away, at the entrance to an arched passageway that led to the playground. The corridor was quite dimly lit. My mouth was suddenly dry. I didn't know what to say, what to do. Luke stepped away from the archway and came towards me. He was smiling. Oh God, I thought, why have I never noticed what a lovely smile he has?

'Hello, Megan,' he said.

'I thought you were still in Germany.'

He shook his head. 'I came back a bit early. Eva told me about this Nativity Play. I didn't want to miss it.'

'You have missed most of it.'

'Well, I got here in time to catch you. That was the important thing.'

Just then, the parents started to come out of the hall. In a few minutes, we'd be completely surrounded and I'd have to go back to Salix House. As though he could read my mind, he said, 'We can't speak here, Megan. Come with me. Let's go and get something to eat.'

'But I can't just leave. I'd have to let everyone know. I think they're expecting me to bring the girls home.'

'Don't worry. Eva will tell the girls and the Fitzpatricks what's happened. Where you've gone.'

'Eva? What's Eva got to do with this?'

He laughed. 'Eva and I are in cahoots. I spoke to her earlier and explained things.'

'Explained what?' I noticed that as we'd been talking, he was walking along the corridor towards the exit doors and I seemed to be walking along with him.

'That I'm going to take you out to dinner. That I wanted to see you.'

He held his hand out to me and I took it. We walked along quiet corridors towards the entrance hall. What had Eva told Luke? *In cahoots!* What a silly expression that was! Didn't I mind the fact that the two of them were arranging my life for me? This explained why she'd practically pushed me out of the hall. Dee and Bridie would be waiting backstage for me to tell them how wonderful they'd been, how well they'd done, but I seemed to want to keep hold of Luke's hand. Eva would explain to them, he'd said. She'd tell them. What would she say?

'Really? Truly? Did she say that?' Dee had taken off her wings and hung them back on the rail ready for tomorrow's performance.

'She did. She said she'd loved it so much and you were both so good that she was going to come and see the whole thing again tomorrow.' Eva was sure she could persuade Megan to do that. She'd be feeling guilty now, knowing that the girls were anxious for her approval. She smiled. Rowena was helping the girls pack up their things and Conor was talking to Tom. 'You were both marvellous and it's easily the best Nativity Play I've seen in my life and I've been to dozens, you know.'

'Did you see the lamb? Everyone laughed when I dropped him,' Bridie said. 'I didn't mean to drop him in the manger, but Mr Shoreley said I must do it again tomorrow because the audience liked it so much. They thought I was *supposed* to drop him. Aren't they silly?'

'I thought you meant to drop him too!' Eva said. 'And Mr Shoreley is right. It was very funny and you ought to do it again tomorrow.'

Bridie beamed with pleasure.

'Are you ready to go, Ma?' Rowena said. 'I do think it's a bit much of Megan to let us down like this. And how come you know anyway? Did she tell you why she was going off?'

'I'll tell you everything in the car. It's lucky Conor's got his car here as well. He can take the girls and we'll go in yours.'

Rowena seemed to Eva to be concentrating extra hard on driving through the snow that had just started to fall but she said, 'Okay, tell me about Megan now, please. I'm listening.'

'Well,' said Eva, 'I'm not sure I know where to begin.'

Rowena sighed. 'I noticed her leaving before the curtain calls. What's up?'

'She went to meet Luke Fielden. He came to school to find her.'

Rowena drew her breath in sharply but continued driving as carefully as before. Without taking her eyes off the road she said, 'How did he know she'd be at school?'

'I told him. We spoke on the phone. He rang the house and asked to speak to me.'

'Good Lord, Ma, I didn't know you were into matchmaking.'

Eva smiled. 'I had no idea either. It's just sort of crept up on everyone. When I looked back on certain conversations I'd had with Luke, it struck me that he might have been keen on her for a while. But I thought that she liked Tom till quite recently, so I didn't say anything. And now I think it's a rather good match, don't you?'

'I have no idea! Honestly, Ma. It's not any of our business is it?' She looked suddenly worried. 'She's not going to go off with him and leave the girls, is she? Do you think she'd do that?'

'I have no idea what she'll do but we don't have to worry about that tonight, surely?'

The restaurant was almost empty when we got there. I was glad I'd dressed up a bit for the Nativity Play because even though it was in the country, you could see it was the kind of place which wouldn't have been happy with jeans and trainers in the evening. Luke had booked a table in the corner.

'I like this place,' he said, 'because the tables are nice and far apart. I hate it when the next table can hear what you're saying.'

'I'm sorry about the other day, Luke. When I ran out . . . I can explain.'

'I was just worried about you. I thought it might have been something I said.'

'No, it wasn't that at all. Well, not entirely.'

The food came and we ate it and all through the starter and most of the first course, I talked. I told Luke everything, every single thing about me, apart from the story of my abortion, and that was because I'd never in my life sat opposite a person who listened to me so attentively. I forgot that I hardly knew him and what he got was my entire life story, or the bits of it that mattered to me. When I'd finished I said, 'I've never done that before. You should have chipped in, told me to shut up. You listen too well.'

'May I ask you something?' he said.

'Of course.'

'It's about Tom. Are you sure it's over? I don't want you to regret anything.'

'I told you. I should never have started anything with Tom. I was on the rebound and he was just . . . *there*. It was wrong of me, but it's okay. We're friends now. He made me feel better when

I was in a really awful state. But that's in the past now.'

'Fine,' he said. Then he took my hand across the table and I felt as if I might faint. 'I want to know everything about you.'

I shouldn't have said what I said next, but it was out of my mouth before I could stop myself. 'Why?' I asked him and he answered. I knew he would. He wasn't the kind of man who'd duck a question.

'Because I liked you from the start.'

'Really?'

'Then when I saw you the second time, I couldn't make a pass at someone who was showing me round a house.' He was smiling. 'I was very keen to buy Salix House and that was, I must confess, more on my mind that day than you were. Though . . .' He stopped.

'Though what?'

'I fancied you the very first time I saw you. When you blocked my car, do you remember? I made up my mind to find out more about you.'

'What did you find out?'

'Not much. Eva told me you'd written an article about her so I looked that up online.'

'That article wasn't exactly as I wrote it. It was . . . well, badly edited. And I Googled you, you know." I didn't tell him that I'd only done this after his last phone call. 'I didn't find out much.'

'I haven't got much of an online presence. That's deliberate.'

'But I saw images of you with lots of lovely women at parties and things.'

He laughed. 'Lots of women, right? Not the same woman over and over again. What do you make of that?'

'Should I make something of it?'

'It means I'm unattached. Those women you found me with were wives of my colleagues and friends at various corporate events. Balls, fundraisers, and so forth.'

'Good,' I said. I couldn't help saying it. Luke had stopped holding my hand and I found myself wishing he hadn't. We were eating dessert. I looked at him and began to wonder what it would be like to kiss him. Suddenly I wished we were out of this place and somewhere alone together. He raised his eyes from his plate and smiled at me.

'Let's go, shall we? I'll get the bill.'

There was no one in the car park. It was quite dark, apart from what little light was spilling out of a tiny window at the back of the restaurant. When we reached his car, I went to the passenger side door and he came with me, to open it. He was standing behind me as I leaned down and then I felt him put his hands on my shoulders and turn me round gently.

'Megan,' he said, or I think he said. I don't know if he said it, or I imagined it. I know he kissed me. Every kiss I'd ever had in my life before was erased from my mind. I don't know how long we stood there. Ages. Seconds. Time had disappeared and I couldn't stop trembling. My arms were around Luke's neck and he leaned forward so that my back was pressed against the car. If I could have made myself dissolve into his body at that moment, I'd have done it. When we pulled apart, he traced the outline of my mouth with one finger and then started to kiss me again: softly this time, then moving on to my hair where he kept on whispering my name. I wanted him to never stop. In the end, we got into the car. Luke glanced at me and put a hand out and touched me briefly.

'I wish,' he said, 'that I didn't have to go back to London tonight. Will you email me? Can we speak on the phone? I'm in meetings, but I'll email. I never write emails but I want to write to you. Okay?'

'Yes,' I said. My voice sounded shaky, uncertain. I was reliving his kisses. I couldn't take in what had just happened.

'Next weekend,' he said. 'Can you be away overnight?'

I knew what he was asking and I nodded. I didn't want to risk speaking. How was the time going to pass till I saw him again? Till next weekend? He said, 'I don't exactly know how I'm going to get through till then,' and I laughed.

'Why's that funny?'

'Because,' I said, 'I was thinking the exact same thing.'

We arrived at Salix House at ten o'clock. When I waved him goodbye from the porch as he drove away, I glanced at my watch again. Ten fifteen. How was it possible for one kiss to last fifteen minutes? It must have been more than one kiss, I thought, as I went upstairs. Thousands of separate kisses merging into one another. I lay down on the bed and the only thing that I could see was Luke. The imprint of his mouth was still there on my swollen lips.

CHAPTER 20

Eva sat at her desk in the study looking at Megan who was sitting on the sofa, typing furiously on her laptop and smiling to herself.

'Is that comfortable?' Eva asked. 'I know they call them laptops but I find it amazing that you can balance it like that on your knees.'

'I don't mind. I'm used to it.' Megan looked up smiling.

'You're happy,' Eva said. 'You can't hide it. It's Luke, isn't it?'

'How do you know? I thought I hadn't given anything away. The girls still think Tom and I are an item.'

'And you're not, of course. I knew that. I could see how you felt about Luke when you told me about his wife and child. What a tragedy!' She looked solemn. 'Also, you're texting much more often than usual. I've noticed that your laptop is always with you and whenever the girls ask you what you're doing, you say: *I'm checking my emails.*'

'I *am* checking them,' Megan said.

'You never used to do that so much before last

353

week. Now, mysteriously there seems to be a great deal of traffic.'

Megan shut the laptop, put it beside her on the sofa and stood up. She went over to Eva at the desk, put an arm around her shoulders and hugged her.

'What a nosy person you are, Eva! Okay, okay. I confess. I get about five emails a day from Luke. He's much more . . . well, much more demonstrative on email than he seems in real life. I've told him everything. Everything about Simon, and the baby and the way I felt about it and Angelika . . . you didn't mind that I told him about your sister?'

'No, of course I don't. Everyone can know the whole truth now. And you must start your relationship knowing as much as possible about one another. I think that's very important.'

'And I answer every single message of his because, in case you didn't know, I can't wait to see him and basically every email says a version of that. I'm in love.'

Eva felt, suddenly, as happy as she could remember feeling for a very long time. 'How lovely. And Rowena told me earlier that you'll be away for the weekend. Let me guess: he's coming back and you're spending it together. Am I right?'

Megan nodded. 'He's coming to fetch me at six o'clock.'

Eva got up. 'I must get ready for supper now, but you have a wonderful time and tell me all about it when you get back, won't you?'

'I wouldn't dream of it,' Megan laughed. 'I don't think it's going to be the kind of weekend I'd want to describe to anyone."

'Excellent,' said Eva. 'That's the best kind of weekend there is.'

FOUR MONTHS LATER

FROM: lissdove@dovedale.com
TO: evacon@btinternet.com
Subject: Catalogue etc

Have just had a brilliant idea! I think it is, anyway. That young woman who inter- viewed you for *lipstick*, whose name escapes me, might be just the person I'm looking for. I want to produce a series of pamphlets for the Museum, about different bits of the collection. It strikes me that she could write the Eva Conway pamphlet. Kind of an extended interview/overview of you and your work. With pictures, natch, of you and the dresses. Hope you approve. If you do, pl. send me her email address and I'll write to her. She'll have time, won't she? Even with the nannying? Let me know.

Hugs, darling Eva,

Lissa

xx

FROM: evacon@btinternet.com
TO: lissdove@dovedale.com
Subject: Catalogue etc
That is a really brilliant idea. I'm sure Megan (Megan Pritchard) will be very pleased indeed. She is not going to be a nanny for much longer. She and Luke Fielden (buyer of Salix House) are getting married in October. He was going to turn S.H. into a spa hotel but now they'll live there together which I am thrilled about. R and C have found a very pleasant house not too far from Frobisher Court and they'll be moving any day now. So your timing couldn't be better. I know Megan wants to go back to freelance journalism very much indeed. Her email is: meganp84@gmail.com
Love, Eva

I was right, Eva thought. That's exactly the right place for the mirror. She glanced up and caught sight of herself sitting at the round table in the dining area of the flat. The mirror, a large antique glass in a wooden frame decorated with swags of carved and gilded ribbons and flowers had become the centrepiece of the room, doubling the space and reflecting everything in a way that seemed to soften every hard edge.

She'd spotted it in a nearby junk shop shortly before she moved into Frobisher Court and bought it at once, liking the slightly wavy reflections she saw in it. The silvering at the back of the glass must be very old, she thought. It gave her enormous satisfaction to know that it could live in her home and be something that made the place more beautiful – something that wasn't a source of anguish and terror. It was hard to believe that she'd been settled here for a whole month, but remembering Salix House and the years when it had been her home was like thinking of a movie she'd once seen, starring someone else. Not her; not the Eva she was now.

Writing to Lissa had turned Eva's mind to thoughts of the wedding. The reception would be at Salix House. Megan wanted bronze velvet for Dee and Bridie's dresses, and Eva approved of that decision, but what about their hair? Ribbons? Flowers? There were still so many things to work out. It was eight o'clock at night and the last light of the April day was still filling the room. Eva felt no need yet to switch on the lamp. She was no longer afraid of twilight, or shadows or mirrors. She was no longer afraid. There are no ghosts here, she thought. Not any more. Not even the ghost of a ghost.

She stroked the heavy white paper spread out on the table in front of her and picked up a pencil. It was time to think about the present she'd promised Megan: a wedding dress which would not only be perfect on the day, but which would have a life when the ceremony was over. An Eva Conway creation.